8/12

# LUSCIOUS

# LUSCIOUS

*Amanda Usen*

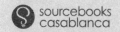

sourcebooks
casablanca

Published by Sourcebooks Casablanca, an imprint of Sourcebooks, Inc.
P.O. Box 4410, Naperville, Illinois 60567-4410
(630) 961-3900
Fax: (630) 961-2168
www.sourcebooks.com

Printed and bound in Canada.
WC 10 9 8 7 6 5 4 3 2 1

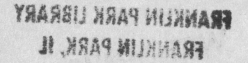

*For Ben, always my hero*

# Chapter 1

"ORDER IN!" THE WAITER DROPPED A TICKET IN THE window.

Irritation spiked in a sudden, sharp wave up the back of Olivia's neck. It was hard to resist the urge to throw something, especially since she had a tomato in one hand and a knife in the other.

She set them both down on her cutting board and took a deep breath. *Not worth it, so not worth it*. Lately, her control felt as thin as the delicate skin of that heirloom tomato. It was only a matter of time before she popped, split wide open, and exposed the mess inside.

She hung the new order with the rest of them, glad the end was in sight. This was it—her last lunch service. Tomorrow, she would leave for Italy. For good, although no one else knew it. The thought made her feel both hopeless and weightless.

Marlene and Joe had everything under control here at Chameleon. They were fantastic chefs, her best friends. She was lucky she didn't have the staffing nightmares her colleagues suffered—no backstabbing, no laziness, no high food cost or pilfering. But she did have two love-struck cooks mooning all over the kitchen. Jealousy, quickly suppressed, tasted bitter in her mouth and guilt made her eyes sting.

*Move*, she told herself, furiously kicking slippery chunks of fallen zucchini under her station. Her kitchen staff was off-site working the Norton Women in Business lunch, so it was all up to her today. Standing still wasn't going to get her through lunch service.

Her eyes darted up and down the empty hot line before they settled on the growing line of lunch tickets. What to do first? The heat from the stove and the grill pressed against her, holding her in place as she stared blankly at the orders. Oven? Grill? Salads? Indecision kept her stock-still in the middle of the kitchen until the sweet smell of roasting garlic gave her a place to start.

She bent to pull the covered sauté pan of garlic cloves from the oven and walked it into the back kitchen, wrestling her doubts beneath the surface again. "Hot! Coming around!" she called, taking comfort from the familiar warnings even if no one was there to hear it.

As she returned to her station, she shook her head, disgusted. Four lousy tables and she was already sweating, feeling the weeds grow around her before the rush even began. *One plate at a time*, she told herself firmly. She could do this. It was just food. She'd been living and breathing this restaurant her entire life. Her instincts, long ignored, would be enough to get her through the afternoon. Of course, *one plate at a time* worked a heck of a lot better with six pans on the burners and a full staff behind her, a luxury she didn't have, but she could do this. Not as fast as Marlene. Not as effortlessly as Joe, but she could get the job done.

The tasks fell into place in her mind—fire the hot stuff, then make the salads. She picked up her tongs and turned to the stove, pulling pans down from the shelf and cranking the burners beneath them. Oil, vegetables—she checked the orders, added white beans to one pan and rosemary red sauce to another.

She moved down the line to the grill and laid marinated chicken breasts on its hot surface. Doubt flared up to catch her again. She had been a better cook before the Culinary Arts College, before she had met Keith. *I can't believe I almost let him ruin Chameleon. God, I'm such an idiot…*It hurt to think about it. She cranked the heat higher on the stove and cleared her mind.

After lunch service, she'd be free. She'd meet Sean at Johnny's bar to pick up her divorce papers, hop on the plane with Nonna Lucia tomorrow afternoon, and be in Verona by dinner time on Friday. No doubt her mother would put her to work in the Villa Farfalla kitchen. Or maybe her father could use her in the vineyard. Either way, she'd have a job, and it would be far away from Chameleon and her ex-husband.

Olivia tossed vegetables in pans with a practiced flip of her wrist. She gave each chicken breast a quarter turn, then reached into the lowboy refrigerator for shrimp skewers and threw them on the grill. The familiar smell of seared meat and smoking oil put her firmly in the zone. She didn't need to think to do this. In fact, it was better if she didn't. Methodically, she washed her hands, put on gloves, and made the Mediterranean salads. She would figure out how to tell her parents "Thanks for giving me the restaurant, but I suck at running it" during the flight. For now, she just had to focus on cooking lunch for twenty-plus people.

One plate at a time.

―∿―

"Kitchen's closed," Olivia said when the server picked up the last four plates. Every second of lunch service had been torture as she waited for all hell to break loose, but there had been no disasters. She was safe now. Almost free. She wiped sweat from her forehead with the sleeve of her chef coat, wondering if she looked as relieved as she felt.

She began refilling pans for dinner service and wrapping items that wouldn't be needed until lunch tomorrow. Everything she couldn't reuse she plated and put into the window for the servers to devour. Ironic that she was doing the same thing with her life—saving what she might need for later and getting rid of what she no longer could use, a husband, a house, and a job.

She swiftly wiped down the line. Joe and Marlene would be back any minute and she didn't want to be here when they arrived. She wanted to bow out gracefully. No kicking and screaming. No hoping to be begged to stay. Absolutely no drama.

She dropped her apron into the bin and did a quick walk-through. The servers were out front doing their side work, so the back kitchen was empty. She grabbed her purse from the office and removed a manila envelope from its side pocket, then opened her filing cabinet and tucked the envelope inside. The drawer slid shut with a loud click and she wondered what Marlene's reaction would be when she found the power-of-attorney papers. Shock? Relief? Glee?

She took one last look around the office. The walls held decades of memories—old menus, ideas for specials, and dozens of photos, mostly of her and Marlene clowning around on the line. Olivia took one—her favorite, a candid shot from just after high school graduation—and tucked it in her purse. She'd remember the good times, before she had ruined everything by marrying Keith.

She carefully locked the office door behind her. Walking up the small hall to the hot line again, she slid a Sharpie marker out of her chef coat pocket and grabbed a piece of paper. The note she wrote was short.

*Ciao, my friends. Good luck!*

She placed the note on the counter with her restaurant keys. *You are glad to be leaving*, she reminded herself. Her gaze touched the clean, white expanse of cutting boards, the knives hanging on their magnetic strip over the sink, the stove that had been her second home since she was tall enough to peer into a sauté pan. She shut her eyes for a moment, breathing in the unique aromas of Chameleon: the cooking grease, the sharp sting of raw garlic that never washed away, the summery smell of farmers' market tomatoes, fresh basil, and ripe peaches. She wanted to imprint the last moment of belonging in the kitchen that held her childhood.

She opened her eyes and gasped, startled to see Jacques, her dishwasher, carrying a broom and dustpan, ready to sweep the line. Good old Jacques. The grizzled dishwasher had been working at Chameleon even longer than she had.

"Leaving, boss?" he asked, resting the broom in the crook of his arm.

She nodded. Impulsively, she reached up to kiss his rough cheek.

Jacques squeezed her shoulder. "It ain't quittin' when it's time to go."

Her breath caught in her throat. She nodded again, dismayed by the understanding gleam in his dark eyes. "Thank you, my friend. Take care," she said.

"You too, boss."

*Not anymore*, Olivia thought as she walked through the dish room and out the back, for once letting the screen door slam behind her. Jacques's comment made her wonder if he knew she wasn't planning on returning. Did that mean Joe and Marlene knew too? Did everyone? If so, why hadn't they said good-bye? She bit her lip, hard. That was just what she was trying to avoid. No big scene. Chameleon didn't need her anymore, and that was fine, even if it felt like she'd just left most of herself in the kitchen by the stove.

"Oh, shut up," she muttered to herself as she cut through the empty parking lot and crossed the street. She opened the door of the bar, blinking as it shut behind her. There were more people there than she would have expected at three thirty on a Wednesday, but since she was embracing the "it's five o'clock somewhere" rule, who was she to judge? She sat down on a stool, surprised Sean wasn't already waiting for her.

"What can I get you, Olivia?" Johnny asked, slinging a bar towel over his shoulder and crossing his arms.

"An Amstel, please."

"You got it." The tattooed bartender reached into the cooler. "You're out early today."

She nodded. "Actually, I'm out for good. I'm leaving for Italy tomorrow."

"Visiting Mom and Pop?"

"Something like that."

Johnny cocked a ringed eyebrow. "Everything okay?"

She took a swig of the beer he placed in front of her and smiled. "It's better now."

The door opened, making the bar brighter for a moment, and they both glanced over to see who was coming in. Too late, she steeled herself against the sight of Sean and her heart kicked up a notch. When his warm gray eyes met hers, a grin curved his lips and she smiled back.

"I hear rebound sex is excellent," Johnny suggested with a sly chuckle.

She turned back to the bar and took a long drink of her beer. "Unfortunately, I heard that too. He turned me down two months ago."

"No way." The flat-out disbelief in his voice was cold comfort.

"Sad fact."

Johnny was still shaking his head as her lawyer took the stool beside her. "What's up?" Sean asked.

"Nothing," she said, taking a deep breath and then wishing she hadn't as his clean scent filled her lungs. She stifled a growl. He smelled like soap and aftershave, and she smelled like grease, onions, and garlic. No wonder he wasn't interested anymore. His pleasant memories of her in high school had been smothered by the stench of caramelized onions, while hers had been fed by the addictive scent of his high-powered lawyer pheromones.

Sean ordered a beer and paid for her drink too.

She sneaked a peek at him as he leaned over to get something out of his briefcase. As always, he looked amazing. He had a fondness for sharp suits that never looked flashy, just the right touch of *GQ* hot in his black jacket and slacks with a subtle stripe, a crisp white shirt, and an elegant tie. She felt like the ultimate slob sitting next to him in her jeans, stained chef coat, and food-splattered shoes. She closed her eyes and took another breath, forcing her racing thoughts to slam into the brick wall of a memory. She'd tried the seduction bit shortly after she'd hired Sean to finalize her divorce. She'd been lonely, raw, and miserable, and he'd left her alone at her door, looking after him with a bottle of wine in her hand. Clearly, not interested.

Paper brushed her knuckles and she opened her eyes.

"You're all set," Sean said with a nod.

She looked down. *Decree of Divorce* was as far as she got before tears blurred her eyes. "Thank God," she sighed, keeping her eyes on the paper until her vision cleared. She didn't want him to see her tears. "I'm glad that's over."

And she was, mostly. It was one more failure to add to her growing list, but staying in the marriage while her husband gambled away their money and screwed every girl in Norton was a bigger mistake.

"Me too," Sean said, shifting closer to her. He raised his bottle. "Let's celebrate."

Automatically, she clinked her bottle with his and took a sip. "What did you have in mind?"

"Dinner." His gray eyes held steady on hers. "For starters."

She gaped at him. He couldn't possibly mean that the way it sounded, and if he did—no way. He should have said yes the first time. Too little, too late, too bad. "Sorry, I have a lot to get done before I leave tomorrow."

"That's a shame. I thought you might want to spend your last night in town…relaxing."

"Nope." She felt her jaw clench and forced herself to take another drink of her beer.

"You work too much." He gave her a lazy grin.

"That's ironic, coming from you. You're always working."

As if to punctuate her point, his cell phone rang.

He ignored it. "I'd take a break for you. Remember that time in high school when we skipped bio lab and went to Tim Hortons?"

Of course she remembered. Her mother had torn into her at breakfast that morning and she'd arrived at school a blithering, sobbing mess. Sean had taken one look at her and all but dragged her out of class. "I caught holy hell for that. Did you?"

He shook his head. "My mother never paid attention."

Whereas hers had dictated, then monitored nearly every step in her life.

"So how about it?" Sean asked. "Would you like to have dinner with me? We're adults now and can do whatever we want." By the glint in his eyes, she knew she hadn't mistaken his meaning. He really was hitting on her. Furious, she hopped off her bar stool and stuffed the divorce papers into her purse. Damn, he had a lot of nerve propositioning her on her way out of the country.

"Not tonight."

He tilted his head to the side and looked up at her with narrowed eyes. "How about when you get back, then? I'll wait."

He took her hand and another memory hit her: his fingers slowly curling around hers at the park where they used to watch his little brother's baseball games on the rare Saturday afternoons she wasn't working.

They had never had the opportunity to spend much time together elsewhere, but those few times stood out in her memory as golden oases of freedom from school, the restaurant and her mother.

Her heart picked up speed again. She hadn't been crazy to wish there might have been more between them...if she hadn't gone away to school and married Keith.

Slowly, she shook her head. "I think it's too late."

"It's never too late," Sean said. But he let go of her hand.

She picked up her purse. "Thanks for your help," she forced herself to say before she headed for the door.

—⁂—

Sean was just about to leave the office when his phone began ringing. There was no avoiding it. This client hated voice mail. "Good afternoon, Mr. Russo," he said, carefully keeping the frustration from his voice.

"My wife is in Italy," Russo blasted in his ear. "I want you to go over there."

Of course he did. "Mr. Russo, I'll get in touch with your wife's lawyer and we'll work something out—"

"She doesn't have a lawyer. She's being ridiculous. A child. She keeps texting me pictures of all the fancy hotels where she's staying and the designer handbags she's buying, flaunting how she's spending our millions. 'If I don't mind,'" he added in an acid tone.

Sean assumed he minded. "Are you certain divorce is—"

"Certain? I should have done it thirty years ago, before the woman ruined my life with her nonsense. Yes, I want a divorce. The sooner the better."

"Then we need to find a way to serve her with the papers, which is going to be complicated if she's in Italy."

"Go over there. I'll pay for it. She's driving me crazy. My credit card bill is through the roof and I'm starting to have heart palpitations. She's gone too far. I want this to be over."

Sean sighed. All of his clients wanted it to be over. "Mr. Russo—"

"I'm begging you. She's in Venice. Or Vicenza. Something that starts with a *V*. Take her the papers. I don't trust anyone else to get the job done right."

Russo was too busy to go, but assumed Sean could leave at a moment's notice? Actually, he probably could. He'd just wrapped up several cases and he hadn't taken a vacation in…well, ever.

"Think about it and get back to me. Soon." Russo hung up.

Sean dropped his phone in his pocket and finished his beer. Where was Olivia going? Verona? That started with a *V*.

Suddenly the idea of a vacation was a hell of a lot more appealing. He'd waited a long time for Olivia Marconi and going with her would give him a chance to explain why. No way was he going to let her declare it too late when they hadn't had a proper chance together. He dug his phone out of his pocket and called Russo back.

***

Sean tucked his toothbrush, razor, and deodorant into his travel kit. His bag was packed and waiting in his bedroom where his little brother Colin was lounging on his bed, probably counting the minutes until Sean would be gone and he'd have the house to himself. He'd been delighted when Sean came home yesterday and told him he was leaving for Italy.

He picked up his bag and carried it into the bedroom. "You aren't planning any wild parties, right?"

Colin snorted. "Dude, I'm almost twenty-two, not fourteen."

"You threw wild parties when you were fourteen?" That had been the year Sean had left Norton for law school.

"I plead the fifth."

Sean groaned. "Forget it. I'm not going."

Colin rolled off the bed, took the travel kit out of his hand, and tucked it into his attaché case. God, when had he gotten so tall, so wide? It seemed like only yesterday Sean had held his brother's small hand and half-led, half-dragged him into his preschool classroom for his first day of school.

Colin patted him on the shoulder, smirking. "Don't try to pretend you didn't sic Mom and Dave on me for the week. I bet she'll be over here trying to pretend she's a real mother. Cooking. Cleaning. Asking nosy questions." He shuddered dramatically and picked up Sean's bag, thrusting it at him. "You better get out of here or you're going to miss your flight. I promise I won't burn the house down while you're gone."

Reluctantly, Sean took the bag and threw the strap over his shoulder. He wanted to defend their mother, but he couldn't. He had done everything he could to keep their lives together, but what did a twelve-year-old boy know about parenting? Not enough, apparently. Sometimes Sean wondered if a sixth sense had inspired him to go to law school because his brother would need his legal expertise.

Thankfully, it had been months since Colin had come home with a new tattoo or piercing, and nearly three years since the phone had rung in the middle of the night, forcing Sean out of his warm bed and down to the police station to collect him. Their nightmare was almost over—Colin's final probation hearing was Wednesday. After that, Sean could stop waiting for the axe to fall.

Colin could make it until Wednesday without a big-brother babysitter…right? Sean knew it was ridiculous to be so worried. Colin was an adult now. But they were so close to being done with the whole disaster and one wrong move…

He dragged his hand through his hair and sighed. On the other hand, Mr. Russo was a major client who could shoot Sean to stardom with referrals. Or ruin his career.

And in other ways, the timing couldn't be better. He'd been waiting for his chance with Olivia Marconi since high school. She'd offered herself on a platter just before officially asking for her divorce and it took every ounce of willpower Sean possessed to refuse. He would not take advantage of a vulnerable woman. He wanted her to want *him*, not just some guy who wasn't her asshole of a husband. One way or another, he would convince her to give him another chance.

Two birds. One stone.

And Colin could survive without him.

Sean took a deep breath.

"Dude, you're gonna be late," Colin said.

"Oh, shut up. I'm going." He picked up his bag.

Colin followed him downstairs.

Sean checked his pockets for his wallet, passport, cell phone, and keys—all where they should be. He headed for the front door, still shadowed by his brother. Sean turned around and gave him a stern look. "I mean it. Don't do anything stupid. Six more days and you're off probation."

Colin rolled his eyes. "C'mon, bro. Would I do anything stupid?"

They both knew the answer to that, so Sean waited for his promise.

"No parties. No cops. No fun. Just work and no play, I swear. Have a good time, man." Colin's grin was little-boy sweet and made Sean nervous. Maybe he *should* stay for the hearing.

His brother opened the front door and made a shooing motion with his hand.

Sooner or later, Colin had to grow up, right? He wasn't a kid anymore. Maybe standing alone would finally make him realize actions have consequences. Sean forced himself to walk out the door.

He tossed his bag into the backseat of his car. Now that he was on his way, his apprehension about leaving eased. Colin would be fine, and he was right—Sean *had* asked their mother to keep an eye on him this week.

Had he really never taken a vacation? There had never been the time, money, or freedom to go anywhere when they were little, and since then life had been filled with school, work, and, for Colin, community service. Except for one uncomfortable "family" trip to Mexico when their mother had gotten married, they hadn't gone anywhere. The end of Colin's probation would lift a huge weight from his shoulders—he deserved this break.

He didn't think it was going to be difficult to find Mrs. Russo. With the pictures she kept sending her husband, it was clear she wanted to be found. As soon as he gave her the papers, he'd have plenty of time to spend with Olivia. Anticipation built inside him. For as long as he'd known Olivia, she'd never taken a vacation either. They could drink wine, soak up the sun, relax…he stopped that line of thought.

He couldn't think about relaxing until he was on the plane to Italy. For all intents and purposes he was hijacking Olivia's vacation and she hadn't exactly been receptive to suggestion yesterday at Johnny's. Sure, he'd built a career out of his ability to be persuasive, but he'd never used his skills to stage a seduction, at least not on this grand of a scale. He caught sight of himself in the rearview mirror and grinned. No turning back now.

―――⁓⁓―――

Olivia pulled into her driveway. She had spent most of last night cleaning her house top to bottom, fueled by her irritation with Sean. This morning, she had canceled her newspaper, put a hold on her mail, left a set of house keys with the real estate agent, and tied up about a million other loose ends. As soon as she found someone to buy her car, her exodus from Norton would be complete, but she was going to hold off on that until the house sold, figuring she'd have to come back for the closing anyway.

Her cell phone rang. When she saw it was the restaurant, she let it go to voice mail. Chameleon didn't need her and she was cutting it close on time, with only two hours to get home, pick up Nonna, and get to the airport for their flight. She probably shouldn't have stopped for lunch, but hot wings were one thing she was going to miss.

She jumped out of the car and jogged up the path, surprised to find her front door locked. Why wasn't it wide open with Nonna waiting impatiently in the hallway?

She unlocked the door and opened it. "Nonna?" she called.

"Upstairs." Her grandmother's voice drifted lazily down the stairs.

"You ready to go?" Olivia asked as she darted down the hall to her bedroom to grab her suitcase, already packed and waiting. She didn't hear an answer. "Nonna?"

Silence.

The doorbell rang.

She whirled to see Sean, smiling at her through the screen door. Her pulse jumped. *Damn it. You're mad at him, remember?*

She pushed the screen door open. "Hi, Sean. Nonna Lucia and I are just getting ready to leave for the airport. Is there a problem?" She hoped there was nothing wrong with the forms she had stashed in the filing cabinet at the restaurant.

He shook his head, making the afternoon sun glint in his close-clipped blond hair. "Nope, no problems. I'm taking you to the airport," he said cheerfully, pulling the heavy suitcase out of her hand. His fingers pressed against hers briefly and the warmth shot straight up her arm. He was wearing a suit again. Just not fair.

She shook her head. "I thought Big Daddy was taking us."

He set the suitcase on the porch and stepped into the

house. "Something came up," he said easily. "Got any more luggage?" He brushed against her in the narrow hallway, and she caught a whiff of fresh laundry just begging to be rolled in.

For a minute, she couldn't move. Then she left him there and dashed up the stairs. "Nonna is going to be crushed," she called over her shoulder. "I don't think she got to say good-bye to him. I'll get her bags." Sean didn't need to haul Nonna's suitcase down the stairs, especially since he'd already been pressed into service as their last-minute chauffeur. She wished someone had told her they needed a different driver. She would have preferred one of Big Daddy's grandsons, or even a taxi, to Sean. She didn't need the added stress of ignoring the awkwardness between them. The fact that he didn't seem to feel it was even more annoying.

She found Nonna sitting on the bed in the guest room. A quick glance into the closet showed that her suitcase was in exactly the same place it had been this morning. Olivia lifted it. Empty. The fear that had been hovering at the edge of her mind since she reached her locked front door became reality.

"*Cara*, I am not going with you to Verona," her grandmother confirmed softly.

Olivia tossed the suitcase onto the bed. "Nonna, I'll pack for you. We can't miss our plane. Please, hurry!"

"I told you I didn't want to go, Olivia. You didn't listen. I love Benito, and I'm staying here. I'll use my ticket another time."

Olivia put her hands on her hips. "You can't marry Big Daddy, Nonna. He's a mobster!"

"Bah! He's not a mobster. He's just misunderstood."

Olivia counted to ten and silently cursed the timeless appeal of bad boys. Benito Capozzi, aka Big Daddy, was indeed a mobster, and her grandmother knew it. He ran the local casino as well as several other questionable businesses in town. He'd also sabotaged Chameleon at the beginning of the summer, which had a huge part in Olivia's incipient meltdown. Big Daddy's complete devotion to her grandmother was the only thing that had kept Olivia from hiding shrimp shells in his limo. Well, that and the fact that his chauffeur never fell asleep in the car.

Olivia tried again. "Mom is going to kill you."

"Ah, your mamma. She doesn't scare me." Nonna straightened her slim shoulders.

Olivia groaned. Easy for her to say.

Her grandmother's lips curved in a girlish smile. "And who said anything about getting married? That's for young people. I'll be perfectly happy living in sin." The lilt in her soft voice stopped Olivia from pulling open the dresser drawers and stuffing Nonna's clothes into her suitcase. Instead, she crossed to the bed and scrutinized her grandmother.

Nonna Lucia's eyes shone with happiness, and it wasn't her carefully applied makeup or her smart, pink suit that made her look radiant. Nonna glowed from within. She didn't look a day over sixty-five. Oh, sweet Jesus, she really was in love.

Olivia sank down onto the bed and tried to ignore the panic she felt tightening around her lungs. "Nonna, I need a vacation." And Sean was downstairs waiting. If they missed their flight, she wasn't sure she could hold it together until the next one. "I'm exhausted." *And my marriage failed, and I'm a monster for resenting my best friends, and as it turns out, I'm not a great chef, so I can't do the thing I was planning to do for the rest of my life.* "Please? I need some time to myself. I just can't—I need a break." *A permanent break.*

"Olivia?" Sean's deep voice echoed up the stairs.

"Be right down!" she called, forcing the tight words out of her throat. Now was not the time to start screaming or sobbing, although temptation welled up so hard it made her eyes water. She clamped her mouth shut and forced herself to focus on this problem, just this one.

"I'm taking your suitcase out to the car," Sean yelled up from the foyer.

"You don't have to do that. I'll get it," she yelled back. Olivia heard the screen door swing shut behind him.

Nonna Lucia patted her on the hand. "You go."

"Nonna, I can't leave you alone."

"Olivia, *cara*, I'm a grown woman. I came to check on *you*, remember? I'm not ready to go home just yet. Take your vacation. And, *mio Dio*, give your mother enough to worry about so that she doesn't come here looking for me. I need a break too." Nonna's chocolate brown eyes sparkled.

Olivia hadn't considered that her mother called every day. Sometimes twice. If neither of them appeared at Villa Farfalla, her mother was sure to come looking for them.

Nonna gave her a gentle push. "I'll move into your bedroom while you're gone if you don't mind. I don't like the stairs." Nonna looked thoughtful. "Benito and I will come next week for *la Sagra dell'Uva*. It's been a long time since our last gala. It's time. Go, *cara*. Your man is waiting."

"He's not my man," Olivia said automatically.

Her grandmother snorted. "You forget who you are talking to. I saw him walk by the restaurant twice a day, every day, for four years when you two were in school together. What happened?"

Olivia ignored the question and leaned to hug her, breathing in her lemony scent. "*Ciao*, Nonna."

Her grandmother laughed softly.

Olivia grabbed the keys to her house and car and handed them to Nonna, knowing she'd have to warn her. "I've put the house on the market. The real estate agent's name is Tricia Banner. I'll make sure she knows to call before bringing anyone over."

Her grandmother arched her delicate eyebrows. "Why are you selling your house, *cara*?"

Olivia looked away. "It's time for a change." She heard Sean open the front door, so she stood up. "Don't worry, the market isn't very good right now. I'll make sure you can stay as long as you want. Unless you plan to shack up with Big Daddy?"

Nonna laughed, but she didn't deny it. "*Ti voglio bene*, Olivia. Travel safely. I love you."

"I love you too." Olivia dipped to kiss her grandmother's soft cheek, then strode out of the bedroom carrying the scent of Nonna's lemons in her hair and the ever-present echo of a frustrated shriek in the back of her skull.

―――

"Why are you carrying your briefcase?" Olivia asked. Rather than leave her at the departure curb, Sean had insisted on escorting her into the airport.

"I can't leave these files in the car," he explained, slinging his large leather bag over his shoulder. He rolled her suitcase behind him, forcing her to trail after him with her carry-on.

"You really didn't have to park, Sean. I'm quite capable of getting myself on an airplane."

In fact, she was glad to be traveling alone now. It had been ages since she felt this free from responsibility—no orders to call in, no delivery slips to sign, no schedules to write, no mistakes to explain to anyone. The pressure had been paralyzing. It had been getting harder and harder to choose a task, to make a decision. There had been too many people depending on her to do the right thing every second of the day, until all she wanted to do was crawl into the office and hide under the desk. Getting away from everything was just what she needed.

Sean tugged her driver's license and passport out of her hand, and she let him—more evidence of the passivity that had overtaken her formerly authoritative self. He handed her documents to the skycap. Woodenly, Olivia answered his questions. Yes, she'd packed her bags herself. Yes, they had been in her presence the entire time. She turned her back while she jammed her documents back into her purse so Sean wouldn't see the sudden tears in her eyes. A dull roar filled her ears and she walked a few feet and sat down on a bench.

When had the moment occurred? The actual moment when she surrendered, succumbed to personal inertia and professional paralysis? Had there been a moment? Or had it happened gradually?

Both, she thought, standing up and following Sean as he rolled her bag into the terminal, no longer resenting his company quite as much. It was nice of him to be here for her, especially when he had to be in court. At least, she assumed he had to be in court because he was wearing a dark suit that made his gray eyes look silver. His white shirt was starched and his fashionable tie was knotted perfectly, as per usual. He walked toward security with the air of a man who knew exactly where he was going.

He motioned her in front of him and handed her tickets to the uniformed guard. Sean slipped out of his shoes and put them in a plastic bin.

She stopped taking off her own shoes and turned to him. "What are you doing? You can't go to the gate unless you have a ticket."

His steady gray eyes gleamed. "I do have a ticket. I'm going with you."

# Chapter 2

"No, you are not." Olivia's eyes blazed.

He'd been expecting resistance. "Now that hurts my feelings. I have business in Italy. Come on, we need to keep the line moving."

She stepped to the side. "I don't care about the line. I want to know why you're following me."

Other passengers shot him irritated glances as he doubled back to join her. "Don't you want company?" he asked.

"No, Sean, I don't want company. I want space."

"You can have all the space you want. I promise I'll keep my hands to myself. Mostly." Her eyes widened. "Relax," he urged. "You don't want to cause a scene. We'll only end up delayed."

She shook her head. "I'm not going anywhere until you tell me why you're doing this." She lifted her chin, eyes hard, like jade only colder. Her blond hair fell forward into her face and she brushed it back in a quick gesture, biting her lower lip.

He had fantasized about the taste of her lips for so long that he had made it a rule to keep three solid feet between them while she was married. His heart beat faster as he stepped closer to her, close enough to smell the flowery scent of her hair.

He leaned down to whisper, "Because it's never too late. You put your house on the market and you gave

Marlene power-of-attorney over Chameleon. I know you put all of your financial affairs in order too." As her lawyer, he knew exactly how she had rearranged her finances after the divorce. "You're running away, Olivia, and I'm starting to think you aren't coming back." He paused, feeling his pulse hammer. "So my question is this: Did you think I wouldn't notice, or did you think I wouldn't care?"

He heard the sharp rush of air as she gasped. Fear, or maybe guilt, crossed her expression before she spoke. "I didn't think it was any of your business."

"But you're my client, Olivia, and as such you *are* my business. Speaking of which, how did Marlene react when you gave her those papers?"

Olivia looked away.

Sean pressed his advantage. "You didn't give them to her, did you?"

She didn't answer his question. "I don't want to talk about it."

The security guard had run out of patience with them. Thankfully, Olivia responded to his curt gesture and walked through the metal detector. Sean spoke to her back as she collected her shoes. "Olivia, we have a layover in New York. You can ditch me there if you really want to be alone, I promise." He stepped back, giving her the space she wanted. For now.

"Fine." She swept forward, leaving him behind with her carry-on. Relief and triumph soared within him as he followed her to their gate.

She ignored him until their flight was called and didn't comment when he pointed to their first-class seats. Apparently, a business-upgrade wasn't going to score him any points, but at least they would be more comfortable. He was prepared for a barrage of questions, but she said nothing, instead turning to stare out the tiny window as he took his seat. He waited, allowing his gaze to slide over her with a familiarity he wouldn't dare use if she were paying attention. He longed to soothe the coiled tension from her shoulders, to brush her soft hair away from her face.

"Why are you here, Sean?" She spoke without looking away from the window.

"Same reason you are."

"That's not an answer. Don't give me lawyer double-talk."

She looked at her lap and her hair fell forward again. He caught it with his fingers and tucked it behind her ear. Satisfaction burst through him, but subsided as she froze like a trapped rabbit.

The plane began to taxi, and she gripped the arms of her seat, looking like she might shatter if they hit a bump on the runway. Tired of resisting, he picked up her hand, caressing her knuckles with his thumb. He could feel the strength in her palm, the callus at the base of her index finger, and the rough skin created by constant abuse in the kitchen. They were capable hands, working hands, and sexy as hell.

She turned toward him as they lifted into the air. Her expression was tense, and he ached to smooth the lines between her brows until they disappeared. He wanted her green eyes to be clear and unshadowed, not haunted and bruised. What had prompted her to close up her life like a summer resort in September? People didn't sign over power of attorney and put their house on the market just to take a vacation. She was running away, and he didn't want her to go.

Her green eyes flashed and he knew he had to answer her question somehow. When in doubt, stall—his favorite legal trick. "Olivia, we've got a five-and-a-half hour layover in New York, and I have dinner reservations at Trio. Can we talk then?" He let that sink in.

If he could get her to dinner, maybe he could get her to Italy. Trio was rumored to be the next restaurant in New York to receive three Michelin stars. Reservations were nearly impossible for the average mortal to attain, but Nonna Lucia's position as Big Daddy's girlfriend had distinct privileges. Nonna had also been happy to share Olivia's itinerary, once he had admitted his desire to join her.

"I want to talk now," Olivia insisted.

"Not before I get some wine into you," he countered.

She shook her head slowly. "I don't think so. You and wine have a bizarre effect on me. I don't want to embarrass myself again." Her words hung there, finally acknowledged.

"I didn't say no," he said quietly.

Olivia raised her eyebrows. "Could have fooled me." Her words were bold, but her hand trembled in his.

"I said 'not tonight.' Remember?" Of course she did or she wouldn't have used the exact same phrase yesterday.

She tugged her hand out of his grasp.

Recklessly, Sean reached out to cup her cheek. "Was there an expiration date on your offer?"

―⁓―

Olivia felt her jaw drop. She shut her mouth with a click she hoped was only audible to her. *You bet your ass there's an expiration date*. And it had run out the minute Sean left her house last June and she'd finished that bottle of wine by herself. Actually, no, before that—it had run out the very second she had read rejection in his blank expression and had known her ex-husband was right. She was a cold bitch, and no one else would ever want her.

Olivia gripped his wrist. His hand still framed her face. She tugged on it, but he didn't budge. His eyes flashed from their usual calm gray to hot silver and she paused, startled, a stinging retort caught in her throat.

He covered her mouth with his lips.

For a split second, her body sagged in relief, surrendering so suddenly and profoundly that she felt as if someone had cut her strings. Breath whooshed out of her lungs. Her hands gripped his jacket for balance. His lips moved confidently over hers and his sweet, warm breath filled her mouth.

Sean thrust the armrest out of the way so it no longer divided their seats, and she felt his hand slide into her hair. What should she do? Push him away or pull him closer?

He kissed her again before she could decide.

His hands were warm on her cheeks as he tilted her head to better align his lips with hers. She shut her eyes and let go of all thought. His mouth was soft and firm at the same time. His lips led hers in an easy dance, not giving her a chance to falter.

She felt the tip of his tongue tease her lips and she stiffened, inhaling sharply. Doubt chilled her. She released her grip on his lapel and flattened her palms on his chest, pushing him away. Too much. Too fast.

Sean locked his arms behind her waist and kept her as close as their fastened seat belts would allow. She arched her back and cleared her throat loudly. "It's not very professional to kiss your clients, counselor."

"I'm on vacation." His eyes flashed again, warning her. "And I quit. Kissing is the least of what I want to do to you."

The distance she had put between them seemed to disappear. "Sean, I wasn't…that night, I didn't mean to, I mean, I don't want—"

"Yes, you did. And I hope you still do."

She was frightened by how much she wanted to bury her face in his neck and discover if his shirt would feel soft beneath her cheek or if the dry cleaner's chemicals had left it scratchy and rough. Sean was the genuine article, a good guy, dependable—and a big, fat, glaring contrast to her ex-husband. Sean had always been there for her. It was why she had gravitated toward him in high school and also why she had wanted him to make love to her two months ago. It was damn hard to resist him now. But leaning on Sean wouldn't solve her problems. She didn't want to drag him into her meltdown. Olivia reached behind her and removed his hands from around her waist.

She cleared her throat again but was mercifully saved from speaking by the intercom clicking on as the pilot made an announcement about their cruising altitude. She gathered her thoughts. "Sean, that was two months ago—why now? Why yesterday?"

"I'll tell you during dinner." He pulled the flight magazine from the seat pocket in front of him. "Want one?"

She shook her head in disbelief, angling her body away from him as he opened the magazine. How could he be so blasé about what had just happened between them? Her thoughts felt as scattered as the cirrus clouds beneath them. Why couldn't he have said yes two months ago? They could have had their catastrophe and gotten it over with.

She blinked, rolling her eyes as they began to sting. This situation called for laughter, not tears. He was following her to Italy to have sex with her, and she wasn't even good in bed. The irony was hilarious.

The sudden jolt of the plane touching down on the runway made her jump. How long had she been staring off into space? She hadn't even realized they were descending. When the seat belt light blinked off, she quickly unbuckled and waited for Sean to step aside so she could retrieve her luggage. He lifted it easily from the overhead bin but didn't object when she grasped the handle and tugged it out of his hand. He stood so close behind her she imagined she could feel the line of his long body pressed against her. Her heightened awareness of him became painful as she waited.

She exhaled in relief as the line of passengers began to move. When they reached the humid tunnel, Sean kept pace with her. He caught her arm as they entered the concourse. "Please have dinner with me."

She gave him the first excuse that came to mind. "I'm not dressed for Trio."

He shrugged. "You look perfect." He expertly herded her toward the moving walkway.

She halted and stood firm against the hand he placed on her lower back. All evidence to the contrary, she was not a sheep. "You wore a fancy suit on a transatlantic flight, so that you could take me to dinner in New York?"

"Yes."

"You don't think that's impractical? Or at the very least uncomfortable?"

His grin was as careless as his shrug. "I spend all day in a suit. Doesn't bother me. Casual wear was easier to pack anyway."

Olivia crossed her arms. Curiosity rose inside her. He had followed her, kissed her. Two months ago he had rejected her. Yesterday, he had propositioned her. Why had he changed his mind?

He leaned down to whisper. "Chef's tasting menu." She shivered but didn't take the bait. "Wine pairing," he murmured, urging her forward with an arm around her waist now.

Olivia dug in her heels and stared defiantly at the dry-looking sandwiches in the airport café display.

The air from Sean's sigh stirred the hair at her temple. "Let's make a deal. If I can't convince you it's a good idea to let me go with you to Italy, then I'll fly back to Norton tonight." She glanced up at him. The grim light in his eyes told her that he had conceded more than he wanted to.

"Deal." She took a step toward the walkway, but Sean held her back. His arms encircled her waist. He raised one hand to smooth her hair out of her eyes. Olivia felt her lips part.

A faint smile drifted across his lips. He didn't kiss her again.

# Chapter 3

A GLANCE AROUND THE POSH TRIO DINING ROOM confirmed that she was tragically underdressed. After a closer glance at the food as the maitre d' led them to their table, she didn't care. She couldn't wait to get a look at the menu. The room hummed with quiet murmurs and the clink of silver on china.

"Nothing with strawberries, please," Olivia requested after they had both ordered the five-course chef's tasting menu. Sean cocked an eyebrow. "Allergic," she supplied. Since he had promised to see her safely onto the airplane, with or without him, Olivia ordered wine paired with every course.

"Start talking, counselor." On the taxi ride from the airport, he had expertly ducked her questions and kept her busy talking about Marlene and Joe's upcoming wedding, but it was time to get some answers.

Sean nodded, swirled his pinot noir, and held her eyes with his calm, gray stare. "You were married," he finally said.

"Huh?" Was he serious?

He shrugged. "When you asked me to stay—you were still married to Keith."

She crossed her arms. "In name only."

"Sleeping with clients is unethical, Olivia, especially when you are negotiating a divorce. I don't like Keith, but I couldn't sleep with his wife."

Olivia added that to the list of ways Keith had ruined her life.

Sean's eyes gleamed. "Now, his ex-wife…" he continued. "I am all about sleeping with Keith's ex-wife. Anytime. Any place. Any country. Italy would be perfect." His lips curved in a wicked grin that made her believe she might have misjudged him. Power suits and reassuring courtroom presence notwithstanding, Sean might not be a safe choice after all.

She took a quick sip of wine, choked, then coughed.

He handed her a crystal glass of water. "See, that's why it's simple. I'm using the business I need to conduct in Italy as an excuse to follow you to Verona and indulge in the fantasies I've had about you since high school."

"Seriously?" she gasped.

His nod was slow and definite. "Crush doesn't even begin to describe how I felt about you. You walked into freshman biology and every other girl disappeared."

"But you never asked me out."

"I couldn't ask anyone out." He took a deep breath, released it. "My mother was a drunk and I couldn't leave my little brother home alone with her. I didn't dare bring anyone to the house either. I never knew when she'd be passed out on the couch or having a screaming fit." He shrugged. "The moments I stole with you were the only 'dates' I had until my mom got sober. You must have noticed that I stared at you in study hall, ate lunch at the table next to yours, and walked blocks out of my way so I could pass your parents' restaurant on the way to and from school every day."

She'd noticed—and wondered why he'd never made a move. Now she knew. And it broke her heart that she hadn't been self-confident enough to make an effort herself. It sounded like he'd needed a friend.

Sean cleared his throat, breaking the spell of the past. "But as I said last night, we're adults now. I don't have to take care of my little brother. You don't have to work. We're headed for one of the most romantic countries in the world, and I've wanted you for at least half as long as I've been alive. Put me out of my misery and say yes, Olivia."

The waiter set a plate in front of her.

She tore her eyes away from Sean's disturbing gaze and looked down at the table. Pure, professional awe eclipsed her personal freak-out. Well, professional awe and her well-developed gift for denial.

For a full minute, she stared at her plate. Then she picked up the fork farthest to her left and delicately assembled a bite of the exquisite smoked salmon salad, making sure to get a taste of every component onto her fork, particularly the preserved lemons. Food, she understood. Food, she could handle. She did not have the same confidence regarding this familiar stranger in front of her. She stole a quick glance across the table. Sean was frowning.

"What?" Olivia asked.

He picked up his fork and speared a shrimp on his plate. "Nothing."

---

Sean chewed, but he didn't really taste the food in his mouth. Oh, he was smooth, all right. Smooth like the freakin' Alps, no doubt about it. He didn't want her pity, he wanted to seduce her, but Olivia looked more bowled over by the food on the plate in front of her than by his proposition.

She had initially responded to his kiss on the plane but then froze in his arms. That did not bode well for his plan. He shook his head slightly, taking another bite and watching Olivia savor her food. She smiled a little every time her lips closed around the fork. Anticipation swirled inside of him as he thought about all the other ways he wanted to bring her pleasure. Her kiss had been so sweet—raw response mixed with hesitation. He wanted to kiss her again, over and over until she relaxed and opened to him. He wanted to know if their bodies would fit together as perfectly as their mouths—but first he had to convince her.

Olivia sighed and set her fork down with a clink. Immediately, a busboy swooped in to retrieve their empty plates. She took a long drink of her wine, then folded her hands in front of her on the white tablecloth. She met his eyes squarely. "I think you'd better tell me more about those high school fantasies, counselor."

His pulse jumped. Maybe he had a chance, after all. "Are you sure you don't want me to whisper them in your ear on the airplane?" She couldn't say no after they were in the air.

"Positive." She tipped her chin up, so her eyelids were at half-mast. Her expectant expression made him think of her head on a pillow, gazing down at him while he…

"Last chance to avoid shocking our waiter," he warned.

"You can't shock a waiter in a place like this."

Sean was certain she was incorrect, but out of public decency, he kept his voice low. He began to weave a fantasy, noticing that every server who passed within earshot of their table discreetly slowed his steps. Olivia attempted to taste the next course delivered by a wide-eyed waiter but dropped her fork with a clatter when Sean mentioned blindfold and gondola in the same breath. Still, he had to give her credit. After dropping her fork, she had focused her attention entirely on him and had barely twitched a muscle.

As he neared the end of his pitch, Olivia's head was cocked to the side and her eyes were glazed. He'd thrown in everything but the kitchen sink, hoping that something might pique her interest. She cleared her throat and straightened in her chair. "There aren't any gondolas in Verona. The canals are in Venice."

"A balcony would work. Plenty of those, right?"

Olivia picked up her fork, color rising in her cheeks. "I wouldn't have pegged you for the kinky type."

He lifted one eyebrow, unable to prevent the corners of his mouth from turning up. He encouraged his buttoned-down, by-the-book, technicality driven, Type-A, loophole lawyer image. He enjoyed arguing a point, any point, just for the sheer fun of it. He liked to be right. He liked to be in control. He liked to win. It had been impressed on him at a very early age that all of these things were necessary for survival, but the bedroom was not a courtroom. Control was necessary up to a point, of course, but buttoned-down lawyer guy disappeared with his tie.

She leaned forward. "Sean, I just don't get it. You had a prime opportunity last summer—"

"I told you, you were married."

"I've been under the impression that guys don't give that detail a lot of thought."

"Some guys don't." He shrugged. "I'm not your ex-husband."

She flinched and dropped her gaze. After a second, her eyes met his again. "You want me to believe you've been dying to have sex with me? That you rejected me a couple of months ago because I was barely married, but now you want to take me to Italy and blindfold me in a freaking gondola?" Her voice was soft, belying the intensity of her words. "Give me one good goddamn reason."

Sean let the desire that had sharpened inside him for years roll across his face. He reached across the table and brushed her hair out of her eyes. "I'll make you glad you did."

Her nostrils flared. "A better reason than that."

He hesitated.

He never put anyone on the stand unless he knew exactly what they were going to say, and that went double for his personal life. He had no idea how Olivia would react to the information he was about to give to her, and that made him nervous. Unfortunately, this felt like his last chance to convince her to let him join her.

"Your mother is expecting me," he said reluctantly.

The color drained out of her cheeks. For a minute, he thought she might fling her fresh glass of wine in his face. When she didn't even glance at the food the waiter gingerly placed in front of her, Sean knew he was in serious trouble.

"You called my mother?" Her voice rose unevenly.

"I'm afraid she'll be very disappointed if I don't arrive at Villa Farfalla. I got the impression she's eager for American tourists to discover the delights of her hospitality."

"No doubt."

"The villa sounds amazing. A sprawling estate, a vineyard, cooking classes with a famous chef, wine tours, a private spa…" Sean was actually looking forward to spending a week there, as long as he didn't have to do it from a shallow grave dug by Olivia, which is where it looked like he was headed.

"Spare me the propaganda. My mother is a brilliant businesswoman, but if you think I'm difficult, wait until you meet her. No detail escapes her attention."

Sean covered his elation with a frown. "Do you think she'll check your bed every night? That would put a kink in my plans."

"Your plans are kinky enough," she said darkly.

Sean chuckled. "C'mon, it'll be fun." He leaned across the table to take her hand. "I didn't mention I was arriving with you, but if I cancel my reservation, I'll feel compelled to give your mother a reason."

"That's blackmail."

"So sue me. I get free legal representation." Olivia's green eyes reminded Sean of the sky just before a tornado ripped across the horizon—lush, eerie, and dangerous to life and limb. He squeezed her hand. "All you have to do is say yes, Olivia."

―⁓―

Sean's thumb in her palm was making it very difficult to think. Each time it stroked across her hand, new tingles would start in another area of her body. Was it the wine or just him? Had she eaten anything for breakfast or lunch?

She shook her head. What had he asked her again? *Right*. How could she forget?

Sean wanted her to say yes. He had spun her well-deserved meltdown into a kinky, sun-kissed, wine-soaked vacation in a picturesque villa and almost made her believe it could happen.

He had no idea what he was walking into. For that matter, neither did Olivia. Her father would likely accept her behavior with his usual good humor, but her mother was another story. Her mother was going to go ballistic. In fact, having a human shield might not be such a bad idea. Maybe her mom wouldn't kill her in front of a guest.

Olivia concentrated on her tingling palm. Under the table, her toes began to curl. In all of her twenty-nine years, no one had ever made her toes curl. Certainly not her ex-husband, although by all reports he'd curled the toes of every other female who let him. For the first time, Olivia could see what all the fuss was about. She smiled into her wineglass. Maybe...

Not.

She knew from experience sex was not the easy romp Sean had just described to her. It was complicated. Embarrassing and confusing. Her smile flatlined. Better not to turn this into anything it wasn't.

Sean was still caressing her hand and waiting patiently. Well, he could wait, the cocky bastard. Any decision she made would be based on practicality, and she would not allow her judgment to be affected by her tingling palm or any other tingling parts either. Just to be safe, she pulled her hand away from him and picked up her fork, finally noticing the fresh plate in front of her.

"Olivia?"

"Patience, counselor. Jury's out for dinner."

—ᴍᴍ—

Exactly three hours and five incomparable courses later, her eyes flew wide as she caught sight of the digits on the bill that had just been delivered across the table. She barely managed to swallow the "Holy shit" that was on the tip of her tongue. She really couldn't let him—

"Don't even think about it." Sean frowned as she reached for her purse. He tucked his credit card into the check cover. "Would I bring you here if I expected you to pay for it? No way. It's my pleasure. Did you enjoy your dinner?"

"You have to ask?" She was pretty sure she had moaned aloud more than once.

"I just wanted to hear you say it."

"It was fabulous, Sean. Thank you. But are you sure you don't want me to—"

He shook his head and smiled at her, displaying the dimple in his chin. The irresistible dimple. In fact, she wanted to touch it. Sean caught the hand she raised toward him and pulled her out of her chair.

"Time to get back to the airport, darlin'. Italy is waiting." The question in his voice gave her pause. Or it would have, if she hadn't spent the last few hours replacing her blood with wine and then diverting all of it away from her brain and to her stomach, which was now busy digesting hundreds of dollars of prime seafood and extremely fine wine.

The pro and con list she had made in her head during dinner had come up dead even, but the wine was making her feel decidedly optimistic. She giggled as she allowed Sean to lead her out of the restaurant and into a waiting taxi. Her messy meltdown suddenly seemed less necessary than enjoying the company of the guy climbing into the taxi next to her. The guy with the dimpled chin and the fancy suit, the accommodating credit card, and the admitted desire for kinky sex.

Normally, that would have freaked her right out. She was not a kinky sex kind of girl. She was a boring sex kind of girl. An on-your-back-and-hold-still-until-it's-over girl. Frigid. Like ice.

A disappointment.

Forget it.

Olivia sat up straight on the taxi seat, lips tight, blood cold. She brushed her bangs out of her eyes and turned to Sean, ready to tell him no. All the wine in the world couldn't make her agree to do something that was guaranteed to bring more failure. One more failure would break her, which was the whole reason she was leaving in the first place.

Sean caught her fingers in his warm hand and brought them to his lips. Heat shot from her knuckles to her nipples and then, yes, lower. Tingling, swelling heat. Not ice. Not ice at all, in fact.

"Hmm," she mumbled as he leaned toward her.

She had never felt like this before. Sean smiled into her eyes just before his lips brushed hers, and she saw the silvery flash again. Her body responded, going loose and melting.

From an intellectual standpoint, this was fascinating. She felt like an observer, watching very strange behavior. Olivia Marconi did not make out in the back seat of a taxi. She had always been the good one, gingerly perched on the front bumper of whatever car

Marlene had been making out in. She was the lookout. The best friend.

Olivia Marconi certainly did not moan and press into the bold hand on her knee. Her panties did not slip wetly between her thighs. She did not throw her head back to invite teeth to graze her throat.

Olivia Marconi had clearly been missing out.

Sean's soft mouth on hers translated a foreign language. His thrusting tongue, no longer intimidating, explained the rules of an exciting new game. His hand on her breast awakened a fresh desire. Was it just the wine? If so, a bottle of wine per day could have saved her marriage.

She stiffened, brain trying to seize command of her renegade body. *This is not a good idea. I can't do this.* Sean pulled her closer, and it was impossible to reject the smile she could feel on his lips. He was still asking, seducing, waiting for her to answer. He wasn't Keith, and she suddenly didn't want to be the old Olivia. She wanted to say yes, wanted it badly enough to risk disaster.

Distantly, very distantly, she knew it was crazy to do any heavy thinking when her brain felt like it was operating six solid inches above her body, but Sean's lips felt heavenly. Like, astral heavenly. In fact, it didn't seem necessary to think at all when his mouth moved across hers and his tongue flirted in a way that made her heart pound.

She was tired of thinking all the time—sick to death of being terrified of her inadequacy while pretending everything was fine, that she was happy, successful. There wasn't anything Marlene couldn't do better at Chameleon. Nothing Joe couldn't do more efficiently. The restaurant was better off without her, but where did that leave her? She hadn't thought any further than Italy and the relief escape would bring her. What happened next?

With shock, she realized she didn't feel like crying anymore. Her hands fisted in Sean's jacket. *Damn it*. She couldn't even have a proper meltdown; it wasn't her style. Her approach was more along the lines of tighten the bolt until the wrench broke and make sure that sucker never cut loose again. The breakdown she had been planning wasn't going to happen unless she checked into a mental institution, and she just wasn't that far gone. Not quite. Not yet.

She needed to come up with a new plan for the rest of her life. The alcohol had cut through the fog that had kept her immobilized for months. What did she want? She had no idea. It was easier to name the things she didn't want—Keith, Chameleon, and failure, damn it. Her mother would just have to understand. Maybe Sean could provide a distraction while she decided how to break the news. His lips drifted over her jaw, feeding her hope. Yes, he was a very good distraction. Even if it was the wine talking, there was plenty of wine in Italy. She'd be well supplied.

"I've made my decision, counselor."

Sean froze against her. "Will you let me come with you?"

"Far be it from me to deny you an Italian vacation."

"So you're saying—"

*God help me*. "I'm saying yes."

# Chapter 4

OLIVIA WOKE SLOWLY. HER HEAD THROBBED. HER mouth was dry. She tried to stretch and found that she couldn't move anything but her neck, and even that felt like it was made of cement. She muffled a groan as she eased herself upright a quarter inch at a time.

Strong, warm fingers pressed firmly against the ache in her neck. A hand released the buckle at her waist and she sagged in her seat, resting her head against the vinyl side of the plane. She let Sean work the knots out of her shoulders for a few delicious minutes, but there wasn't enough residual alcohol in her system to let him continue indefinitely.

She turned around.

"Better?" he asked.

"Not even close."

"Take these."

He handed her a travel packet of ibuprofen and water. She hoped there was enough in the bottle to wash down the unfortunate sweat sock that seemed to be lodged in her throat.

"Hair of the dog?" Sean suggested slyly.

"Hell no, I'm never drinking again."

"That wasn't what I meant." Sean held her still and kissed her so thoroughly that Olivia was sure he'd find half a sweat sock in his mouth when she pulled away from him.

"You got me drunk," she accused.

"I didn't drink the wine for you, darlin'."

"Temporary insanity."

"Whatever gets you through the flight," he quipped.

"I'll be right back." She pointed at the airplane lavatory, needing a moment alone to assess the damage from wine consumption, bloating, and dehydration.

She made her way to the bathroom and locked the door behind her, peering hesitantly into the mirror. Not completely tragic. Her blond hair always looked exactly the same. Her skin was clear, although she looked faintly green under the punishing fluorescent light. She looked into her eyes, trying to puzzle out how she felt by gazing at her reflection. No clue.

She used the bathroom, washed her hands, then fished a tinted lip balm out of her purse and stroked it over her dry lips. She'd better get some more water into her body soon. Wine could only take a girl so far. She gulped to think about where it had taken her in the taxi.

The prospect of spending a week in her parents' house fooling around with Sean seemed improbable in the sobering light of the airplane lavatory. His interest was flattering—beyond flattering—but an affair spelled catastrophe. Was there any way to pretend that whole conversation hadn't happened?

Olivia turned to the door and caught a whiff of Sean's aftershave trapped in the crease of her neck. His scent shot a thrill straight through her. She lingered for another minute, reliving his kiss. She shivered, saw his eyes flash silver in her memory, wanted to kiss him again. Sean had made her feel like a different woman— someone adventurous, exciting, and carefree.

Could she be that woman with him?

Sadly, tragically, unfortunately, no. She couldn't fake sexy. She was still the same woman he'd rejected. Sure, he'd said it was because she was married and from the intensity in his kiss she could almost believe it, but that didn't mean it was worth the risk of disappointment. Hers or his. Resolutely, she unlocked the bathroom door.

—∿∿—

The door to the airplane lavatory opened and Olivia walked toward him. Her frown told him to expect trouble. Desire kept him still as she brushed by his knees and sat down beside him. His heart sped when her arm brushed his. She fastened her seat belt and stared straight ahead. "Listen, about what happened in the taxi…" she began.

He said nothing, waiting to see where she was taking her argument.

"I can't do this. It's just not possible. I, uh, the whole sex thing—it's not something I can do."

Sean reached out with two fingers to turn her face to his. "Can't do? Or won't do?"

Anguish shone bright in her eyes. "I have it on good authority that sleeping with me only rates slightly higher than watching grass grow." Her lips twisted in a self-deprecating smile.

*Her bastard ex-husband convinced her she is bad in bed?* Half the marital estate was too good for him. They should have taken him to the cleaners for making Olivia feel inadequate. Sean cupped her jaw, bringing her closer, wanting to reassure her in the most direct way possible. "Good thing I don't plan for us to sleep much."

She held him off with a hand on his chest. "I can't

handle any more complications, Sean. I can't—" Her teeth dug into her lower lip as she stared at him, mute and miserable.

He smoothed escaping strands of blond hair against her cheek and leaned toward her until their mouths were a whisper apart. "Of course you can," he murmured against her mouth as he closed the distance between them. Her lips were soft, and she tasted faintly of grapes. "It doesn't have to be complicated. It's just a vacation."

Her body relaxed beneath his palms, which had come to rest on her neck and her waist. She sighed, and he moved his lips to her eyelids then her cheeks. Her eyes opened. She looked at him with deep green eyes gone sleepy and he kissed her lips again, a quick, hard, possessive kiss, before he settled back in his seat.

Whatever Olivia believed about her sex appeal, he knew better. A simple kiss from her set him on fire, and he couldn't imagine what making love with her would be like. In fact, he'd better not even try or he was going to scare the flight attendant, who was approaching with her snack cart. Her ex-husband was an idiot, and he couldn't wait to prove him wrong. He'd spend the week showing her exactly how wrong, in as many ways as he could imagine, in even more ways than he had suggested in the restaurant in New York.

He glanced over at Olivia, who was pretending to be asleep again. He watched a pulse beat faintly in her neck. He itched to press his lips to that spot and feel the blood flowing through her veins. He couldn't believe his luck. He was on a plane to Italy with Olivia Marconi and there was nothing to keep them apart anymore.

As he'd mentioned in the restaurant, he hadn't wanted

any of his high school friends to meet his mother. He'd also been afraid they might tell their parents what was going on at his house. He'd worried every day that Child and Family Services would arrive on the doorstep and plunk him and Colin in foster homes. Keeping their lives together had been more important to him than dating or making close friends, but by the time Colin had been old enough to fend for himself, Olivia had been busy with college and the restaurant, then away at culinary school.

He remembered getting drunk when she came home from culinary school engaged to Keith. He'd been thrilled when she'd appeared in his office looking for a lawyer to handle Chameleon. His specialty was divorce law, but he knew enough about everything else to handle her business, and it gave him an excuse to talk to her now and then. Of course, handling her divorce had been an absolute pleasure—and ignoring her when she had hit on him had been the hardest thing he'd ever done.

Olivia sighed and turned her head. Her body slipped sideways, so he caught her with his arm and nestled her head on his shoulder. His heart thudded in his chest and he couldn't help a sigh of utter contentment. Her scent, fresh and flowery, drifted up to him, and he leaned to press his lips to her sleek blond hair.

# Chapter 5

THE LATE AFTERNOON SUNLIGHT IN ITALY WAS brilliant, as if God had put a lot of work into this part of the world and wanted it brightly displayed. Rectangular and pale, the enormous stone structure of Villa Farfalla graced the blue sky with its peaked, red-tiled roof. Gardens, greener than she had been expecting from late August in Verona, stretched out on either side of the house. The rounded Roman archways and tall, shuttered windows looked like romantic eyes on the front of the building. Patio furniture lazed on the front porch where cheery white umbrellas shaded the wrought-iron tables and chairs. The pictures her mother displayed on the website didn't do it justice—Villa Farfalla was stunning.

Too bad she was in no mood to admire the scenery. She had been panicking since the moment their plane touched down in Paris. She had spent their layover stress eating pastries, and the flight to Verona had been too short. Now they were pulling into the driveway. What was she going to say when her parents wanted to know how long she was staying? How was she going to explain Sean? What was she going to do after she told them she was finished with Chameleon? How on earth was she going to explain her apathy in the kitchen? Her cooking mojo had all but deserted her and there was no way her mother wouldn't notice. Her mother hated idle hands in the kitchen. What had she been thinking? She should have taken off for the Caribbean instead.

The taxi slowed, then stopped. She chewed on her lip and peered out the window.

Sean opened his door and slid out of the taxi. She could hear him thanking and paying the driver. Now their luggage was on the curb, waiting. Sean opened her door.

She fought off the anxiety that froze her muscles and slowly climbed out of the car. Sean tugged her out of the way and slammed the door behind her. The taxi sped off, raising dust from the dry road.

He put his bag over his shoulder and rolled her carry-on and suitcase behind him. "Let's go."

"Give me a minute," she muttered.

It was ridiculous to drag her feet after traveling for nearly twenty hours, but she wasn't ready to face her parents. Unfortunately, her hesitation didn't register with Sean. He motioned for her to precede him, then herded her up the walk toward the round archway that shadowed the door.

"Let me take something," she begged, needing to do something with her hands.

"I've got it. Go ahead. Open the door." Her feet felt heavy and her heart fluttered as she tugged on the elaborate brass handle.

It was cooler inside.

"Mamma?" she called.

"Olivia!" Her mother's voice flew from the back of the house, and her stout body barreled through a swinging door and into the foyer a bare moment later. She enfolded Olivia in her arms and the smell of basil and yeast was overpowering. The bones of her mother's shoulders were curved, felt brittle, and there was a new slackness to her middle, as well as a lot more silver in her blond hair. It had only been two years—why did her mother seem so much older?

Her mother squeezed her tighter. "You're not eating enough." The familiar criticism provoked instant regression. *Too skinny, too slow, too—*

Her mother stiffened. Olivia felt her mother's head swivel back and forth and knew she was searching over her shoulder. Her mother held her at arms length. "Where is your Nonna?" Her brown eyes were sharp. "And who is this?"

"Uh—" Olivia bit back a hysterical giggle as she quickly rejected several possibilities, trying to think of a delicate way to phrase Nonna's situation. She should have thought about *this* on the plane. "Well…Nonna met an old friend in Norton…and she wasn't quite ready to come home yet. She's coming for the Gala next weekend, I think." There. That sounded pretty good.

Her mother cocked her head to the side. Her gaze intensified. Olivia felt like the truth was plain on her face, inscribed on her forehead for her mother to read. *Nonna's shacked up with a mobster.* Finally, her mother blinked hard and let go.

Olivia stepped back to allow Sean room to hold out his hand to her mother. "This is Sean Kindred, my lawyer, and your new guest."

Her mother frowned. "Mr. Kindred! I wasn't expecting you to arrive with my daughter."

"It was a surprise for her too," he said.

*Understatement of the year there*, Olivia thought.

She heard a door swing open near the back of the house and looked up, hoping it was her father, usually only a few beats behind her mother. Instead, a dark-haired man wearing a black chef coat swept through the dining room and entered the hall. He stopped behind her mother, who gave him a broad smile and presented him with a flourish that instantly put Olivia's *uh-oh* meter on high alert.

"This—is Alessandro Bellin, our chef. A man who can cook."

Oh boy, she had walked into that one. Subtle, her mother was not. No wonder she'd given Sean the stink eye. She already had Olivia's next man lined up. Alessandro Bellin, the man who could cook, must have her mother's blessing in the kitchen, unlike Olivia's ex-husband who had repeatedly earned her scorn.

Alessandro took the hand she held out to him politely and used it to draw her forward to kiss her soundly on both cheeks in the Italian fashion. He brought the heat of the kitchen with him. The chef looked down at her, still holding her hand, making her wonder if he knew about her mother's romantic hopes for them.

"I have heard so much about you, Olivia." His English was subtly accented and made Olivia think of the elegant way snakes move, sinuous and mesmerizing. She couldn't fault her mother's taste in potential boyfriends, that was for sure. The chef had a full-lipped James Dean pout, a sexy mouth that looked as if it ought to have a cigarette dangling from it at all times. His brown, almost black, eyes danced beneath brows too elegant for a man's face, and his distinctly Roman nose was only eclipsed by the strength of his proud chin. He looked every inch the chef, God's gift to the kitchen and the world.

Inwardly, she groaned. Just what she needed— someone making her feel even less capable than she already felt. No doubt he was one of those old school protocol-conscious nightmares too.

Alessandro turned to Sean with a cordial nod, but he still didn't release Olivia. "Welcome to Villa Farfalla," he said in a tone that felt as proprietary as his grip on her arm.

---

Sheer perversity made Sean take Olivia's hand and pull her away from Bellin.

"I'll show you your *rooms*," Mrs. Marconi said, stressing the last word intentionally, he was certain. He wondered when and if she would connect him with the boy who had often cut through the parking lot of their restaurant, hoping for a glimpse of her daughter. Once, he'd even saved up enough cash for him and Colin to go in for dinner, just so he could watch Olivia bus tables. Colin had been about five and behaved badly, knocking over his water glass and dropping food all over the floor. Sean had avoided any attempt to eat there again after that.

Mrs. Marconi tugged her daughter away from his side and pulled her toward the stairs, leaving Sean to contend with their bags. Olivia shot a helpless glance over her shoulder, shrugging in apology and snagging her carry-on as her mother corralled her.

"I must get back to my stove." The chef shot him a look of amusement and disappeared toward the back again.

Sean threw his bag onto his shoulder and lifted Olivia's heavy suitcase. He trudged after them, trying not to outwardly fume. The chef had clearly been hitting on her.

"Where's Papà?" he heard Olivia ask as he reached the top of the stairs, somewhat behind them.

He didn't hear the response. The upstairs hall branched left and right. He went right, toward the sound of voices and stopped in front of an open door. A four-poster bed dominated the room, which was heavy on antiques and brocade. Sean set Olivia's suitcase inside the door.

"Mr. Kindred, if you'll follow me." Mrs. Marconi ushered him swiftly out the door.

They continued down the hall past several closed doors.

She stopped in front of the corner suite and unlocked the door, gesturing for him to precede her into the room.

The first thing he noticed was that his bed was even bigger than Olivia's. He stifled a grin. When he had booked it yesterday, the Montecchi Suite had been the only room available, probably because of the exorbitant price. He set his bag next to the bed and turned to thank his hostess.

She handed him the key. "I hope you will enjoy your stay with us, Mr. Kindred. Villa Farfalla guests are immersed in Italian culture from the moment they arrive at our estate. You can learn our language, as much as you wish, and our chef will be more than happy to instruct you on all aspects of the traditional foods that will be served to you each day." *Yeah, I'll just bet he will*, Sean thought as she continued. "My husband conducts daily tours of our small winery, which exports our private label wine to the United States. Our full-service spa, Bella Farfalla, is just down the hall. My niece, Giovanna, is an excellent massage therapist and aesthetician. I'll be happy to introduce the two of you at dinner. A staff member will always be available should you have any questions and Olivia is too busy in the kitchen."

Before Sean could muster more than a bemused nod, she gave him a tight smile and turned her back, stepping out of the room and closing the heavy door. Closing him in, he thought.

Sean crossed the room to the doors that led out onto a small balcony overlooking the back of the estate. He flipped the bolt and stepped out into the hot afternoon sun. He shrugged out of his jacket and unknotted his tie, tossing both onto one of the small chairs on the balcony.

Looking over the edge, he saw a tiled patio that wrapped around the back of the villa. Off to the side, a small garden boasted bright splashes of color. As he had half expected, a hammock swung in the shade of two trees. The vineyard stretched behind the house and down the hill as far as he could see. Just below the escarpment, he saw a well-camouflaged building that he guessed must be the winery. It appeared to be growing out of the hill, making him wonder if the wine cellars stretched behind the structure into the earth. Another building, more of a barn really, sat just at the edge of the vineyard. He turned his thoughts back to his immediate surroundings.

Villa Farfalla was posh, beyond posh. Everything around him underscored the casual luxury of people who took money for granted. He'd had no idea Olivia's family was so wealthy, but she must be used to it. She hadn't batted an eye at the wide expanse of pink marble casting a rosy glow over the foyer or the chandeliers dripping with jewels. She hadn't caught her breath, as he had, at the size of her bed or the opulence of her room.

He rubbed his eyes with his fists. His big bed was calling to him in a serious way. Jet lag was making him feel dizzy, but he wanted to get himself on the local schedule as fast as possible.

He checked his cell phone again, as he had a dozen times since they landed. Still no signal. His service provider had apparently lied. He'd have to figure out how to get a working cell phone as soon as possible. He trusted Colin to stay out of trouble but he didn't want to be out of touch, and he needed a working cell phone to keep in touch with Mr. Russo. He'd left the villa's number with his client, but time was of the essence. Who knew how long Mrs. Russo would stay in the Veneto region? He didn't want to have to chase her down to the tip of Italy's boot.

He heard a noise in his room so he ducked back through the doors, half expecting to see the talented Giovanna, sent by Mamma Marconi and armed with oil, hot towels, and strong hands. With relief, he saw Olivia poking her head in his room.

She shut the door behind her, scowling. "My presence has been commanded in the kitchen. I haven't even been in the building for ten minutes, and I get called in to work. My mother is something else."

"Terrifying," he agreed.

"You think so too, huh? Glad I'm not the only one." She joined him at the balcony doors and looked out the window.

"I'm sure she just wants you in the kitchen so she can spend some time with you."

Olivia's sigh turned into a choked laugh. "Give me a break, Sean. She wants free labor."

He shrugged. "So don't go." He put his arm around her shoulders and squeezed, intending to offer comfort, but she gave a little groan and leaned into him, making him want to offer more.

"Of course I'm going. I have to go. If I don't, it will upset the order of the universe. I spent a zillion years in school getting a business degree and a culinary degree because she told me to. Why would I balk at a little kitchen duty?"

"Why don't you get a massage in the spa instead? Your mother would approve. She was just in here extolling the skills of Giovanna. Your cousin, I presume?"

Olivia turned to face him. "Gia's here? I haven't seen her in years. She's always traveling."

He drew her forward against his chest and wrapped his arms around her, seeking the tight knots in her shoulders with his fingers. She froze and he thought she would pull away, but then his fingers hit a tight spot and she gasped and pressed closer, resting her head on his shoulder.

They stood silently for long minutes as his hands moved over her strong back. Her muscles were long and lean, ribs and shoulder blades prominent beneath her flesh. "You're not eating enough." He mimicked her mother's disapproving tone.

She giggled and he felt her tension ease a bit under his hands. Satisfaction glowed inside him. "That's better," he said.

She raised her face. Her eyes asked a silent question and no force on earth could have made him disappoint her. He bent his head and touched his lips to hers in a kiss so soft it felt like floating, yet so intense he hardened immediately. Need clawed his throat and the taste of her breath made him groan. He wasn't the only one. Olivia wrapped her arms around his neck. Her whimper blanked his mind to everything except the desire to get closer to her. He steadied her body with his and took slow steps toward the bed.

Dimly, he registered a sound in the periphery of his awareness but ignored it. When they bumped the mattress, he bent to lay her down, not losing contact with her mouth even for an instant. He stretched out on top of her, carefully sheltering her from the weight of his body. Her mouth opened under gentle pressure and her thighs widened to make room for him. He poured his gratitude for her welcome into his kiss, worshipping each delicate curve of her mouth with his lips and tongue. He reached for the bottom of her shirt, intending to pull it over her head.

She froze. "Sean—"

The noise at his periphery sounded closer and he realized it wasn't his pulse hammering in his ears.

"Mr. Kindred?" he heard Mrs. Marconi call, a second before the rapid knock came at his door again.

Olivia gasped, eyes wide.

Sean rolled to the side. "Quick—hide." She slithered over the edge of the bed and dropped onto the floor, ducking her head. He took a moment to straighten his clothing, betting the door would open before he reached it. He was right.

"Oh!" Mrs. Marconi exclaimed as he caught the door and prevented it from opening fully. "You startled me!" Her arms were full of folded towels.

"I could say the same."

"I wanted to make sure you had enough towels."

"Never too many, thank you." He held out his arms for the towels.

She dropped them into his arms. "Have you seen my daughter?" she asked, her voice sharp with suspicion.

He didn't confirm or deny, but he smiled and let the door swing wide enough for her to take a look around the empty suite. "Have you tried *her* room?"

She flushed. "Naturally."

He smiled. "If I see her, I'll let her know you're looking for her."

"*Grazie*." She spun on her heel, heading for the stairs. This time he locked the door.

He tossed the towels onto the bed and walked around to the other side where Olivia was sitting cross-legged on the floor, eyes dark. He held out his hand.

She stood without his help. "I better get down to the kitchen."

Disappointment flared inside him. "Tell her you're too tired from the trip."

"I slept the whole way here," she said.

"Your mother doesn't know that."

Olivia snorted. "My mother knows everything. Just ask her."

"Not everything. At the moment, she doesn't know where you are." He pointed at the towels on the bed. "If my memory of the website serves me correctly, there's an enormous Jacuzzi tub in my bathroom and I now have more towels than I could possibly use all by myself. Why don't we take a dip?"

She cleared her throat. "Sean, I don't think—"

"You think too much," he countered softly, closing the gap between them.

She held up her hand. "I'm sorry if I led you on, but I told you I'm not good at this. I just can't..."

Her tortured expression brought him back to his senses. "You'd better go to the kitchen then."

She blanched, making him instantly regret his harsh tone. He swallowed, wanting to reassure her. "I'm sorry, Olivia."

"It's okay." She nodded too quickly for him to believe she meant it. She kept her eyes on the floor, making him wonder what she was thinking. He was used to seeing her meet every situation head-on, with her eyes open and her head up. Again, he wondered. "What happened during your marriage, Olivia?"

Her eyes flew to his, and he saw something stir in their depths. "You handled the divorce, counselor. Weren't you paying attention?"

"Yes, I know Keith was unfaithful. We cited him for adultery and he didn't contest it. But what really happened? Did he do something to you?"

Olivia's laugh was a sharp burst of air. She shook her head. "No, he sure didn't. Not a thing."

Something in her voice made him want more answers, even though her expression was forbidding. "But you were intimate, right?"

Her eyebrows flew upward. "That is none of your business."

"Don't give me that."

She crossed her arms. "Define intimate."

"You had sex."

She burst out laughing again. "Keith had sex with everyone. That was the problem."

"Smart ass. You had sex with each other," he corrected.

She nodded, but her smile was sad. "At the beginning. When I found out he was sleeping around, I didn't want him touching me. No great loss. It wasn't…I didn't…" She sighed.

"Ah." It was inadequate but it filled the silence while he gathered his courage. "So that night when you asked me to stay, you were…" Words failed him again. His face must have said it for him.

"Desperate? Pathetic? Giving it one more shot?"

"And I—"

She cut him off. "Yeah, you did. Or as the case may be, didn't. But it's okay. It's fine."

No, it wasn't okay, and it sure as hell wasn't fine because she was sad, and at this moment he would do anything to remove the grief from her eyes, to erase the devastation that had been haunting her expression for months now. He reached for her again, but she stepped back.

"You told me to go to the kitchen, remember?"

He deserved that. He was reassured by the color in her cheeks and fire in her eyes, but he didn't want her to leave the room thinking about that night. "You can run, but you can't hide." He forced a teasing smile. "I've got plans, remember? I've said it before, but I'll say it again. Your ex-husband is an idiot. Whatever we do together will be unlike anything you've ever experienced, I guarantee it. So, fine, go down to the kitchen, but you can't escape my high school fantasies forever."

He pointed at the towels on the bed. "However, if you want to knot those suckers together to make a rope, we can escape from the balcony together. Your mother will never know."

She laughed and the happy sound made him smile too. "Not a half bad idea, Romeo, but I think I'll just suck it up." She paused at the door. "You'll be okay on your own?"

"Sure," he said casually. Better to be alone than in the kitchen watching Chef Smarmy put the moves on her. "I'm on vacation, after all. I can think of a half a dozen things to do until dinnertime. Hey, if I order a snack from room service, will you be the one to bring it up?"

"Only if you want me to poison it," she said as she unlocked the door and pulled it open.

# Chapter 6

OLIVIA SANK DOWN ONTO THE BENCH AT THE TRESTLE table in the upper kitchen and closed her eyes. Her body still ached from the effects of Sean's kisses. What had he said? *Whatever we do together will be unlike anything you experienced with him.* She shivered. No doubt. She was sure he was good in bed, but she was an utter disaster.

*A disaster according to whom?* The question popped into her head, and she considered it. Keith had been the one who didn't want to kiss her, didn't want to make love to her, and eventually stopped coming home to her. Keith had subsequently proven himself to be an authority on absolutely nothing. Was it wishful thinking to hope he was wrong about other things too?

She searched her memory, going back to their years in culinary school, trying to remember what had made her believe in Keith in the first place. He had come on strong, overcoming her reservations with fast-talking charm. He'd been a rule bender, a fast worker in the kitchen, a teacher's pet, and good girl that she was, she'd admired those qualities immensely.

Keith had convinced her he could run Chameleon, made her think that if they married, all her worries would be over. She had discovered too late that his slick charm disguised inability. He took shortcuts that ruined the food, insisting the fastest way to do something was the best way.

It had taken her two years to see through his façade and when she had, her restaurant had been in shambles — one more reason to be grateful to Marlene. Marlene had stuck around through two years of hell with Keith in charge and now she was in Norton cleaning up his mess. No, she was cleaning up Olivia's mess. She scrubbed her face against her palms as shame made her cheeks burn.

She had run away, and worse — she didn't want to go back. A real boss would have stuck around to earn back the respect of the staff, not fled. She needed to regain her self-respect, not indulge in a senseless affair with another man who made her feel weak and inadequate.

*Nice try.* Olivia sighed, catching herself in the lie. Sean *did* make her feel weak, but only in the knees. When he had laid her on the bed, his strength had made her feel strong too. His weight on top of her had made her feel protected and powerful. He didn't make her feel inadequate. He made her feel invincible, but maybe that was the problem. She didn't trust her own judgment anymore. The intense desire to be with Sean could be another sign of her imminent personal apocalypse.

So, where, exactly, did that leave her? Well, let's see — she was in Italy with a man who wanted to make love to her. She'd been summoned to the kitchen by her mother who was probably going to kill her. She had a boatload of guilt from her failed marriage, a stalled career, and no bright, shiny plan for her future. She felt her wheels begin to spin. What was she going to do?

Abruptly, she decided not to panic. The old Olivia would panic. The new Olivia, the one who had just been making out with Sean, was going to figure this out. Somehow. She sat up straight on the bench and pulled her shoulders back, taking a deep breath, letting the air fill her chest, forcing it lower, into her belly. She blew it out. One more slow breath.

She could do this. One plate at a time, right?

Sean was in his room, so she could ignore him for the moment. The rest of her life could wait too. That left her in the kitchen, alone, not a bad place to be at all. Olivia looked around.

The trestle table at which she sat was the focal point of the upper level. A wine bar sat against the near wall with bottles racked up to the ceiling. A narrow table-like ledge circled the room. There were high stools placed at intervals to create intimate seating arrangements. The top level gave the effect of a tiny restaurant dining room with a roomy chef's table in the center.

Her bird's-eye view of the empty lower level showed a more traditional production kitchen with stainless steel tables, another small dish room, and refrigerators, ovens, and stoves on both ends of the cooking space. She could easily picture smooth workflow from refrigerator to workstation, from workstation to table, from table to dish room.

The outer wall of the lower kitchen was made entirely of windows, filling the room with natural light. The windows, combined with the stainless steel tables, coolers and ovens gave the kitchen a sophisticated feel while the exquisite copper pots and sauté pans hanging above the stoves and the warm colors on the walls gave the room welcoming charm. The kitchen had been painted in shades of yellow that made her think of wheat waving in the wind. The burgundy and umber accents were reminiscent of red wine and rich, dark soil. The split-level teaching kitchen was beautiful as well as functional, with every piece of equipment placed for maximum efficiency. There was no arguing with the fact that her mother was a genius.

She heard a door slam and a voice getting rapidly louder. She wiped her fingers under her eyes, smoothed her ponytail, and stood, ready to face whoever was approaching. The upper-level door swung open, crashing into the wall, and Alessandro stormed into the kitchen, snarling into his cell phone. When he saw her, he stopped.

She watched cautiously as Alessandro made a visible effort to control himself. He spoke so quickly she could only understand about every other word of the Italian he spoke as he ended the call.

He dropped the phone in his pocket. "*Ciao*, Olivia. Are you looking for your mother?"

She offered him a brief smile. "I'm looking for someone to tell me what I can do to help with dinner," she explained.

"Is that so?" His eyebrows arched.

"I *can* cook," she assured him, wincing as her defensive tone brought a patronizing smile to his face.

"Of course you can, but everything is already prepared for dinner tonight…unless you'd like to chop some herbs?" he asked, in the manner of someone appeasing a child.

"Sure." She felt the smile congeal on her face.

He handed her a stainless steel bowl from the dish room. "The garden is along the side of the villa. We need parsley, rosemary, and basil. Do you know them?"

She blinked, thinking she had misunderstood his accented English, then realized he had indeed just asked her if she could identify parsley. "I'm sure I'll figure it out." She narrowed her eyes. There was always something to be done in the kitchen. Always. Why was he wasting her time picking herbs?

"Chef Alessandro?" she called as he strode down the shallow stairs and headed for the stoves. He turned his head and raised an eyebrow. "What's for dinner?" she asked.

"Some simple vegetables, cheeses and meats for antipasti, gnocchi, osso buco, and lavender gelato for *dolci*."

"Can I assume we'll have a gremolata with the osso buco?"

He swung around to face her fully. "Naturally."

"Is it done?"

"Of course."

"Just checking," she said, giving him a sunny smile as she headed out the door to pick herbs she now knew he didn't even need. Well, at least it was work she could do well. She snorted softly. No chance of failure here.

The herb garden at the side of the house was well-tended and neatly labeled in English and Italian. Only an idiot could fail to bring back the correct varieties. She picked until the bowl was full. He hadn't told her how much to gather and she wasn't about to go back into the kitchen to ask.

She moved down the row and began plucking the blooms from lavender gone to flower. It was too pretty to ignore and would look lovely as a garnish on his gelato. A drizzle of lavender honey would be perfect too, but she stopped the thought. Not her job, not her problem. She was just the herb girl. Still, she'd leave the flowers in the kitchen and see if they appeared on the table. She sighed, resigned to kitchen scut work while Alessandro looked down his Roman nose at her.

The sun was just beginning to drop as she turned back toward the kitchen door. A glass of wine sounded like heaven, but she didn't dare treat herself until the herbs were chopped. She entered the kitchen and set her bowl down on a workstation. Cutting boards, spatulas, tongs, towels, and wooden spoons were neatly lined up on a shelf under the counter. She reached for a towel, wet it, and laid it on the table underneath her cutting board to keep it from slipping. Then she pulled open the drawer in front of her, knowing without a doubt she'd find a razor-sharp chef's knife. Her mother thought of everything.

She set to work stripping rosemary leaves from stems. The sharp piney scent mingled with the smell of warm sunshine and reminded her of Sean's aftershave. Heat rose to her cheeks as she began to chop. Of course he would have to smell like something edible.

When the rosemary was finished, she used the flat of the blade to scrape it into a ramekin. She began to strip the leaves from the parsley stems. When she had a fluffy pile in front of her, she compressed it into a tight bundle and began to chop it into bits.

Alessandro entered the kitchen and paused beside her, just inside her comfort zone. She glanced at him, then back at her cutting board.

"You are as talented as your mother claims," he declared.

She kept her head down so he couldn't see her roll her eyes. It was freakin' parsley, after all. When she had her expression under control, she looked up at him but she kept her knife moving swiftly and evenly through the parsley. "Thank you. Perhaps you'll find some use for me," she managed to say without irony.

A sound drew their attention to the back door. Joy raced through her when she saw her father.

"Papà!" Olivia dropped the knife on the cutting board and launched herself at the man coming through the door.

She buried her face in his shirt. He held her tight as she tunneled into his arms. He smelled like sweat and earth, like wine and sunshine on clean skin. Oh, thank God, he was here. She hadn't known until this minute she needed him, hadn't known she needed shoring up until the dam broke and she finally wept on his shoulder. Chuckling softly, he drew her sobbing toward the back door.

The feel of his wide palm patting her back made her cry harder. How many times had he comforted her after some childhood disaster? How many days had she come home from school and told him all her miseries while he made her a snack in the kitchen at the restaurant? If only her current troubles could be so easily cured with a big plate of spaghetti. Her stomach rumbled.

Her father looked over his shoulder. "We'll have espresso and biscotti," he said to Alessandro.

More tears came to her eyes when her father treated her like an honored guest. "I have to finish the herbs, Papà."

His laugh was full of disdain. "What are you going to do with the herbs, *cara*, wash them with your tears? Cook if you like but leave the herbs to Marco, our dishwasher. He doesn't have enough to keep him busy at the moment." He led her out onto the back patio to a padded wrought-iron lounge chair. He sat, pulling her down beside him. "I heard you brought a man with you."

Olivia gulped. The door opened and Alessandro strode out with a tray. She waited for him to set it on the small table in front of them and go back into the kitchen. She picked up her tiny cup and sniffed, relishing the scent of the hot, rich brew. "Sean is my lawyer."

"Oh?"

"Yes." Olivia sipped too quickly and burned her tongue.

Her father raised an eyebrow. "You think that's a good idea?"

"No." She never lied to her father. It was a waste of time. She wasn't sure what else to add, though. She cleared her throat, paused.

He spoke first. "Why don't you take a break, *cara*? Let it settle. Give your heart time to heal. I assume that's why you're crying?"

Olivia gave a quick nod. Wise words. Good words. She should do that. Her heart was only half the problem, though. Her life was the other half. How on earth was she going to tell her parents she wanted to quit the restaurant? Every project they started turned into a huge success. Her mother would make Villa Farfalla famous. Her father had taken over the winery and was already exporting wine, whereas she wanted to hand over their family business to Marlene and Joe and…what? What did she want to do? The sense memory of Sean's kiss swept through her. *Other than that*, she told herself sternly.

She schooled her expression as her father's face became stern.

He crossed his arms, still scowling. "Your marriage… it is over?"

"The divorce is now final." Olivia looked down, examining the tile under her feet. Keith's utter betrayal had motivated Olivia to make it happen quickly. Two months and they were done. Finished.

It shouldn't make her heart ache, but it did.

"I'm sorry, *cara*."

"I never should have married him." She closed her eyes and shook her head. "I feel like an idiot." She slumped and let her head rest on the back of the chair. Her father touched her arm. She opened her eyes, dreading the judgment she expected to see. Instead, she saw sympathy.

"He was very charming, *tesoro*. He fooled us too. We don't blame you. In fact, we blame ourselves. We should have been there for you. We wanted to give you the chance to make Chameleon yours. We didn't want to interfere…"

"I know, Papà. I appreciate that." *But I failed*. She closed her eyes against the pain that knowledge caused. His approval felt like warm sunshine after a long Norton winter and she didn't want to step out of the light.

He grasped her hands. "You shouldn't have had to go through that by yourself."

"I wasn't alone. I had Marlene. I don't know what I'd do without her." So true.

Her father's smile was proud. "How is my other girl?"

"Fabulous as ever. You should see her and Joe on the line together. I swear they remind me of you and Mamma. They're that good."

"I'm glad she's happy." He gave her a searching look. "I want you to be happy too."

"I'm happy to be here, Papà. That's enough for me now."

She was glad when he turned to look out over the vineyard, and a wide grin softened his face. "Would you like to come check the grapes with me? It's nearly time to harvest the Amarone."

His excitement made her smile, but she shook her head. "Tomorrow."

He kissed her cheek before he rose and strode toward the vineyard. His passion for the vines reminded her of the way Marlene talked about Chameleon. Olivia sat up straight in her chair, lifting her face to the evening breeze. She inhaled deeply, smelling grass and the faintest hint of growing grapes in the air. Her espresso was cold, but she bolted it, licking the bitter brew from her lips. Cooking smells wafted across the patio. Wonder stirred inside her as she realized that for the first time in a very long time, the smell of food didn't make her feel tired.

---

Sean picked up the phone next to his bed and dialed for the operator, glad he could still access the contacts in his cell phone. When an operator came on the line, he recited Russo's number and waited for the call to go through.

"Mr. Russo, this is Sean Kindred," he said when Russo picked up.

"Why haven't you been answering your cell phone?" Russo sounded harried, as usual.

"No signal. I'm getting another phone tomorrow, and I'll text you the number as soon as I can. Do you have any information for me?" He hoped to keep this conversation brief.

"Marilyn is in Padua. At the Hotel Loggia Antica. Five hundred bucks a night."

Sean stifled a smile. Mrs. Russo knew just how to push her husband's buttons. "I'll Google it. Maybe I can catch her tomorrow."

"Why not tonight?'

"Jet-lagged. Why don't you send any new messages or pictures to my email? I'm sure I can find a computer around here somewhere."

"I'll do that. Let me know as soon as you have news." Russo hung up.

Sean replaced the phone on the table and left his room. As he descended the stairs, he admired the family photographs that lined the stairwell. He paused to take a look at a photograph of a hawk-faced boy picking grapes, wondering if that was Olivia's grandfather. The sun-dappled vineyard seemed to stretch for miles along-side him. There was so much peace and contentment in the photo that Sean stared at it for a long time before he continued down the stairs and out the front door, turning left to loop around the side of the villa. He could just see the roof of the building he had spotted from his bedroom window, so he continued along the path until he reached stone steps cut into the hillside.

The air was warm and smelled sweet. The lush green grass and tall evergreen trees glowed beneath the late afternoon sun. The cloudless blue sky looked full of promise. He checked his cell phone again, as if it would suddenly, magically, get a signal. So much for interna-tional roaming. He followed the steps down the escarp-ment until he reached the front porch of the building set in the hill. Business hours were chalked on a sign out front, so he assumed he didn't need to knock. A bell tinkled as he opened the door. He stepped inside.

The room was empty.

"Hello?" Silence.

He shut the door and looked around the long, narrow room. The walls held racks of wine bottles. Colorful displays featured all manners of corkscrews, diffusers, decanters, chillers, and everything relating to the enjoyment of wine. A wine list was chalked on the wall behind a small bar that showcased more beautiful rose-colored marble. Padded wooden stools sat at the bar and the atmosphere invited him to take a seat and choose a sample, although there was no one behind the bar to serve him.

He spotted a door at the back of the room and moved toward it. From the outside, the structure looked larger than could be explained by this shallow room. There must be more to see.

He knocked once before he turned the knob. Cautiously, he poked his head through the doorway. Still no sign of life, except for a quiet whooshing noise. He stepped into a narrow, dim hallway and peered into the first open door on his left.

It looked like a laboratory. Beakers, pipettes, and test tubes were scattered over the long counter. Cabinets lined the wall above the workstation. At the back of the room, racks held unfamiliar equipment. To his right, cardboard boxes were stacked to the ceiling and a basket held labels and packing tape. This must be where the wine was tested and later shipped.

He continued down the hall. The next room held a computer, a desk, a bank of filing cabinets, and a couple of chairs. Perhaps he could find someone to let him use the computer to check his email. He found two more doors at the end of the hall. The one at the very end was locked. He turned to the right and cautiously stepped into the last room.

A muffled sob broke the silence and he froze, half-way into the small kitchen. A dark-haired woman sat on a small stool next to an industrial-sized dishwasher. Her head was down.

The door whooshed shut behind him.

She looked up and gasped.

"I'm sorry." He offered a small smile of contrition. "I didn't see anyone out front, so I…"

She hurriedly wiped her eyes and ran her hands through her dark, curly hair. "I wasn't expected any visitors today! I'm so sorry. I came back here to wash glasses."

He shrugged. "It's okay. I'm not really a visitor. I came with Olivia Marconi."

She wiped her hands on a towel and rose, smiling. "I'm Olivia's cousin, Giovanna."

"Sean Kindred." He took her hand.

"Ah—the American. Zia Anna Maria mentioned you already." She chuckled.

"That can't be good. I didn't get the impression she liked me very much."

Giovanna's grin got wider and her dark eyes flashed with humor. "She's basically harmless." She pulled the handle of the dishwasher up and eased a steaming rack out of its middle. She slid a new rack into place and pulled the handle down to start the cycle again. "Come on, it's happy hour. Isn't that what you call it in America? In Verona, every hour is happy."

"I could tell that by your tears." He hoped she wouldn't take offense at his gentle teasing, and he was glad when she laughed and led him back down the hall to the tasting room.

She gestured toward the stools at the marble counter as she walked behind it. "Have a seat." She reached for two glasses, grabbing a bottle from the line up on the bar. "This one always cheers me up. High alcohol content."

The red wine swirled into the glasses. When she was finished pouring, she set the bottle down and raised her glass.

"*Salute!*"

He took a sip. It was full-bodied in the way he expected a red wine to be, but it didn't turn his cheeks inside out or suck all the moisture from his mouth. "What am I drinking?"

"Valpolicella, naturally. The lifeblood of Verona."

He tilted his head to the side, deciding that alcohol and jet lag made an interesting combination. He tried to count how many hours he'd been up, failed, and took another sip of wine. "I like it."

She nodded. "I've been all over the world and never found a wine I love more than this one."

"All over the world? I've barely been out of New York."

"New York is nice. I spent summers with the Marconis in Norton until I was thirteen. Then I went to boarding school. After that, University and beauty school. Lately, I've been traveling, but I'm broke. And tired. Getting old I guess. Anyway, I decided to come home and help Zia and find a nice Italian husband." She made a face. "So far it's not going as planned, but I think that's because I'm only attracted to wicked men."

Hence the tears, he supposed.

He picked up the bottle and poured more wine in her glass. "*Salute*," he said and she laughed. "I thought Verona was full of romance and happily-ever-afters, the home of Romeo and Juliet…"

She peered over the top of her glass at him. "Have you ever *read* Romeo and Juliet? Everyone dies!" She sighed. "Every time I hope it will end differently. I want Romeo to get the Friar's message. I want Juliet to wake up faster, so that Romeo doesn't drink the poison. I want *someone* to survive. It never happens, and each time the pain is exquisite. I love that play. Such passion."

"I think you just summed up your thing for wicked men right there. The ending is always the same." He smiled. "You must like it."

"I think you might be right." She tilted her glass and he watched her savor the garnet-colored liquid. She licked her lips. "Fortunately, wine is the sure cure for a broken heart."

"I thought it was time that healed all wounds."

"Wine is faster." She reached for a clean glass and pulled another bottle of wine out from under the counter. As she opened the bottle, Sean saw a familiar-looking hand-drawn butterfly on the label.

"Taste this." She poured red wine into the glass and handed it to him.

He sipped. "What am I tasting for?"

"Beauty and complexity—like the flight of a butterfly. The wine should take you on a journey and leave you feeling breathless and still—the way you feel when a butterfly lands on your hand. You can't hold it; you can only enjoy it. *Vivi nel presente!* Live in the moment."

He sipped. The wine was good but not awe inspiring. "I'm no wine expert, but I'm not getting that from this."

She poured the wine into the sink. "It just needs time."

"That label looks familiar. Is this one of your exports?" he asked.

She shook her head. "This is Zio Paolo's first Amarone, for private sampling only. It's too young to drink; really it shouldn't even be in a bottle yet. The rest of the vintage is still in barrels but we tapped a few bottles just for kicks. You might have seen one of our Valpolicella labels. Zio began exporting those last year."

He winced, realizing he must have seen the label the night Olivia had served him wine and asked him to stay with her.

Giovanna leaned toward him to whisper, even though there was no one else in the room. "Zio Paolo is going to recreate *La Farfalla*, I just know it." She sat back, looking pleased with herself.

"The butterfly?" he asked. "Like the one on the label?"

"Not just a butterfly. *The* Butterfly. The most incredible wine Verona has ever tasted. The one that gave the villa its name."

Her enthusiasm was catching. "Tell me more."

She refreshed their glasses. "Over fifty years ago an exquisite wine was created. The vintner had such high hopes for it, he named it La Farfalla—the Butterfly. Of course, no one knew what it would become because Amarone needs at least two years to mature—but it became the perfect Amarone."

"What's Amarone?" he asked.

"The king of Valpolicellas. Complex. Special. Valpolicella is best drunk young, but the Amarone can take age, and when certain techniques are employed, it can withstand decades. La Farfalla is such a wine."

Intrigued, Sean asked, "What kind of techniques are you talking about?"

She raised her hands. "No one knows. The vintner's son got old man Conti's daughter pregnant just before the vintage had been tasted. There was a huge scandal, a shotgun wedding was planned, and then the vintner and his son disappeared. That season the grapes were picked, dried, fermented. The wine was barreled and bottled, but it wasn't the same. Neither was the Conti family. Sofia's heart was broken and La Farfalla's secret was lost."

"That must have been devastating."

"The Conti family continued to make wine, but eventually La Farfalla came to mean something entirely different here in Verona. It means…gone, like the vintner, like the vintage. Ironically, Sofia Conti's daughter ended up getting pregnant out of wedlock many years later—by a grape picker who moved on with the harvest. You can see why the butterfly thing stuck, hmm?"

"Why didn't they change the name of the villa?"

Her laugh was dry. "It doesn't work that way around here. Everyone knows everything. When Nonna bought the estate from Sofia a couple years ago—"

Sean raised his glass. "Wait, I thought the villa had been in the family for years."

Giovanna shook her head. "That's just what it says on the website."

Sean chuckled. "Nice."

"Our family has always lived in Verona, but the villa and the vineyards belonged to the Contis. Nonna bought the estate and moved back here with Zia Anna Maria and Zio Paolo when Olivia took over the restaurant in New York. They are trying to reclaim the name La Farfalla and make it mean something beautiful again. Unfortunately, it's been one problem after another lately."

"Really?" It looked pretty successful to him. "What kind of problems?"

"Cash flow. Staffing. Broken equipment. Bad luck. Nothing unusual for starting up a new business, but it's been two years, and the newness has worn off. I think Zia has bitten off more than she can chew. That's part of the reason I came home, although Zia would probably drink poison before she'd actually ask anyone for help."

"That reminds me of someone else I know. Like mother like daughter?" he asked.

"Exactly."

He nodded, thoughts returning to her story. "What happened to Sofia and her daughter?" he asked.

"Old Sofia passed away just after Nonna bought the estate. The daughter had been gone for years—an accident, I think. I don't remember."

"And her child?"

"A son." She cleared her throat. "Too long a tale for now. Unless you want another glass of wine?"

Sean shook his head. The room moved with him. "Better not."

"Ah, well." She picked up their empty glasses and set them in a rack under the counter.

She pulled a cell phone out of her pocket and glanced at the display. "Oh! It's almost time for dinner. I'll walk with you so I can see Olivia again, but I won't be able to join you for dinner. I have a date."

Sean gave her a look. "Another wicked man?"

"I'm optimistic about this one." She tucked her phone into her pocket. "Speaking of eternal optimism, tomorrow night is the last performance of *Roméo e Giulietta* at the Arena. You and Olivia should go."

"That's a wonderful idea. Is it easy to get tickets?"

"Zia always has tickets."

"Great." Sean pulled his own cell phone out of his pocket and showed it to her. "No signal," he said. "Any advice?"

She grinned. "I can't tell you how many times that's happened to me in foreign countries. You need to pick up an Italian phone in the market and get a new phone number for your stay here. American phones rarely work in Italy, no matter what they tell you back in the States. Even if you could get it to work, the bill would give you a heart attack. Better to spend a few Euros on a new phone. In fact, buy one before you get here next time. They sell them in the States."

He rolled his eyes. "My carrier told me it wouldn't be a problem as long as I paid the fee." He wondered if there was a chance to kill two birds with one stone. "Any chance there's a market in Padua? I need to catch up with a client, or rather, his wife."

"You're in luck. Padua has an excellent market and it isn't far away."

"Can I walk?" he asked, hoping his luck would hold.

She laughed. "Not quite. Take the train or ask Zio Paolo to give you a ride."

"I'll do that, thanks. Do you think someone will let me use a computer tomorrow?" He'd need a map to find the hotel.

"You can use one now, but you'll be late for dinner."

"Tomorrow is fine. I'm starving." A sudden thought made him smile. "You're the villa masseuse, right?"

She nodded.

"I don't suppose you have time for a new client this week?"

"You don't think Olivia will mind?" Her wicked laugh sent a prickle of apprehension skating just below the surface of his thoughts. A beautiful woman laughing like that should give him ideas, but the only thoughts he had were of Olivia. "Not me—your cousin. She's so tense she practically vibrates. Think you can de-stress her?"

"Absolutely. In fact, I insist. On the house."

"No need for that."

She shook her head. "I don't charge family."

"I'm not family," he countered. "Let me pay for it. Please. I'd love to help fund your future travels."

Her lips twitched. "In that case, are there any other spa services you'd like to arrange for her? If she hasn't changed in the last five years, she's disgustingly beautiful but has been cutting her own hair and nails—with a paring knife."

"Give her whatever she wants or whatever you think she needs."

Giovanna was openly grinning now. "Any particular colors or scents you prefer?"

"This is for her, not me," he reminded her. Or was he reminding himself? The thought of Olivia spending the day getting scrubbed, smoothed, relaxed, and slathered with good-smelling lotions roused something primal inside him. He ignored the temptation to admit he had a thing for painted toenails. "Make her happy."

# Chapter 7

OLIVIA RETURNED TO THE KITCHEN DETERMINED TO finish chopping the herbs before her father emerged from the vineyard for dinner. She stopped short when she saw her mother and Alessandro glaring at each other over the prep table nearest the stove. They ignored her, so she walked silently to her cutting board, thankfully on the other side of the kitchen, and began to work.

Her mother put her hands on her hips. "Don't be ridiculous. Of course you will teach the guests. That's why they are coming—to learn how to cook." Her words were staccato, like the sound of Olivia's knife on the board.

Olivia glanced up to see how Alessandro was taking her mother's tone. Not well. His nostrils flared and he drew himself up to his full height. Even with the table between them, he dwarfed her stout mother, who ignored his huffy display and bent her head to the pasta on the table in front of her.

Oh boy. Why hadn't she fought off the compulsion to return to the kitchen? She would have gladly accepted the guilt for shirking her responsibility in order to avoid this little collision.

"Anna Maria, I'm a chef, not a teacher. I told you that."

"You told me you would do anything necessary."

"And you told me that you would handle the classes if I wrote the menus. I wrote the menus."

"Which makes you the best person to teach them," her mother said, eyes gleaming with satisfaction.

Olivia couldn't prevent the small smile that quirked her lips. She met Alessandro's eyes and was surprised to see he echoed her amusement. So he had a sense of humor, huh? He raised an imperious brow and tossed his head in her mother's direction as if to say, "Impossible, that one." Olivia gave a small shrug of agreement. Her mother laid down the law with impunity and complete comfort. Her arrogance was maddening and admirable at the same time. Alessandro turned on his heel and disappeared into the walk-in cooler. Olivia had used that trick too. She wondered if he would count to ten or twenty.

Her mother glanced up from the bigoli.

Olivia froze. She recognized that look.

Olivia shook her head. "Oh, no." Her heart began to thump.

"*Perfetto!* I can't believe I didn't think of it before." Her mother dusted the flour from her hands.

"Think of what?" Alessandro asked as he stepped out of the walk-in.

"Since Olivia failed to bring her grandmother home, she will take her place and teach the classes with you."

Panic welled up hard in Olivia's chest as she fought to think of words that would convince her mother not to make her do this. This is exactly what she had been trying to escape in New York, the pressure of people looking to her for guidance, for answers, asking her to tell them what to do. She didn't want to be in charge, damn it. She wasn't good at it.

"No." Alessandro crossed his arms. "That isn't

necessary. I'm sure your daughter is a very good cook, but we just met. If I have to do this, I want to do it alone."

His flat refusal should have made her thank her lucky stars but instead it made her hackles rise. Who the hell did he think he was, trying to keep her out of the kitchen? Her knife moved faster on the cutting board. Of course she could teach cooking classes. She might not be familiar with his recipes, but food was food and she could cook anything. She just didn't want to.

Her mother made a sound of utter derision. "You forget your place, Alessandro Bellin. You may be the chef, but this is still my kitchen. My daughter will not be in your way. In fact, you'll be lucky if you can keep up with her."

Olivia caught her breath. *No pressure there.* She looked down at the herbs on her cutting board and saw they were bruised and black from too much chopping.

"I don't think that's going to be a problem," Alessandro said, pointedly staring at the herbs. She pressed her lips together. God, how arrogant could you get? She hid the ruined basil with her hand, then wished she hadn't as her motion drew her mother's glance to her cutting board. She felt her cheeks redden.

"Olivia, what have you done to that poor basil?"

"I killed it, but don't worry. I won't massacre herbs in front of *our* students."

Her mother smiled forgiveness. Oh God, she'd really done it now. The decision to help had clearly been made in some part of her brain that was only capable of action, not intelligent thought. Shit.

She looked over at Alessandro. If looks could kill, the one he was giving her would do the trick. For some reason that made her feel cheerful, and she smiled sweetly in return. Suffering through a cooking class would be worth showing her mother's pet hotshot he wasn't God's gift to the kitchen.

Her mother wrapped the bigoli and put it in the freezer. "You will make a beautiful team. The first class is on Sunday," she said, before she swept up the stairs and out of the kitchen.

Two days? Yikes. Olivia scraped the basil into a plastic container. It couldn't be used for garnish anymore, but it could lend its flavor to something that didn't have to be pretty. She tucked it into the reach-in nearest the stove, trying not to laugh at Alessandro's expression. She'd had a lifetime to get used to her mother's force of will, but poor Alessandro looked a little shell-shocked. She almost felt sorry for him.

Anna Maria Marconi was nearly impossible to thwart, not that Olivia had ever actually tried to go against her mother's wishes. Just as she had told Sean earlier, she had gone to business school and culinary school on her mother's say so. After graduation she had accepted the gift of Chameleon without protest. She had never thought about what to do with her life because her future had been mapped out for her. Well, she was thinking now. Soon, she would know what it was like to cross her mother too.

A sharp ringing broke the tense silence and Alessandro slid a cell phone out of his pocket. "Excuse me," he said, striding toward the patio door.

Olivia watched him through the windows as he paced back and forth outside, frowning. Where was the too-charming chef who had welcomed her to the villa this afternoon? He'd certainly changed his approach when she had dared to enter his kitchen. Territorial chefs drove her nuts. In her recent experience, big egos disguised even bigger insecurities. Keith had been a prime example of that. He'd never wanted help, and she'd been too timid to force the issue, instead letting him destroy her restaurant.

Now she was stuck in the kitchen with a chef who appeared to be even more set in his ways. She glanced at her watch and wondered what Sean had been doing for the past hour. She hoped he'd found his way to the dining room and was enjoying a pre-dinner glass of wine. Even better, she hoped he had one ready for her. A little Dutch courage would mask her anxiety about the cooking classes. *Faking it is what you do best.* She sighed. *Not anymore.*

She heard the patio door swing open and looked up, expecting it to be Alessandro. It was her father. "In the kitchen again, *cara*? I had a feeling I would find you here. There must be wine in the dining room by now. Let's have a glass and celebrate your homecoming."

"My thoughts exactly." *Well, sort of.* She wiped her knife and placed it back in the drawer, then picked up her cutting board, and dropped it into a dish rack. She followed her father up the stairs and through the door he held open for her.

In the dining room, her father lifted a bottle of sparkling wine out of an ice bucket on the sideboard. He wiped it off with a towel, then twisted the bottle. She heard a soft hiss as the cork let go.

When she'd left Norton, she'd been ready to explode but, like the cork her father had just popped, getting away from Chameleon had removed the pressure. Without the weight of her life in Norton dragging her down, she felt possibilities fizzing to her surface like the perlage of bubbles rising in the prosecco.

---

Giovanna took Sean into the villa through a side door. A short hall led them to the casual room he had glimpsed from the foyer when they arrived. There were several comfortable-looking couches, a big-screen TV, and lots of small coffee tables covered with food-related magazines. Bookshelves held cookbooks, and there was a bar along one wall.

He followed her through the room, across the foyer, and into the dining room, where the table was set with china and silver. He counted at least three wineglasses for every plate. Great, just what he needed—more wine. Olivia's parents would be very impressed when he fell face-forward into his plate and began snoring. He spotted Olivia standing near the kitchen with an older man with black hair.

"Olivia!" Giovanna exclaimed and bounded across the dining room.

"Gia!" Olivia wrapped her arms around her cousin. "How are you? God, it's so good to see you. Where have you been hiding since I got here?"

Giovanna laughed, returning the enthusiastic hug. He reached them in time to hear her whisper, "I stay out of the kitchen or your mother puts me to work." Louder, she said, "I work in the tasting room in the afternoons. I can't stay for dinner. I've got a date tonight, but we'll have plenty of time to catch up tomorrow. Your man booked you into the spa." She rubbed her hands together with a gleeful smile.

"He what?" Olivia wheeled around.

Sean shrugged, trying to look nonchalant.

Giovanna grasped Olivia's hand and turned it over. "What have you been doing with your fingernails? Peeling potatoes bare-handed?"

Olivia snatched her fingers out of Gia's grasp and hid them behind her back. "I work with my hands. They don't have to be pretty to get the job done."

"I work with my hands too, but mine don't look like I've put them through a wood chipper."

A low chuckle drew his gaze from the women.

The older man raised his chin. Sean identified him instantly as Olivia's father. His features were harsh, where Olivia's were delicate, but the clear, green eyes branded them both.

Sean held out his hand.

"Papà, this is—"

"I know who this is." Mr. Marconi took his hand. The handshake was so brief as to be insulting. Sean looked to Olivia for a cue and found her glaring at her father. She shot an elbow into Mr. Marconi's side. "Welcome to the villa," he said grudgingly.

"Thank you," Sean said with the same ironic intonation.

Olivia pressed a glass into his hand and he took a grateful sip. It bubbled and fizzed against his tongue. "Champagne?"

He heard a hiss from Mr. Marconi.

"Prosecco," Olivia corrected.

"Right," Sean said. "Italy. Must be the jet lag."

The door to the kitchen swung open and Alessandro

entered carrying a platter in each hand. He set them on the sideboard and silently returned to the kitchen.

Giovanna touched her uncle's shoulder. "Zio, do you still have season tickets to the opera? The last performance of *Roméo e Giulietta* is tomorrow night. Don't you think Olivia should go?"

"An excellent idea!" Mrs. Marconi proclaimed as she entered the room from the central hallway. "You have not seen *Romeo and Juliet* until you have seen it in the Arena, and I have a block of seats reserved for villa guests."

Sean took Olivia's hand. "Sound good?"

"Sure." She smiled up at him, smelling like parsley and another herb he couldn't identify, something that reminded him of black licorice. He leaned closer to see if he could get a better whiff of the elusive scent.

Mrs. Marconi cleared her throat loudly. "I'm sure Alessandro would be delighted to escort you. You can talk about the cooking classes."

Olivia's eyes snapped to her mother. "I'm going with Sean."

"A foursome, then. Giovanna will be happy to go too."

Sean looked at Giovanna. From the look on her face she would be anything but happy to join them, but she didn't protest, at least not aloud. Her dark eyes shot a glare at the chef, though. Was he one of her bad boys? Or was that just wishful thinking because it might keep Bellin away from Olivia?

"That sounds like fun," Sean said cautiously.

"Then it's settled." Mrs. Marconi nodded her head firmly. "Olivia, we have a full house this weekend. I'll need your help in the kitchen during the day tomorrow."

"Of course, Mamma, but—"

"Nonsense!" her father broke in. "She just got here. All work and no play, eh? Let Olivia settle in. Alessandro is capable of doing the work we hired him for, yes?" Sean noticed a subtle threat in his tone, as if the chef, or perhaps his wife, would be in trouble if Alessandro were not capable of accomplishing his tasks.

While Mr. and Mrs. Marconi continued their debate, Sean gave Alessandro the long look of warning that had been boiling inside him all afternoon. The chef shrugged, a faint smile tilting his lips before he turned and headed back to the kitchen.

Sean felt a hand on his arm and he automatically followed Olivia as she dragged him and Giovanna toward the buffet table.

"I'd only put up with that punk for you, cousin," Gia muttered under her breath.

"You could have said no," Olivia whispered furiously back.

"To your mother? Not worth it. I don't have plans tomorrow night, and she knows it. Plus, I love the opera."

Sean left them to argue and grabbed a plate. His mouth watered at the sight of the cured meats, cheeses, and marinated vegetables on the platters. Suddenly, he was starving. He filled a plate and stood back, resting his hip against a dining table chair, and chewed blissfully. Oh, perfection. The olive oil was unbelievable. Fruity. Light and rich at the same time. He paused between bites to clear his palate with a sip of bubbly wine. He reached for another roasted pepper, a slice of mortadella, then a slim wedge of hard cheese. He could make a meal of the offerings on this table.

Alessandro entered the dining room. "*Il primo piatto* is served."

"Alessandro isn't joining us?" Sean asked as the chef withdrew to the kitchen.

Mr. Marconi shook his head. "He prefers to serve."

As the group began to settle around the dining room table, Giovanna hugged her cousin again. "I must go. I'm late for my date. See you tomorrow!" She grabbed an olive on her way out of the room.

"I can't believe you booked me into the spa," Olivia groused as she sat down in the chair he held out for her.

He sat beside her. "I thought you would love the idea."

"You did not," she retorted.

"I thought you might enjoy being out of the kitchen?" The plate in front of him held a small pile of round dumplings in a reddish-brown sauce. The scent rising from the plates was rich and meaty. His mouth began to water again. He looked around the table and picked up his fork, waiting for everyone to be seated before he took a bite.

Mrs. Marconi ignored her food and glared at her husband. "Olivia doesn't have time for the spa. I need her help in the kitchen."

Olivia gave him a look that said "See?" and picked up her fork.

"She didn't come here to work, Anna Maria." Her father's voice was stern.

"Of course she did. What else is she going to do?" Mrs. Marconi's confusion sounded sincere. Sean kept his head down and speared one of the little pillows on his plate. He popped it into his mouth. Delicious. He hadn't been sure what to expect from the unprepossessing pile of rugged dumplings, but they were fantastic, lightly tossed with a tomato-based meat sauce that had an intriguing sweetness. "What is it?" he whispered to Olivia.

"Gnocchi," Olivia said.

"A Veronese specialty," Mrs. Marconi added.

"Fabulous," Sean assured them both. If the rest of the food was this good, he was going to eat himself silly this week.

He took a sip of the red wine he found in his glass. When had that been poured? The light, peppery wine was a magnificent match for the rich gnocchi. He felt eyes on him and he looked up and shrugged. "It's so simple, but it's perfect."

Olivia's father nodded grudgingly from the other side of the table. He held up his glass. "Simplicity is the soul of Italian cooking. Flavor. Color. Texture. Some foods become something more when they are eaten together…and with the right wine…bliss."

Sean nodded in wholehearted agreement. He felt like he already had one strike against him and he was glad they had found something to agree on. "Giovanna told me you are recreating a wine. How is it going?"

"Slowly." Mr. Marconi's brow became even more hooded over his sharp eyes. *Make that two strikes*, Sean thought philosophically, returning his attention to his food.

Olivia stepped into the breech. "I'm so happy she's here. I've missed her."

"She probably won't stay long, but it's nice to have her," Mrs. Marconi said. "Spend the morning with your cousin, Olivia," she relented. "You can help me in the afternoon."

Sean sat back in his chair as Alessandro removed the plates from the table. He smiled at the chef, feeling magnanimous. "The gnocchi was excellent, Alessandro. What was in the sauce? Veal?"

The chef shook his head. "No. A Veronese delicacy." He smiled and returned to the kitchen for the next course.

When Alessandro returned, he carried three plates stacked on his left arm and another in his right hand.

"Osso buco," Olivia whispered. "Veal shank and polenta."

The rich scent of buttery polenta rose from the plate. The meat fell apart at the touch of his fork and he took a bite. Even with the fresh herbs and lemon zest sprinkled around the edges of the plate, it was indecently rich. Suddenly, he was starving again.

He hated to admit that Bellin's food was every bit as good as the meal he and Olivia had enjoyed in New York. Actually, it was better. For all the technical brilliance and artful elegance of the foams and spumes, Sean much preferred food grounded in simple tradition. He swirled the red wine in his glass and sniffed, anticipating the way it would wrap itself around the flavors already in his mouth. He took a sip and let the liquid flow over his tongue before he swallowed.

"How is Chameleon, Olivia?" Mrs. Marconi asked.

"Joe and Marlene have it covered. Those two are like lightning in the kitchen." Olivia picked at her veal shank. She cleared her throat and set her fork down on her plate. "Mamma, I—"

The door to the kitchen flew open with a bang and Alessandro entered the dining room, carrying an open bottle of wine and a pitcher of water. Sean leaned aside to allow him to pour yet another glass. Surprisingly, he didn't feel drunk, just very mellow. "Thank you," he murmured, taking Olivia's hand under the table. She didn't pull away and that small victory filled him with pleasure. Her hand felt strong. Her fingers were long and delicately shaped. He rubbed the hollows between her knuckles and caressed the space between each finger. He rested his fingertips on the pulse in her wrist and felt it beat, slow and steady.

Mrs. Marconi raised her glass. "Yes, Olivia? Were you saying something?"

Olivia shook her head. Tentatively, her fingers began to explore his in return, a whisper-light caress that made him forget to eat, his attention completely focused on the subtle dance of their hands beneath the table. It seemed to him as if their hands were making love. Did she feel that way too or was he reading too much into a little hand-holding? Her thumb slid into his palm in an unmistakably sensual motion.

He forced himself to move his fork to his mouth and eat.

Mrs. Marconi was speaking and Sean hoped he was managing to nod and smile in all the right places. His thoughts were miles away from the events of the upcoming week and his heart beat unevenly in his chest. Clearly the alcohol had stripped his inhibitions because it was taking every ounce of self-control he possessed to keep from pulling Olivia away from the table. He wanted nothing more than to finish what they'd started that afternoon, before her mother had knocked on the door.

Alessandro removed his plate from the table and Sean realized he'd eaten every bite without tasting a thing.

Now that was tragic. Olivia was carrying on a conversation with her father. He brushed his palm over the back of her hand and watched a tiny shiver shake her before Alessandro stepped between them to deliver dessert, and Sean was forced to drop her hand.

Sean couldn't imagine having room for more food, but he didn't want to seem rude. He nudged some purple flowers out of the way with his spoon.

"It's lavender. Edible, I swear," Olivia whispered.

He arched an eyebrow at her and scooped up one bite of the pale purple ice cream. He raised the spoon to his lips. From its appearance, he expected it to be grapey, but the flavor was complex, more floral than fruity. The grape was there, but it hummed in the background, more scent than taste.

"I love it." He took another bite because he couldn't stop himself. He wanted more of the flowery perfume that hit his tongue and his nose at the same time. "It reminds me of something." He closed his eyes and took several deep breaths, trying to pull the scent from his memory. Whatever it was, it was giving him an erection. His eyes popped open at the realization.

He glanced at Olivia. She gave him a tiny smile. "I picked the flowers today. I'm glad Alessandro found a use for them."

"Beautiful," Sean said, not talking about the flowers. He smiled and took her hand beneath the table again.

—∿∿—

Olivia had no idea hand-holding could be so erotic. The way Sean's fingers glided down her palm should be illegal. She swallowed, wondering if he could tell her heart was racing. From the slight curve of his lips, she imagined he could. She stole another sideways glance and saw he was watching her eat her ice cream. His eyes held a wicked gleam. Her parents seemed oblivious to the play happening under the table. Her father was staring out the window at the vineyard and her mother was busy outlining Olivia's list of responsibilities for the week.

"Our guests arrive at various times tomorrow. We also have a morning tour of the vineyard followed by a five-course lunch for the Garden Club. I'm sure Alessandro has the lunch under control, but you can help with dinner after you're done with your cousin. I'd appreciate it if you didn't stay out too late after the opera tomorrow because the cooking classes start on Sunday, and we'll be in the kitchen for most of the day. A limited room-service menu will be available tomorrow for anyone who prefers to eat in their room."

Olivia blinked hard and picked up her spoon. It was hard to shift into work gear when Sean's fingers were making her head buzz. The wine wasn't helping her either.

Alessandro silently placed tiny cups of espresso next to each of them. "I'm afraid I must take the afternoon off tomorrow. A family emergency."

Mrs. Marconi's eyes sharpened. "Dinner isn't going to make itself."

Alessandro shrugged. "I am sorry. It can't be helped. I will make everything ahead of time and come back to serve it."

"I'll handle dinner, Mamma," Olivia volunteered, surprised she felt no panic at the thought of working in the unfamiliar kitchen. *Wine to the rescue once again.*

"I said I will be back to serve it," Alessandro repeated.

Naturally, the herb girl couldn't be counted on to cook.

She took a bite of gelato and nearly swooned in spite of her irritation. It was sweet and flowery with just enough acidity from the grapes to balance out the rich cream. She could almost forgive Alessandro's arrogance if he could create food with this much subtlety. At least he had the skill to back up his superior attitude.

Her mother crossed her arms and sat back in her chair. "The villa will be completely full by tomorrow night and we have a very busy week ahead of us. Cooking classes, wine and cheese seminars, vineyard tours, trips into Verona and Padua. We also have to get ready for *la Sagra dell'Uva* this weekend. I'm so glad you're here to help, Olivia."

The weight of her mother's expectations was heavy but familiar. Olivia sipped her espresso, feeling pleasantly numb around the lips. The pastries she'd scarfed in Paris couldn't stand up to the wine. Counting their dinner last night in New York, she'd had more alcohol than food in the past twenty-four hours. Was it only last night? Their Trio dinner felt like it had been last week.

She could probably blame that on the wine too. Prosecco. Valpolicella. Amarone. It was no wonder she was feeling light-headed. No doubt her father would insist on Recioto after dessert. Maybe she could drink it lying down. Her head began to whirl.

"I need some air." She stood carefully and Sean stood beside her, ever the gentleman. "I'll be right back to help with the dishes, Mamma."

"No need, *cara*. Marco will get them," her father said.

"Wonderful." Olivia didn't expect to receive an offer

like that very often, so she made her way toward the front door, intending to lie down on one of the lounge chairs, because it was closer than her bedroom and she wouldn't have to climb any stairs.

"Thank you for dinner," she heard Sean murmur to her parents. Would he follow her to the porch? Did she want him to follow her?

She pushed open the front door and let it shut behind her. As she felt the warm tile under her bare feet, she realized she'd left her sandals lying under the dining room table. She'd have to remember to fetch them before guests arrived. She lowered herself onto a lounger and stretched in relief. Maybe she would sleep here. Maybe she would spend the week here.

She heard the front door open. She kept her eyes closed, hearing Sean groan as he lay down on the lounger next to hers.

She giggled. "I know, right? I'm never going to move again."

He took her hand in his. They lay together, separately, linked by their lazily intertwined fingers. She was exhausted, yet every nerve was alert, attuned to the man beside her. She could almost sense the blood pulsing through his body.

"Can we sleep here?" he asked.

"No," she sighed. "But the thought of staggering up to my room is more than I can handle."

"I'll help you." He seemed to be marshaling the effort to move but then he groaned again, surrendering. "In a minute."

"More espresso, maybe?"

"I'll explode. That lavender ice cream was spectacular."

Olivia turned her head to the side and opened her eyes. In the moonlight, his eyes were silvery. She caught her breath. He was beautiful—and at the end of the week, he'd be gone.

Her lassitude began to dissipate.

She slowly sat up, still holding his hand. "I use lavender shampoo, you know."

"That must be why I liked the ice cream so much."

Maybe it would be different with Sean. Maybe some of those fascinating things she'd heard happened to other women would happen to her. She knew one thing for certain—they would never happen if she didn't give it a try at least. She would never have a better opportunity to experiment. So what if it ended in epic failure? He was leaving. The disaster would be short-lived. And if it was good…they had a week to enjoy it.

Sean's eyes were half shut as he watched her, but she knew he was waiting to see what she would do. It was his way, to wait. The expression in his eyes always seemed to say *your move*, and suddenly it seemed like a cowardly way to operate. Anger chased away her exhaustion. Naturally, he wanted her to make the first move, while he lay there safely removed, taking none of the risks.

She pulled her hand out of his and stood. She didn't know how to stage a seduction, not if he was just going to lie there. She couldn't do this alone. "Good night, Sean." She turned to walk toward the house.

He chuckled softly. "Coward."

She looked over her shoulder. His grin made her feel exposed. "I was just thinking the same thing about you."

Swiftly, he rose to stand behind her and wrapped his

arms around her waist. An involuntary shiver shook her. She swallowed, trapped between the lounge chair and his body, unable to move forward or back. His large palm firmly cupped her small breast, making her nipple peak under his fingers. She twisted in embarrassment. Her ex-husband had preferred big breasts; what if Sean did too?

His arms tightened around her, stilling her movement, holding her immobile until she became aware of his arousal. He pressed his face to the curve of her neck and kissed her. His breath puffed softly against her neck. Longing swept through her, bringing tears to her eyes.

Best just to get it out there. He couldn't be disappointed if he wasn't expecting much. "I've never felt this way before, Sean. I don't know what to do."

A laugh shuddered through his frame. She stiffened. Was he laughing at her?

She pushed against his arm and he caught her hands and held them. "I've never felt this way either, Olivia. Not like this. I don't care about anything else when I'm with you. It scares the hell out of me." His rough voice reassured her.

She stopped struggling. She wanted to turn around and look at him, but God, what would she do then? "I don't know how to do this," she whispered.

He kissed her neck again, raising goose bumps. "Relax, Olivia. You don't have to do anything at all." His arms tightened around her. "Although I can think of a number of things I'd like you to do, we don't have to rush. I would love to just kiss you. But not right now."

"Why not now?" she asked, surprising herself and wresting a rough chuckle from Sean.

"Let me rephrase that. Not right here. Your parents don't seem to care for me and that chef gives me the creeps. Want to make a run for it?"

*Yes*, she thought, and then *no*. There was no turning back from a premeditated dash up to his bedroom. But to deny him now would make her feel like even more of a failure.

He turned her gently in his arms and pulled her body into his. They fit together. Pressed against him, she felt soft and womanly, desired. His hands coasted slowly over her hips, up her back, to her shoulders, and down again, molding her body firmly to his. Her head fell forward to rest on his shoulder, her lips a fraction away from his neck. He smelled of clean skin and faint aftershave. Her awareness of him grew with every breath. This was Sean, she reminded herself—solid, dependable, thoughtful Sean.

She raised her head. The rising moon lit his blond hair and she reached up to brush her palm across his head. She half expected the glow to rub off on her hand. She touched his cheek, watching him watch her. There would be no faking it with Sean. He was too observant. He'd guess, or he'd know.

Was that what she wanted? She moved restlessly against him. He moved with her, making her gasp. *If he kisses me, I'll say yes.*

His eyes flashed as if he had read her mind, and his lips descended.

# Chapter 8

SEAN KEPT THE KISS GENTLE, ALTHOUGH THE URGE TO lower her to the lounge chair and cover her body with his pounded through him. His desire for her had been a constant in his life for so many years that it was hard to go slow, but her uncertainty made him cautious. He wanted to erase her doubts before anything more happened between them, and that wouldn't happen if he rushed her.

He focused on her lips, responsive to every movement of his mouth. She followed his lead but didn't try to take charge of their kiss. As long as he had known her, Olivia had been deliberate and controlled in her words and actions. She was direct, but not a risk taker. Was that because she was afraid of doing the wrong thing? After meeting her mother, he could understand how that might be the case. Maybe her idiot ex-husband had convinced her she made mistakes in the bedroom too.

Her arms crept around his waist and he didn't muffle the low groan that ripped from his throat. He wanted her to know what she did to him and give her a good idea of what he wanted to do to her. He could sense her passion, tightly controlled, and he wanted to free it.

He pressed against her until there was no space between them. His body throbbed. She probably wasn't aware of her slight forward thrust, but he sensed every motion of her hips, felt every rapid beat of her heart and involuntary shiver, heard every sigh and gasp. He hoped they could move this conversation to a room with a securely locked door soon. For some reason, she didn't think she could do this, but he was determined to prove to her, beyond a shadow of a morning-after doubt, that she could. He would make her feel safe enough to lose control—to take control.

As if she had sensed his thought, her mouth opened under his and he felt the tip of her tongue touch his lip. He followed her invitation. Their tongues met, stroked. They shared a breath. He groaned again. If she continued to kiss him like this, she was going to wind up beneath him on the lounger despite his best intentions and the proximity of her parents.

The strangled noise she made so closely mirrored the protestation of his restrained desire that he almost ignored it, but he couldn't ignore the hand she placed on his chest when she pushed.

He released her. With relief, he saw her eyes held desire not doubt. "Everything okay?" he asked.

"Yes, but I can't, we can't…" She gestured around the patio. "My parents."

"Thank God," he breathed. "Your room or mine?"

"Mine is closer."

"Let's go." He grabbed her hand and pulled her toward the house, wondering if they could get past the kitchen, through the foyer, and up the stairs without running into anyone. Her lips were swollen with his kisses, her silky hair had tracks from his fingers in it, and her eyes were shining. He wasn't in any more presentable shape—the front of his pants was distinctly tented.

*Baseball, roadkill, starving orphans on lifeboats*, he chanted silently.

They entered the house. It was silent. He sighed in relief. They tiptoed down the hall. The sudden clatter of the dish washing machine as they passed the kitchen door made them both freeze.

Olivia giggled.

"Shh," he warned and tugged her down the hall. He held up a hand before he stepped into the foyer. Looking cautiously left and right, he motioned her quickly up the stairs. She darted in front of him. At the sound of voices in the dining room, she stifled a shriek and broke into a sprint.

The voices got louder and she sagged against the banister, giggling. A chuckle bubbled up inside him. For God's sake, they were both adults. He grabbed her hand and pulled her up the stairs, although it was almost worth getting busted if sneaking around like a teenager put a smile like that on her face. Almost.

They careened to a stop in front of her door. Laughter shook her shoulders and it took her three tries to get it unlocked. "Hurry," he urged, making her laugh harder.

The voices rose in the stairwell just as she twisted the knob. They fell into her room and he shut the door behind them, checking to make sure it locked.

The room was dark, lit only by the moonlight streaming through the lace curtains. Olivia walked over to the bed, still laughing softly. Her hair shone and he admired the smooth, white curve of her cheek as she turned to smile at him. He crossed the room and bent to turn on the lamp beside the bed.

No longer smiling, she put her hand on his arm. "I like it dark."

He shook his head. Olivia wanted to cling to the safety of the dark. She wanted to hide, but he wanted to show her there was nothing to fear. He took a step toward her.

She took a step back and stumbled. He caught her around the waist, holding her until she regained her balance. She pushed against his hands and lurched again, forcing him to grip her more tightly.

Damn, he'd forgotten about all the wine they had drunk tonight. Disappointment surged through him, killing his desire. He gave her a gentle shove down onto the bed and sat beside her, stroking her soft hair away from her face.

He looked down into her eyes, gone dark with doubt again. "Are you all right?" he asked.

She shook her head. "I'm not sure. Part of me wants to do this more than you can possibly imagine, and when I get enough wine in me, it seems like a really excellent idea. But I can only keep myself fooled for so long before I remember…well…" She paused and he would have given anything to know what memories were passing through her head that made her look so sad and defeated. "It's too big a risk. I don't have a lot of people in my circle, Sean. My ex-husband is a total loss. Marlene and Joe are wrapped up in each other. It's obvious I don't have the easiest relationship with my mother. I don't want to do anything that might damage our friendship." Her fingers clutched his hand. "I might need a friend when my mother disowns me and kicks me out of the villa."

"Why would she do that?"

"She doesn't tolerate fools or failure. It's pretty much her way or the highway and always has been. I'm picking the highway, Sean. I just came here to tell her. You're right—I can't go back to Chameleon. I'm not even sure I want to go back to New York."

For once, being right didn't make him happy. "So what are you going to do?"

She shrugged. "I haven't decided. Travel? Eat, pray, run?"

"Running away isn't going to solve any of your problems, Olivia."

"Are you sure? Because it's a hell of a relief." Her jaw tightened. "I'm so glad to be out of Norton, I almost feel like a different person. A person who could do... this. But you're right. Running away doesn't change anything. And I'd like for us to stay friends."

"So you think if we make love we won't be friends anymore?" he asked.

Her lips curved in a wry twist. "That seems to be how it works out for me."

Sean paused, thinking. "Yeah, pretty much me too." But that wasn't how he wanted it to turn out with Olivia. The rules that had applied to other women didn't seem to apply to her. If she had been any other woman, they would be naked right now. His casual relationships hadn't suffered from a drunken roll in the sheets, but he owed Olivia more than a one-night stand. And he didn't want her to have any reason for regrets—or excuses. He kicked off his shoes, then slung an arm around her shoulders in a casual embrace and drew her toward the pillows.

"What are you doing?" she asked, keeping one arm stiff and perpendicular to the mattress.

He pulled it out from under her and caught her to his chest. "Being friendly." He settled back onto the pillows and wrapped his arms around her. Slowly, her arm crept around his waist. His heart began a steady thump as she fit herself into his side. He hugged her and sighed.

"I'm no pro at this either. I've never had a serious relationship because I didn't want anything to pull my focus away from my responsibilities to my clients or my family.

She snuggled closer. "Tell me more about your family."

He took a deep breath. How could he explain his childhood? He was trying to make her feel better, not making a play for sympathy. There was no way to put it delicately, so he just laid it out. "My dad died when I was young and that's when my mom started drinking. There was an insurance policy, so there was plenty of money." He snorted. "To buy more vodka. She lost touch with what was going on and I figured out pretty quick that if I wanted to go to college then my grades had better be perfect. You may have noticed I didn't socialize much in high school."

She nodded. He was grateful not to see pity in her eyes, just acceptance. It made it easier to tell her the rest. "You remember my younger brother, right?"

He felt her nod, so he continued. "Colin's twenty-one now, but when Dad died he was just a little guy. My mom couldn't deal with him."

She raised her head. "So what did you do?"

"Research. I found a universal Pre-K program that was free, and I made an arrangement with his teacher to watch him every day until I got done with school. Whenever mom was sober enough, I took her with me so the teacher wouldn't ask too many questions. It wasn't a great solution, but it got us through that year. The next year he went to kindergarten, and it was easier. I was terrified someone would discover what was going on at home and put us both in foster care."

"Don't you think that might have been easier for you?"

He shook his head. "I'd already lost my father and most of my mother. There was no way I was going to lose Colin too."

"When did your mother stop drinking?" she asked.

"A neighbor took her to church one Sunday and she found God. Then he took her to her first AA meeting. She's been sober for ten years and that helpful neighbor is my stepfather now."

"A happy ending?" she asked.

"He's a good guy. Solid. They got married the year I went to law school, so I didn't have to worry about him trying to play daddy to me, but Colin was just at that age, you know? Teenage boys are crazy, but teenage boys with religious recovering-alcoholic moms and new know-it-all stepfathers are absolutely impossible."

"How would you know? You didn't get to be a crazy teenager. You had to take care of Colin."

"I didn't have a choice," he said. "We were both a wreck, but we held each other together. Taking care of him kept me from exploding, although I guess I'm not the exploding type. Colin, on the other hand, he's always been a live wire, and when I got a scholarship and moved to Syracuse for law school, he didn't have anybody to ground him anymore."

Sean looked away, afraid to see the blame in her eyes. "I thought he would be fine. Mom was doing really well and she basically told me it was time to stop being so territorial about Colin, that he wasn't my child, he was my brother and it was time to start acting like it."

Olivia gasped. "Are you kidding me? If you hadn't stepped up to the plate she wouldn't have had a family to take care of when she stopped drinking."

Her outrage made him realize how angry he had been with his mother. "But she was right. She was sober. She was stable. And if I didn't step out of the way, she was never going to get her son back." He sighed and looked down at her.

Her eyes were wide green pools. "I don't like the look on your face. What happened?"

Sean shrugged. "Colin hooked up with a lousy crowd. His grades tanked." He swallowed, remembering the last straw. "He came home with a tattoo. A piercing a few weeks later—you can imagine, just what you'd expect from a kid trying to get attention."

"Did it work?"

"Sure, Mom and Dave kept getting stricter and stricter. Colin kept getting wilder and wilder."

"What would you have done in their place?"

"Probably the same thing, but we had a bond. Mom and Dave didn't have a prayer. I came home at Christmas and saw it wasn't going well, but by the time the school year was over, Colin wouldn't listen to me either."

"What happened to your bond?"

He shook his head. "He was fourteen, just starting a new school, and I had left him with mom and squeaky-clean Dave and trotted off to law school thinking my work was done. I barely recognized him anymore. He'd practically turned into a thug. He hated the whole world and me along with it."

"It ain't easy being a teenager."

"Or living with one. He got caught driving drunk when he was eighteen. It wasn't the first time, and Mom and Dave kicked him out. Thank God I'm a lawyer, and I can pull a few strings once in a while. I managed to get him prosecuted as a youthful offender and he got three years probation. He lives with me now."

"Some people would call that enabling." Her voice was sleepy.

"Yeah, maybe," he said, kissing her forehead. "But he's a good kid, and I didn't want him going to jail. I've been terrified for three years. Any little mistake would send him to jail, and I wouldn't be able to do anything about it."

"Is his time almost up?"

"This week. His last hearing is Wednesday."

"Don't you want to be there?" she asked.

*Not as much as I want to be here with you.*

He shook his head and she brought her arm up to clasp his shoulder and shifted. Now she was all but lying on top of him. Her body was warm and her breath was slow and even. He held her close and breathed the flowers in her hair. A small smile crossed her lips as her eyes drifted shut and she fell heavily into sleep. His heart ached.

Sean closed his eyes too, wanting to give in to his fatigue. But if he didn't move now, he'd be out until morning and Olivia's mother was sure to come knocking. Slowly, one limb at a time, he untangled their bodies, regretting every inch of chill that claimed him.

He covered her with the blanket at the end of the bed and flipped as much of the comforter over her as he could. He turned off the light and picked up his shoes. He walked quietly toward the door. The hallway was empty and the house quiet. He checked to make sure the door had locked behind him and ghosted down the hall to his own room. Once inside, he dropped his shoes by the door and stripped on his way to the bed. Crawling under the covers, he stretched out on his back and recalled the feel of Olivia, warm and trusting.

# Chapter 9

OLIVIA WOKE SLOWLY TO A SHARP RAP ON HER DOOR. Ten o'clock. She hoped whoever was knocking had coffee and lots of it. Her stomach growled. Ditto for food.

As she climbed out of the tangled covers, she realized she was fully dressed. The night before came rushing back to her. She'd fallen asleep on Sean? Absolutely classic.

She hesitated, wondering who was on the other side of her door. Was it her mother or Sean? Her cheeks heated. Had he left angry? She brushed her bangs out of her eyes and opened the door.

Sean stood waiting in the hall and he was smiling. She covered her relief with the first thing that came into her head. "Why is it I always wake up hungry when I stuff myself at dinner?"

He stepped into her room. "I don't know, but I was starving too. I have croissants and cappuccino." His eyes held a memory. Did he mean to finish what they had begun last night? Her heart did a lazy somersault in her chest.

He set the tray on the desk. "Don't shoot the messenger, but your cousin wants you in the spa *immediatamente*. I'm off to the Padua market because my cell phone isn't working. Is yours?"

"I don't know. I haven't checked," she said, amazed that it had been so easy to cut the tie to Chameleon.

She crossed the room and dug through her purse. "No signal."

"I'll get you one too, then."

Olivia shook her head. "Marlene and Nonna have the number here. I don't want to hear from anyone else just yet."

He shrugged. "Your call."

She reached for a croissant. "Can you stay and eat with me?"

He shook his head. "Your father is waiting."

She nearly dropped the pastry.

He grinned. "That was my response too. I was planning to call a taxi, but he insisted."

Her father had been uncharacteristically rude to Sean at dinner last night and then Sean had followed her away from the table—there was no telling what her father thought about what had happened between them. He would have been right too, if she hadn't fallen asleep. "Watch out. I haven't had a chance to tell him to be nice to you yet." She took a bite of the croissant, chewed, and swallowed. "Listen, about last night—"

"No worries."

That didn't make her feel any better, especially when his eyes gleamed. Uh-oh. She dropped the croissant onto the tray and reached for her coffee. She wasn't having this discussion without caffeine in her system. She took a sip and sighed, sinking down into the desk chair. There was nothing like Italian coffee.

"Well, I can see I'm no longer needed," Sean teased.

"Coffee first and always," she insisted, hoping to forestall further discussion.

"I'll remember that." He leaned down to brush her

hair away from her face and damned if she didn't lean into the press of his fingers against her cheek. Her anxiety disappeared, replaced with a sense of comfort.

He bent to press a kiss on her forehead. Her body responded, going alert and tingly. She blinked up at him—stupidly, she was sure. What the hell was happening to her?

"I don't understand it either," he said a little grimly. "But I feel exactly the same way. I'll see you later, okay?"

She nodded and raised her cup to her lips to cover her expression. She watched his back as he left. As the door clicked shut behind him, she lowered her cup and sighed.

Abruptly, she laughed at herself, sitting in her chair and mooning over Sean like a lovesick schoolgirl, like Juliet. She might as well repair to the balcony.

*Move*, she told herself. Her cousin was waiting and so was her mother. First coffee, then a shower, because she wasn't going to present herself to Giovanna with travel scum all over her.

Should she have accepted Sean's offer to get her a cell phone? Technically, she was still in charge of the restaurant, although she had no doubt Marlene and Joe were doing fine. It was easy to picture them working together like clockwork while the orders flew in and then making out like teenagers when the board was clear, just as they had been doing all summer.

Olivia took a deep drink of cappuccino. She felt a time bomb ticking away inside her head, counting down the minutes until she had to tell her parents she didn't want the restaurant anymore. Last night at dinner, she had begun her confession, but then Sean had taken her hand and she had decided to wait. She didn't want to ruin his vacation, and waiting until the end of the week would give her time to chop, dice, stir, and bake her way into her mother's good favor. She could imagine how it must look to her parents—freshly divorced and arriving at Villa Farfalla with a new man. The femme fatale image was so far from the truth it made her smile. She couldn't even stay awake to be seduced, let alone do the seducing herself.

She stepped into the bathroom and gazed around with wide eyes at the enormous expanse of pale tile on the floors and darker tile on the walls. Was that a marble countertop? She ran her hand over the smooth, cold surface. The shower was walled in with glass and had dual showerheads and a bench. There was a Jacuzzi tub tucked into an alcove. She sniffed the shampoo and smiled. Lavender.

After a heavenly shower and one more croissant, Olivia made her way to the salon and found her cousin frowning at a computer screen. "Scowling will give you wrinkles." Olivia held out the basket she brought. "Croissant?"

"Croissants will make you fat," her cousin retorted. She pushed away from the simple secretary's desk that graced the tiny reception area.

"This is all the space Mamma gave you to work with?" Olivia asked.

"Just wait." Gia grinned and led her behind a creamy velvet curtain and into a white room filled with sunlight.

"Oh, much better," Olivia said.

Clean white sheets and pale wood dominated the décor. Water burbled gently from a fountain of pebbles in the corner. A bathroom with a shower and an even more elaborate tub than the one in her room was off to one side. There were only a few pictures on the walls, black and white photos of stark landscapes that complemented the simplicity of the room.

The only splash of color in the room was a beautiful, tasseled, Oriental rug in jewel tones. Gia caught the direction of her gaze. "I long for austerity," she said. "But I just can't quite give up my colors."

"Nor should you. Where did you find it?"

"Turkey. An absolute steal, but it cost a fortune to have it shipped here."

"Worth it."

"I think so too." Giovanna narrowed her eyes. "Sooo...let's see what we've got to work with."

Olivia took a step back. "Really, Gia, let's not go overboard. I don't need all the bells and whistles. I'm sure Mamma wants me in the kitchen as soon as possible..."

"If she wants you, she can come get you. Until then, I've got my orders." She pointed to the bathroom and scooped a lush robe from a pile near the fountain. "By the time I get done with you, you'll thank me."

Olivia opened her mouth to protest, but her cousin cut her off with a stern glare. "Your man was right. Your stress level is making my teeth vibrate. Consider it an act of mercy and do it for me. Just a massage and a manicure." She glanced down at Olivia's feet and added, "Pedicure too, probably."

"He's not my man" was all Olivia could muster in reply.

"Right." Her cousin snorted. "Then I'm sure you'll say no to a bikini wax."

Olivia closed her eyes for a moment, defeated. When she opened them, her cousin was grinning smugly.

"I want the bikini wax," Olivia admitted.

"I know. Sugar's already hot," Gia said cheerfully. "We'll do that first so the pain doesn't ruin your massage buzz."

Olivia touched her cousin's arm. "I've missed you, cousin."

Giovanna wrapped her arms around her in a tight squeeze. "Of course you did. Now strip!"

———

Sean found Mr. Marconi waiting for him in the foyer. He nodded a greeting, which the smaller man returned. "Would it be possible to use a computer before we go?" Sean asked.

"Certainly." Mr. Marconi led him down the hall to an office, typed a password, and gestured at the chair. "Be my guest. Let me know when you are ready to leave."

"Thank you very much."

Sean opened Google, and as he began typing, other recent searches auto-filled in. Someone must have been researching osso buco recipes. And gnocchi. A familiar name flashed on the screen. Capozzi. As in Benito, Nonna Lucia's boyfriend?

He clicked the link and caught his breath at the title of the article, "La Farfalla Dies With Its Maker." His curiosity had been piqued by Gia's story yesterday. He scanned the text and discovered Pasquale Capozzi had been the vintner at Villa Farfalla in 1955, the year of the La Farfalla vintage. This particular article had been published six months ago and detailed the life of a man who had apparently done everything in his power to stay out of the spotlight. The Conti family had searched high and low for him after the 1955 vintage had been tasted, but he never came forward. Capozzi had lived out his years alone in a remote cabin in the Alps, apparently deserted by the son who had ruined his career. He never made wine again, and his secret had died with him.

Sean heard Mr. Marconi's voice in the hall and remembered he was keeping him waiting. He quickly checked his email and found nothing new from Russo, so he Googled the Hotel Loggia Antica. A minute later, he printed a map, then closed the browser.

He found Mr. Marconi in the driveway, waiting next to a black sedan. Sean took the passenger seat. "Sure is hot," he said, hoping he didn't sound as inane as he thought he did.

"Not for long," Mr. Marconi's voice was gruff.

Sean forged ahead. "Well, I appreciate the ride. I have business in Padua, and my cell phone isn't working. Giovanna suggested I buy another one in the market."

Mr. Marconi frowned. "I don't have a use for cell phones. I prefer to stay connected to the earth, not the air. I don't understand why everyone is always on their phones these days."

"I need to stay in touch," Sean said, annoyed that he felt the need to justify himself.

Mr. Marconi nodded agreeably, but his eyes were sharp. He started the car. "So how is it you come to Italy with my daughter?"

Sean felt his lips curve thinly. "A happy coincidence. I need to meet with a client and Olivia was already coming to Italy."

"This isn't the first time you've chased after my daughter," Mr. Marconi said, leaving Sean in no doubt that he remembered the boy who had walked past his restaurant so many times.

"As her lawyer, you should know she doesn't need another man to complicate her life."

"I agree with you there." Out of politeness, Sean resisted the urge to say more.

Olivia's father slowed the car to a crawl as they came up to the main road. "I don't mean to insult you, Mr. Kindred. I'm sure you are an honorable man, but I'm thinking of my daughter. I don't understand why you booked a room in the villa since you were traveling with Olivia. Surely she would extend our hospitality to you. Didn't she know you were coming?"

"No," Sean said tersely. "She did not."

"Does she want you here?" the man asked bluntly, making a slow turn onto the main road.

"Have you asked her that?" The lawyer in him knew just how to handle cross-examinations.

Mr. Marconi shook his head. "Not in so many words."

"Well, why don't you do that first? I'd like to know myself."

Mr. Marconi snorted.

Sean could understand the man's plight. He wanted the best for his only child. Sean wanted the best for her too, but their understanding of her needs was necessarily different. He certainly wasn't going to get into that discussion, so he settled for saying, "I don't want to hurt Olivia."

"So don't. Go back to New York. Leave her alone."

"I can't do that."

Silence settled between them, a silence that Mr. Marconi seemed to have no intention of breaking again. Sean steeled himself. "How long to Padua?"

"About an hour."

That was a lot of silence.

———

Mr. Marconi pulled the car over to the side of the road and parked. "Here you are." He gestured at a street lined with green and white umbrellas. The Padua market looked prosperous and welcoming, but Sean was too tense to enjoy the hustle and bustle. The hour in the car had felt like a week.

Olivia's father cleared his throat. "Mr. Kindred, there is no delicate way to make this offer, so I will just say it. I want you to go back to New York. In fact, I'm willing to pay your travel expenses if you quietly take your leave of my home and my daughter. She's been through enough, and I don't want her getting hurt again."

Sean opened the car door. "Thank you for the ride. I'll call a taxi for my return trip." Even if it cost him a small fortune. There was no way he was going to spend another hour in the car with Olivia's father.

"Your trip to the airport?" Mr. Marconi suggested.

Sean ignored the glint of humor he saw in the other man's eyes. He did not want to like this man. "No, not today. I think my leaving her would hurt her too." Sean shut the car door and began to walk toward the market.

He felt a tight knot of frustration in his center. Her father was wrong. He wasn't going to hurt her. In fact, she was more likely to hurt him. Holding Olivia in his arms last night had been so peaceful, and he hated to be reminded that their affair could be short. What if she decided to stay in Italy? What if he couldn't convince her to come back to New York with him?

Sean set off into the market, looking for a street sign. According to his map, the Hotel Loggia Antica was near the Piazza Dante. He passed displays of vegetables, scanning the tables for electronics. Finding the hotel was his first priority but if he happened to see a phone he would certainly stop. He paused to admire a stall filled with nothing but different varieties of the red lettuce they had eaten at dinner last night, then slowed in front of a stall displaying so many kinds of cured meat products that it looked like the walls had been papered with sausage. The next stall offered a hard squash that looked like a pumpkin. "*Zucche! Zucche!*" the seller called out to him.

He shook his head politely. "Hotel Loggia Antica?" The woman pointed down the way. Just past a booth filled with artichokes, strings of garlic, and about twenty vegetables he couldn't identify, he spotted a stack of cell phone boxes. He approached the stall.

A young girl talked on her own cell phone as she sat behind the table. "*Telefono?*" he asked.

She looked up at him. "*Documenti?*"

He shook his head apologetically. "English?" he asked.

She released a long-suffering sigh and said something in rapid Italian. "*Ciao*," she said into her phone and pushed a button. "Are you from Italy?" she said slowly.

"No, I need a telephone because I can't get a signal." He held up his phone. "Do you have something like this?"

"Yes, but I can't sell it to you unless you can prove you live here or you show me a passport."

His passport was in his room at the villa. "Are you kidding me?" he asked.

Her phone signaled a text. "I'm sorry, but no," she said, looking about as sorry as a teenager with an unread text message can look. Sean tried not to glare at her as she told him that it wasn't her fault that rules were rules and her employers, indeed the government itself, required *documenti* for every cell phone sold, that no, it wasn't just her. Her competitors would also be unable to sell him a phone. And no, he didn't look like a terrorist but she didn't want to lose her job.

Having no polite response, Sean simply nodded. "Is this the way to the Hotel Loggia Antica?" he gestured down the street.

"Yes, right there." She pointed at a building across the square, clearly impatient to get back to her conversation.

He crossed the piazza and took the stairs by twos, nodding his thanks to the hotel doorman. The Hotel Loggia Antica was almost as nice as Villa Farfalla. Mrs. Russo had excellent taste in accommodations. He approached the front desk. "Hello, I'm looking for Marilyn Russo. Could you tell her someone is here to see her, please?"

"Certainly, sir."

The divorce papers were tucked in his pocket. Hopefully his ruse would get Mrs. Russo into the lobby, and he could deliver them without incident. Then he would decide whether to try his luck with another phone vendor or head back to the villa for his passport. Was it worth paying a fortune in taxi fares to stay in touch with Mr. Russo and his family? Maybe he could find the train Gia had mentioned.

The clerk hung up the phone with a smile. "She is coming."

"*Grazie*." Sean walked over to the seating arrangement in the middle of the lobby and took a seat next to a tall potted plant. A few minutes later, a woman rushed into the lobby. He knew Mrs. Russo was in her fifties, but this woman looked much younger. Her auburn hair was twisted on top of her head and she was wearing high heels. Her blue dress swirled around her ankles as she whirled to look where the desk clerk was pointing—at him.

Sean moved into her line of sight. As their eyes met, she looked puzzled. Then her face crumpled and she pressed a hand to her lips. Sean felt like someone had punched him in the stomach as he realized she must have been expecting her husband. He forced himself to approach the front desk.

"Mrs. Russo?" he said softly. "I'm Sean Kindred. Your husband sent me."

Her shoulders straightened. "I realize that now."

"I'm sorry…I didn't think…I guess I wasn't thinking, but I'm sorry for misleading you." He took a breath and pulled the divorce papers out of his pocket. "I'm your husband's lawyer. He wants a divorce."

She cleared her throat. "Yes, I know he does."

Her sudden smile stunned him. He blinked and felt like a cad as he held out the papers.

Mrs. Russo shook her head and kept her hands at her sides. "He's not going to get it until after my vacation. I told him that before I left New York."

"How long is your vacation going to be?" he said, already fearing the answer.

"I haven't decided."

Sean had to ask, "Why on earth do you want to stay married to him if he wants a divorce?"

"Because I love him." Her voice broke on the last word.

"I'm sorry," he said again, and she nodded.

"Me too. But I'm not going to throw away twenty-eight years of marriage because Tony won't take a vacation. He works too much and he doesn't know how to relax. It's ruining our marriage—"

Sean held up the papers again. "Are you sure it hasn't already ruined your marriage?"

"Tony is an idiot."

Sean nodded in agreement. "You can do better than him."

She patted him on the cheek. "But I want Tony. I picked him, and I'm keeping him. Whether he knows it or not—he's keeping me too."

"I'm sorry for being the bearer of bad news, Mrs. Russo." Sean pressed the papers into her hand and turned toward the door.

She caught his arm. "What are you going to tell Tony?"

"I'm going to tell him I delivered the papers." He'd also tell him that he should keep his wife, not that Russo would listen to him.

"Would you tell him one more thing?" She gave him an impish smile.

Sean raised his eyebrows and waited. Nothing good could come from a smile like that.

"Tell him I won't contest the divorce if he takes a two-week vacation in Italy. I just know he'd love it here as much as I do. Have you seen much of Padua?" she asked.

"I'm staying in Verona at Villa Farfalla," he said.

"I've heard wonderful things about that place! When you speak with Tony, tell him to book a room there, please."

Sean bit back a chuckle. Mrs. Russo was as relentless as her husband. Maybe they were perfectly matched after all. "I'll send him an email when I get back to the villa. I imagine he'll need some time to get used to the idea before I talk to him."

"Tony's like that," Mrs. Russo said complacently, and he heard the truth of twenty-eight years ring in her voice.

Sean pulled his wallet out of his pocket and gave her his card. "Keep in touch."

She shook his hand. "Thank you for your help. I hope we'll see you at the villa."

"Good luck," he said and meant it.

He stopped at the front desk to pocket a hotel card in case he needed to contact her again. Then he stepped outside and headed back toward the market. Russo was going to be furious, but he wasn't sure he cared. To be perfectly honest, he wasn't sure he wanted to be his lawyer anymore. It was hard to believe the lovely woman he had just met had been driving Mr. Russo crazy. It seemed more likely the other way around.

Slowly he became aware of music. He followed the cheerful sound and found several musicians set up outside a café. His stomach growled, so he sat down at an empty table. *Vivi nel presente.* He might as well have lunch while he figured out what to do about his phone.

# Chapter 10

OLIVIA STAGGERED OUT OF THE SPA. HER MUSCLES felt like room temperature butter, soft and malleable. Her nails were gorgeous, fingertips buffed to a natural shine and toes painted a racy dark red. Her stomach ached from giggling for hours as her cousin entertained her with even racier stories from her love life. As Olivia reached the bottom of the stairs, she fought the urge to hook a sharp left and keep walking, to continue out the back door and into the vineyard. So far her day had been stress free. That would end once she joined her mother in the kitchen. She stopped in the hall and took a deep breath.

The desire to please her mother was too strong for her to actually walk out the door, but just for a minute, she indulged the fantasy. What would she do? Where would she go?

She could spend the day lying in the vineyard watching the grapes grow. Or maybe she would walk into the village. A long lunch in a cute *trattoria* sounded very appealing.

The back door opened and she jumped.

"*Ciao, cara*. How was your morning?" her father asked, stepping into the hall.

"Peaceful. I was just on my way to help Mamma."

His face softened and a teasing light entered his dark green eyes. "I can see you're in a big hurry."

Olivia turned toward the kitchen but her father touched her arm, holding her back. "You don't look like you've had a peaceful morning, *tesoro*."

"I'm fine. Just gearing up to chop some more herbs."

"Bah! Why don't you play in the vineyard with me instead? It is lovely among the vines." The kindness in his eyes made her feel weak. She shook her head.

"I can't. Mamma is expecting me."

"And what's the worst thing that could happen if you disappointed her?"

Olivia opened her mouth to answer before she realized she didn't know. She had never deliberately defied her mother. She pressed her lips together, frowning.

"Your Mamma loves you," he said.

"Of course she does." That wasn't the sort of thing a daughter needed to be told. She glanced out the door behind him, looking for Sean. "How was your morning? Did Sean find a phone?"

"I wouldn't know." Her father crossed his arms. He looked like he was trying not to laugh.

"Where is he?" she asked, suspicious.

"In Padua."

"You left him there?" she exclaimed.

"He's a big boy. He'll find his way back."

"Papà, he doesn't speak Italian! How is he going to—" She broke off. "Go get him."

Her father's truculent expression told her he would do no such thing. Logically, she knew Sean could get back to the villa fairly easily. Someone would speak English and help him find the train but it had been a dirty trick. "Fine. Be that way. But when he does make it back on his own, you have to promise to be nice to him."

A calculating grin creased her father's tanned face. "Only if he makes it back before dinner."

"Then you have to be nice to him for the rest of the week," she countered.

"It's a deal." He held out his hand and they shook. "But I can't speak for your mother."

He kissed her cheek and headed toward the front of the house, chuckling. Olivia entered the kitchen and saw a young man clearing the chef's table. His back was to her as he lifted a heavy tray onto his shoulder. She stepped out of the way, nodding a greeting as he passed. Below, she could see her mother deftly rolling pasta dough while Alessandro hovered over the stove, stirring something with a long wooden spoon. The kitchen smelled like garlic and roasting vegetables. She felt a twinge of guilt for spending the morning getting pounded like veal while they had been busy serving up lunch. She tugged an apron from the stack in the dish room and joined them.

"*Ciao*, Olivia," her mother said as she stepped down the stairs.

"*Ciao*, Mamma. What's on the menu today? Do you have a list ready for me?"

Her mother turned to Alessandro.

He untied his apron. "Ask Marco. I gave the list to him." He gestured toward the young man who had been clearing the chef's table, who was now leaning on the table and laughing with two women wearing black pants and white shirts. Her mother made a beeline for the stairs. To get the list? To put the waitstaff back to work? Alessandro glowered and threw his apron in the linen bin. He moved toward the glass door.

She followed him. "Alessandro, I'm here to help. I don't plan to stay long, but I'd like to be useful while I'm here. Isn't there something I can do while you're gone?"

He turned to face her. The proud lines of his face softened. Olivia waited, hoping he would accept her olive branch, but the sudden ring of his cell phone ruined the moment. His face hardened again. "Nothing," he said.

Olivia crossed her arms. "What about the class tomorrow?"

"What about it? The people will come. We will cook." His hand moved toward his pocket. "*Un momento*," he said sharply into his phone. He turned back to her and jerked his chin toward the stove. "Make soup for *primo piatto* if you want something to do."

Olivia had taught occasional cooking classes at Chameleon. They were a ton of work, and it was far easier to have a good bit of the prep done ahead of time. Amateur chefs were interested in the exciting parts of cooking not the scut work. It was fun to peel one potato; it was not fun to peel two bags of them. It had taken both her and Marlene, prepping at warp speed the day before the class, to get everything ready to roll. There was no way in hell she was going to show up and wing it tomorrow.

She stepped in front of him. "Where's the menu for the class?"

He pointed impatiently at the chalkboard next to the stairs.

"What time will you be back?" she asked, refusing to allow him to intimidate her.

He waved his cell phone at her. "*Mi scusi*."

She shrugged and stepped aside. The patio door

slammed behind him. What on earth was wrong with that guy? As her mother had said, dinner wasn't going to make itself and she wanted to help. Well, she was done being polite and trying not to step on his toes. She'd run her own kitchen for years, and she didn't need him to tell her how to make dinner.

She walked back to the stove, automatically taking stock of what was cooking on the burners. Polenta? He'd left polenta sitting on the stove and walked out the door? The bottom of that pot was going to be scorched as hell. She killed the flame and poured the cornmeal pudding into a pan, being careful not to scrape the bottom or sides. After pressing plastic wrap to the top of the pudding, she cleaned out the pot, then put it back on the stove with some baking soda in the bottom to cook off the mess.

She carried the polenta to the walk-in and found two enormous pans of lasagna sitting on the shelf. That was enough to feed fifty people. He clearly intended to serve it as the entrée, but Italians customarily served lasagna for *primo piatto*. Was he catering to American tastes? And what had he planned for dessert?

She found *amaretti* cookies cooling on the baker's rack. She pulled one from the parchment and took a bite. It was delicious—sweet and fragrant with almond paste, crisp on the outside, and chewy in the center. She grabbed another cookie.

She supposed she could spend the rest of the day lolling around her room, but damned if she'd be thrown out of the kitchen because Chef Alessandro didn't think she was big enough to play with the grown-ups. She was used to being busy, and she'd had enough relaxation this morning to last her a month. Shaking her head, she studied the chalkboard for the next day's menu: *sottaceti* and bruschetta, risotto, *bollito misto* with *la peara* and *torta sabbiosa*.

She had to admit that Alessandro had a gift for menu planning. It wasn't easy to create a four-course menu that was simple to prepare yet impressive to serve. As far as she could tell, he hadn't used any ingredients that cost the earth either. That was good for the villa and even better for the guests who might wish to repeat the dinner at home. The menu was simple yet rich. Light and refreshing. The colors would be beautiful, as much a feast for the eyes as for the palate. *Bastard*. She rolled her eyes. *Alessandro Bellin, the man who can cook*. And bake, she thought, swallowing the last bite of cookie. Still, he didn't have to be such an ass.

She returned to the stove, assuming the lazily bubbling stock was meant for soup since she hadn't seen an older batch in the walk-in. She grabbed a strainer, a large pot, and a smaller pot to use as a ladle. She began to strain the hot stock.

Her mother appeared on the stairs just as she was deciding she probably shouldn't try to lift the pot off the stove by herself. "Perfect timing," Olivia said with a smile.

Her mother descended the stairs and stepped into place beside her. Together, they lifted the heavy stockpot and poured the rest of the steaming liquid through the strainer. When the pot was empty, her mother carried it to the dish room while Olivia dumped the discarded vegetables into the garbage can.

"Can I do something with your pasta?" Olivia asked, when her mother returned.

"I'll take care of it."

Olivia nodded and set up a cutting board as her mother began to wrap up the dough. An easy peace settled between them, so different from the agitation Olivia usually felt in her mother's kitchen.

"What are you working on, *cara*?" her mother asked.

"Alessandro asked me to make soup. I'd also like to get a few things done for tomorrow's class, if that's all right with you."

"Go ahead, *cara*. Do whatever you think is necessary. I'd help you but I need to double-check the rooms and make our guests comfortable when they arrive. I also promised your father I'd find someone to fix his tractor. I swear it seems like something new breaks every week." Her mother wiped her hands on her side towel and turned to go.

At the bottom of the stairs, she paused. Olivia looked up from the pan she was wrapping in plastic and waited for her mother to speak, sure that whatever she was going to say would ruin their fragile camaraderie. She braced herself.

"Thank you, *cara*." Her mother gave her a brief nod and swept up the stairs.

Olivia stared after her, bemused. Well, that was a first. She couldn't remember the last time her mother had thanked her for anything. She was always too busy rushing off to organize the next task. Right now, Olivia could hear her voice in the dish room, probably adding to Marco's list. Her mother expected everyone to share her goals. Anyone standing still was put to work. She smiled, remembering the many times when they were teenagers that she and Marlene had tried to

artichokes, an offer she gratefully accepted, so she could focus on inventing a soup.

She walked over to the sink where the strained beef stock was sitting in an ice bath. She couldn't resist dipping a spoon into the still steaming liquid. She blew carefully, then sipped, amazed by the pure beef essence.

The flavors were all right there, but not overpowering. The stock had backbone, but would effortlessly adapt itself to a soup or risotto without adding aggressive notes of onion, celery, or carrot.

It was perfect. Inspiring, even.

It would make a beautiful soup. Suddenly she wanted to make a more elaborate dessert too, something to complement the *amaretti* cookies, something creamy, but light. Something…sexy? She let ideas play in her mind as she headed for the walk-in.

Ice cream? No, they'd had that last night and it wouldn't have time to freeze.

As she passed the stairs, she noticed a pile of pumpkins in a basket on the floor. Would crème brûlée, a favorite at Chameleon, be too heavy after lasagna? The *zucche* would be delicious roasted, pureed, baked in the thinnest sheet of custard, and coated with an amber ice of caramelized sugar. Crème brûlée was easy to make, but did she have enough time to cook the pumpkins? She eyed the clock. Barely, but if she ran out of time they could eat them tomorrow.

Enough doubts. Nothing ventured, nothing gained. It had been a long time since she had felt truly inspired to cook and she was going to go for it.

Swiftly, she attacked the pumpkins to get them ready for roasting. When they were in the oven, she cruised the walk-in, looking for inspiration for her soup. It needed to be gloriously simple, a soup that would tease the appetite but leave room for the substantial lasagna, something that would showcase the purity of the broth but also stimulate the imagination. Perhaps if she made an excellent soup, the peace between her and her mother would continue until the end of the week when she told her about Chameleon.

She felt chilled, although the walk-in was only forty degrees. Even if she made the best soup in Italy, her mother was not going to be happy with her. Resolutely, she focused on the joy again. Who wouldn't be optimistic at the sight of the beautiful array of vegetables in the cooler? The radicchio looked like a bouquet of crumpled purple roses; so convoluted and crisp, it burst with life. The fennel fronds were soft and feathery. She wanted to brush them against her skin. Even the more common produce like celery and carrots seemed firmer, brighter and sharper. Her mother could write the book on fresh, local, and seasonal, that was for sure. She gathered what she needed and took it back to her station.

She worked slowly and deliberately, humming a bit as her knife worked through the vegetables to make the *battuto*, so much like the French *mirepoix*, but finer and with garlic, of course. The *battuto* reduced celery, carrot, and onion to their essences and then carried them through the dish. With guilt, she realized she hadn't made one since her basic skills class at the Culinary Arts College.

As she chopped, a prickle of anxiety made her heart stutter in her chest. What if she couldn't finish her soup in time? What if it was unremarkable? What if her custard scrambled? Or was pale and wan? Insipid? For a moment her knife stopped moving and she felt locked in place by the same kind of pressure that had paralyzed her in New York. *Stop it. It's just food.* No one was expecting anything of her. She could walk out of the kitchen right now having accomplished more than had been asked of her.

With surprise, she realized she didn't want to leave. She *wanted* to cook. Her heart skipped another beat, but this time it was because of excitement. She began to chop again, remembering how much pleasure Sean had taken in the simple Italian meal last night. She wanted it to be her food that brought him pleasure. *Only her food?*

No, not just her food. As soon as she got the custards in the oven, she would go to the tasting room and ask Gia to pair wines with tonight's menu, although she was going to make sure they didn't drink too much tonight. *Maybe then she could finally get laid.* The thought popped into her head and she froze, then she laughed, surprised she felt no panic.

She distinctly remembered the utter relaxation she had felt as she fit her body to his right before she fell asleep. *Right before you used him as a bed, you mean.* If she had gotten any closer to him, they would have become one person.

*Exactly. The beast with two backs.*

She snorted. Naturally, the first bit of Shakespeare that came to her would be that one. Her hands had been busy with the knife while she was thinking, and the *battuto* was ready. She heated olive oil in the pan to fry the pancetta. When it was crispy, she removed it and began to sweat the vegetables. The fragrance of her childhood wrapped itself around her. She chopped fennel and more garlic, glorying in the beauty of the simple ingredients.

As she julienned the remaining carrots for the sheer pleasure of feeling her knife move, she felt an ease she hadn't enjoyed for months, maybe years. She felt drunk with the joy of creating something without worrying about how much it was costing, how long it was taking, or if her time wouldn't be better spent doing something else.

Keeping Chameleon in the black had slowly eaten away her joy for cooking. Making a dish for the pure luxury of the experience or the quality of the products had fallen off her radar when she was faced with the necessities of employee scheduling and calculating food costs and payroll. It hadn't helped that after Marlene left the line and moved to the bakeshop, she'd been afraid to leave Keith alone. All the denial in the world couldn't hide the fact that he couldn't hit medium rare with a baseball bat. They had been racking up customer complaints right and left before she'd fired him.

Leaving all that carnage behind her was a revelation. Time, usually her biggest enemy in the kitchen, now felt like a welcome challenge. She felt energized by her race against the clock.

She added crushed red pepper flakes to the soup and stepped back to reach for a tasting spoon. Suddenly, she was fiercely glad she was alone. She could do this. She dipped the spoon into the soup, blew on it for the necessary seconds to avoid scalding her tongue, and then tasted it.

*Perfetto.*

A smile curved her lips. It would be even better after it had a chance to simmer. Eagerly, she crossed the room to check on the squash. It was soft and smelled like caramelized sugar already, so she pulled it out of the oven to cool a bit. She rummaged in a drawer for a pencil and paper to make a few quick calculations. She would have to adjust her basic custard recipe to allow for the added liquid of the pumpkin puree.

Should she add some booze too? Amaretto would match the almond in the cookies. The custard would be rich, yet ephemeral, singing the top notes of spice and sweetness yet echoing comforting chords of crunchy caramelized sugar. It would need one more flavor, she decided, to even begin to compare with the complexity of Alessandro's lavender ice cream.

She spun on her heel, searching the kitchen for inspiration. An herb? A spice? She walked over to the spice rack and searched the labels. Vanilla bean? Never a bad choice, but not what she needed tonight. Not fennel either; it might fight with the amaretto.

Star anise? Maybe. It might be too strong of a flavor. Or it could be perfect, providing an interesting counterpoint to the amaretto and almond. It was a risk.

She grabbed the container and headed for the stove, hoping Sean would make it back in time for dinner.

---

Sean pillowed his chin on his hands and stared across the piazza, admiring the elaborate frescoes painted on the buildings. He had switched from espresso to wine during lunch and the second glass had probably been a mistake. It was well past noon and warm enough to make him sleepy but not quite hot enough to make him sweat. The red and white striped umbrella above his table shaded him from the worst of the sun and the musicians continued to play, seemingly tireless.

He watched two men argue at a café across the piazza. The younger man looked exactly like Alessandro Bellin. He squinted and realized it was Alessandro.

He studied the men, taking note of the chef's aggressive body language and the way his hands flashed in front of him as he spoke. The other man was much more relaxed, almost indolent. The man stood and leaned across the table, getting within a breath of the chef's face. Sean's fatigue disappeared. He wondered what the man was saying as Alessandro slowly drew an envelope out of his pocket and tossed it onto the table.

The older man picked up the envelope and tucked it into his jacket. He rose and flicked the back of his fingers under his chin in a broad arc. Sean had never seen anyone use that particular gesture but it looked insulting as hell, and it didn't take years of observing people in the courtroom to know the chef had just lost that argument.

The older man turned his back and walked away. Before he had taken three steps, two men rose from the next table and followed him, one on each side. They were an intimidating trio, all in dark suits despite the heat of the day. In fact, they looked like Mafia gangsters as they cut across the piazza and disappeared into an alley.

He hesitated for a moment, pitting his dislike of the chef against his need to get back to the villa. Practicality won. He pushed away from his table, leaving enough euros to cover his bill. He crossed the piazza and stopped at Alessandro's table. "Alessandro—I thought that was you."

The chef nodded, not looking at all happy to see him.

Sean stuck with it. "If I had known you were coming this way I would have asked you for a ride to Padua. In fact, I was hoping you might be able to give me a ride back to the villa. I didn't want to ask Mr. Marconi to wait for me. Big mistake, as it turns out. The shop girl wouldn't sell me a phone, so my entire trip was wasted."

Finally, Alessandro seemed to notice him. "Why wouldn't she sell you a phone?"

"Because I didn't bring my passport with me." The disgust in his voice sparked a wry smile from Alessandro.

"Did you offer her *una bustarella*?"

"A what?"

"A little envelope. A bribe. You're in Italy, remember."

The chef stood and walked away from the table, motioning for Sean to follow him. He seemed to know where he was going and led Sean right back to the same cell phone display he had visited earlier. Sean hung back, wondering if the girl would recognize him.

Alessandro greeted her and removed his own cell phone from his pocket. He held it up, smiling. The girl smiled back and handed him a box. Their conversation was fast and Sean wasn't close enough to hear it. She blushed as she made change, darting quick glances through her thick, black eyelashes.

She did not ask for his *documenti*, he noticed sourly.

"*Ciao! Grazie!*" Alessandro blew her a kiss and walked over to Sean.

Alessandro led him away from the stall.

Sean gave him a hundred euro. *"Thank you*. Is this enough?"

The chef nodded and tucked the bill into his pocket, handing over the bag containing the cell phone. "My car is this way."

He followed Alessandro to a black Fiat parked on the sidewalk. Sean climbed into the low-slung car, tugged his new phone out of the bag, and swiftly unboxed it. He opened the directions. They were in Italian, of course.

"Let me help." Alessandro took the phone out of his hand and snapped it together in two easy motions. After checking the number he'd been given, he dialed, listened for a few moments, and pressed several buttons.

"There." Alessandro handed the phone back to him. "If you run out of minutes, it's easy to buy more."

"Thanks. I feel like an idiot."

Alessandro shrugged. "It's just technology. They make it difficult on purpose."

Sean fiddled with his phone until he found his new number. Had he misjudged the chef? Alessandro was being awfully helpful. He began to compose a text to his mother and brother, almost dropping the phone as Alessandro pulled out into the street. Brakes screeched. The chef ignored the noise and accelerated until the Fiat hovered three inches from the bumper of the car in front of them. Funny, Sean hadn't noticed the roads were this narrow when Mr. Marconi was driving.

He checked his seat belt as Alessandro zipped around the car in front of them and began gaining on his next target. At least they'd get back to the villa faster.

Alessandro swerved around the next car, then took a hairpin turn at eighty kilometers an hour.

Sean swallowed a sigh of relief as the road straightened in front of them.

"Was that your family back in the piazza?" Sean asked.

For a long minute he thought the chef wasn't going to answer him. "No," Alessandro finally said.

Sean watched him. "My mistake—I thought you said you had a family emergency."

"My business is none of yours." The chef's voice was cold, his expression imperious.

"I guess it just seems strange that you would take time off when guests are due to arrive, especially when Olivia has to cover for you." Was Alessandro part of the staffing problems Gia had mentioned?

Sean felt the car accelerate. It was probably stupid to pick a fight with a guy driving a hundred and thirty kilometers per hour but he really didn't care. Olivia's parents may not have given him a warm welcome, but Villa Farfalla was charming and he wanted it to succeed for Olivia's sake. "I wonder what Mr. and Mrs. Marconi would think about their chef sneaking off for a long lunch in Padua?"

Alessandro gave him a brief glare. "I'd prefer you not tell them."

The chef wanted his silence? Well, he wanted something too. "Well I'd prefer you stay away from Olivia," he warned.

Alessandro shrugged, glancing over at him. "I can't keep her out of the kitchen. Can you?"

A sharp thump sounded beneath the car and Sean heard the unmistakable bang of a tire exploding. The car jerked to the right. Alessandro spun the wheel and they skidded to a halt on the side of the road, inches from a ditch.

"I hope you have a spare," Sean said grimly.

"That was the spare."

# Chapter 11

OLIVIA PULLED HER VELVETY SMOOTH PUMPKIN custards from the oven. She set the water bath on a table and carefully removed each ramekin, wiping them gently before she placed them on a sheet tray to cool. She was glad that the Culinary Arts College had insisted that every good chef needed to perfect crème brûlée just in case the pastry chef ever got sick.

She looked at the clock—an hour to spare. Technically, the crème brûlées should come to room temperature before she chilled them, but she didn't have *that* much time. She'd have to put them in the walk-in.

Speaking of time, where was Alessandro? He had said he'd be back in time to finish dinner. She didn't mind covering for him. In fact, she'd enjoyed herself, but shouldn't someone try to call him? It was almost six o'clock, and Sean wasn't back yet either. Damn it, she'd wanted to win that bet with her father and prove Sean could take care of himself.

She put the lasagna in the oven and pulled three trays of *antipasto* out of the reach-in. Her julienned carrots added a splash of color to the platters and they tasted even better than they looked tossed with fresh tarragon vinaigrette.

She carried the *antipasto* platters upstairs and poked her head into the dining room to catch Elena's eye. The server followed her back into the kitchen.

"Ready for these?" Olivia asked.

Elena nodded. "*Grazie*. Where is Alessandro?" Her brown eyes were wide.

Olivia held up her hands. "I have no idea, but don't tell my mother."

The girl laughed and picked up the platters. Olivia went back downstairs for the other tray. It would be much easier to serve dinner if the guests were seated in the upper kitchen area at the trestle table. She selfishly hoped they only used the formal dining room on the first night of their stay.

Elena met her on the stairs and traded the last platter for a glass of wine. "*Grazie*," Olivia said, touched by her thoughtfulness.

Elena smiled and headed back into the dining room. Olivia checked her soup. It smelled good enough to make her stomach rumble. Quickly, she chopped some bright green chard and threw it into the pot. Tomorrow, the greens would darken and she could add tomatoes and beans and serve it as minestrone. Of course, tomorrow, Alessandro might not let her back in his kitchen after the liberties she had taken today.

She heard a car drive around the side of the villa. Two doors slammed.

The chef swept into the kitchen first followed by Sean.

Alessandro made a beeline for the oven and the stove.

"What on earth took you so long?" she asked.

"Flat tire," Sean said. "We had to wait for the tow truck to bring a new one."

"You two were together?"

"I ran into him in the Piazza Dante, and begged a ride back to the villa," Sean explained.

She shook her head. "I'm so sorry my father abandoned you, but I'm glad you made it back in time for
dinner." She dropped her voice to a whisper. "I bet Papà
you would, so now he has to be nice to you for the rest
of the week."

Sean burst out laughing. "Nice work."

Alessandro looked up from the pot he was stirring.
"Thank you for making *il primo piatto*. Your soup
smells magnificent."

"The soup is only as good as the stock, and yours
was fantastic."

Color rose in Alessandro's cheeks.

Sean took Olivia's hand. The memory of their dinner
last night swept through her, raising her awareness of
him. She imagined she felt the air press against her as
he edged closer. She cleared her throat. "Go change for
dinner. We've got guests in the house."

Alessandro adjusted his chef coat. "I'll get to work."

"No way. This is my meal now. Too many chefs spoil
the broth. You can take a seat in the dining room."

He frowned. "I don't eat with your family."

"You do tonight. We've got a double date, remember? The opera? Go make yourself presentable. I hope
you brought other clothes to work today."

He nodded, looking reluctant.

"Ten minutes," she warned. "Soup's on."

<hr/>

A half hour later everyone was seated at the dining
room table, chatting and getting to know each other.
She took a seat beside Sean. "Where's Papà?" she
asked her mother.

"Checking the vines," her mother said, smiling at Alessandro. She was clearly delighted to have him at the table and Olivia could understand why as the newly arrived guests clamored for his attention.

"This is fantastic." The woman on her other side exclaimed.

"Thank you." Olivia returned her grin, glad she had taken the time to introduce herself to the guests while Sean and Alessandro were changing. Mrs. Schmidt and her husband were from Germany. They had spent the summer studying wine-making in the Valpolicella region, and Villa Farfalla was the last stop on their tour. Olivia spooned up a bite of the rich broth. It was rather fantastic.

The clink of spoons replaced the chatter as the other guests dipped into their soup. One couple had come all the way from Australia on their honeymoon, and Olivia could sympathize with their jet-lagged stasis. The husband's eyes were glazed as his hand mechanically moved his spoon from bowl to mouth. His wife sagged slightly in her chair. The four middle-aged American couples sitting at the far end of the table were traveling together and ate in comfortable silence.

Olivia concentrated on finishing her soup so she could serve the main course. Every so often, Sean would brush against her and she would have to remind herself to keep eating. Her physical awareness of him was reaching ridiculous levels. Her skin felt tingly. She was conscious of every breath she took, and she could actually feel each hard beat of her heart.

Across the table, Alessandro charmed the guests like he had been doing it every night. Even the exhausted wife perked up a bit when he told her about the classes planned for tomorrow. He urged them to get plenty of rest, absolving them of any responsibility for social interaction that evening. The Germans fired questions at him, picking his brain about the grape varietals used to make the villa's Amarone and Valpolicella and whether he thought they had a chance of reproducing the villa's famous La Farfalla. Just as Olivia was about to rescue him by suggesting they wait for her father to arrive, Alessandro began answering their questions. Her mother didn't interrupt, so she assumed he must be correct.

She left the table to return to the kitchen, glad she had pulled the lasagna out of the oven before serving the soup. It was now at the perfect temperature. She carried it up to the trestle table where Rosa and Elena were waiting to carry plates out to the dining room. As she portioned fat slices of lasagna, the smell of basil, garlic, eggplant, and rich cheese made her mouth water. The servers loaded their trays and headed for the dining room.

A sound in the lower kitchen caught her attention. Her father entered from the patio and joined her at the table, looking pleased.

"Happy grapes out there?" Olivia asked.

"Extremely. Sorry I'm late. I'll wash up and meet you at the table. Make me a plate?"

"Of course."

Her father headed for the hand sink and Olivia carried the last three plates out herself. Alessandro was still holding court, regaling the table with stories from his misspent youth. Olivia wondered why her parents didn't insist he dine with the guests every night. His easy charm encapsulated exactly what her mother was trying to achieve at Villa Farfalla.

The guests continued to talk and eat as she made her excuses and returned to the kitchen to torch the crème brûlées.

The deep orange custard looked gorgeous covered with amber sugar. She placed each ramekin on a plate with two *amaretti* cookies, wondering if she needed another garnish. Berries? Almonds? No, the perfect sheen of caramel was divine, no need to detract from the complexity of her flavors.

Sean came down the stairs just as she finished the last plate. "Can I help?"

"Nope, all done. The servers will get them. I was just headed back upstairs."

He walked around the table to stand behind her. His hands touched her hips and she felt him lower his face into the curve of her neck. He breathed deeply, making her shiver. "You smell delicious. Like citrus and spice."

Her knees gave out and she sagged against him. He cradled her against his chest. "Tired?"

"Not at all. I don't know why, but working in the kitchen today felt amazing. I felt…liberated. Not as hopeless as I've been feeling in Norton." Her sudden burst of inspiration could have something to do with the beauty of Villa Farfalla, but she had a feeling it had more to do with the man standing behind her.

She turned to face him. "Are you ready for *Romeo and Juliet* tonight?" She asked and then made a gagging noise.

He cocked his head to the side. "Don't you like the play?"

"I hate it," she said cheerfully.

"Then why are we going?" He looked confused.

"Duh—because it's in the Arena."

He laughed and bent his head to kiss her. She sank into him, reaching up to caress his broad shoulders. She dared to slip one hand beneath the collar of his shirt. His warm skin sparked a craving to feel more, to be closer. She opened her mouth. His tongue flirted with hers, teasing her. Did he want more too? Oh God, she hoped he did.

She raised herself on tiptoe to fit herself more perfectly into his tall frame, and he groaned, twisting to lean against the edge of the table, taking her body with him, pulling her forward, thrilling her with his strength. Heat flared inside her as he lifted one of her thighs to his waist. She pressed eagerly against him, wrapping her arms around his neck and brushing her hips against him in a tentative caress, captivated by the blooming pleasure that had taken over her body. The tip of one shoe connected her to the earth. The rest of her felt sky bound.

The sound of a throat clearing brought her crashing back down to the ground. She looked over Sean's shoulder to see her cousin smirking at them from the door, with Rosa and Elena standing behind her.

Gia raised one eyebrow. "I thought you two might need a hand," she said. "But I think maybe you need a room instead."

Her cousin gestured to the servers and they hurried forward with their trays. Gia picked up the two dessert plates that didn't fit on their large trays. She balanced the plates in one hand, the other she put on her hip. "Hurry up you two—it's almost eight and we need to get to the Arena."

"Let's skip it," Sean whispered, eyes gleaming. "You don't like the play anyway."

"I heard that. Don't even think about it," Gia warned from the stairs. "I'm not going without you, and your mother just told the Germans we would take them with us. You two are going to have to control yourselves for another couple hours." She headed back to the dining room.

Olivia hid her face in his chest and giggled. "Well, that was awkward."

She felt Sean's shrug. "Better Gia than your father. He offered to pay for my trip back to the States this morning."

"He did not!"

Sean laughed. "Daddy's little girl, huh?"

She sighed. "I'm sorry. Good thing I won that bet."

"No kidding. Otherwise he might try to run me off with a shotgun."

"A tractor is more his style these days. You're lucky his is broken." She grabbed his hand and pulled him toward the stairs. "C'mon, dessert awaits."

---

Sean picked up his spoon and cracked the sugar shell on top of his dessert. Mmm, pumpkin, as spicy and comforting as Thanksgiving memories. He sighed as other flavors teased his palate. Almond? Yes, and something more elusive and unexpected, like the lavender last night. He looked up to see Olivia watching him.

"Luscious," he said, taking another bite. She smiled around her spoon and he couldn't take his eyes off her mouth. He had completely lost interest in the opera tonight. Their kiss in the kitchen had made him want to toss her over his shoulder and carry her upstairs for a private performance instead.

"There's a flavor I don't recognize," Alessandro said from across the table.

"Star anise," Olivia supplied.

"A masterful touch." Alessandro's smile was a little too close to flirting for Sean's liking, and he gave the chef a long look. Alessandro shrugged and popped a cookie in his mouth.

Gia glanced at her cell phone. "Eat up, folks," she said. "I don't want to miss a single note."

Seeing her cell reminded Sean that he hadn't gotten in touch with Mr. Russo yet. He polished off his custard in a few bites and pushed away from the table. "I know we're in a hurry, but can I run upstairs for a minute? I need to get in touch with a client."

Olivia stood too. "I'm going to change my clothes. Meet you all out front?"

"Ten minutes," Gia warned.

Olivia paused at the head of the table to kiss her father's cheek. "Remember your promise," she whispered, loud enough for Sean to hear.

Mr. Marconi raised one dark eyebrow. He pinned Sean with a direct gaze, so much like the expression on his daughter's face that Sean looked back and forth between them with amusement.

Mr. Marconi nodded sharply. "Come to the winery tomorrow for the tour."

Olivia winked at him. Her grin was smug.

"Thank you, sir. I would love that." His chest tightened. When had this man's approval begun to mean

something to him? Olivia grabbed his hand and tugged
him out of the room.

# Chapter 12

"WOW." OLIVIA STOPPED, STUNNED BY THE MAJESTY OF the huge structure. The Arena walls curved across the darkening sky and hundreds of archways watched over the surrounding piazza like ancient, vigilant eyes. Most of the arched doorways were shut by simple wrought-iron grates but a few were open so that theatergoers could stream through the entrances. The last remnant of the original outer wall jutted proudly toward the sky as if declaring itself the victor.

The gate attendant took their tickets and handed each person a *libretto* and a small candle.

"Come on!" Gia urged, catching Olivia's hands and pulling her forward. "I know where we're going."

Olivia followed her into a stone corridor with crumbling walls and a high ceiling. It was dark and cool in the hallway. Sean took her hand as she began to climb the stone steps, and she was glad she had something to hold on to as they crested the staircase. Her head spun. "Whoa." A dizzying sea of people stretched left, right, and center, surrounding an elaborate stage.

Gia led them to the left and up another stone stairway. Sound rose around them as they climbed. Olivia noticed that many people were perched on the simple stone steps, miles away from the enormous stage. "How will we be able to hear anything?"

"The acoustics are perfect. We'll hear every note," Gia promised.

Her cousin stopped and gestured for them to take their seats. The Germans slid in first, then Sean, Olivia, and Gia. Alessandro took the last seat in their row.

Olivia sat down, glad that her seat was padded. Two hours sitting on a rock would kill her back. "What is this for?" She waved her candle.

Her cousin's excited smile made her look like a teenager. She held out a lighter and touched it to the wick of Olivia's candle first, then her own. "Look around us."

Olivia raised her head and saw that other people were lighting their candles too. As night fell around them, the Arena began to glow with thousands of small candles. The tiny lights made her feel reverent. She swallowed a lump in her throat. "Do they do this at every performance?"

Gia nodded. "It's tradition. Just think, if you'd come next week, you would have missed it. The opera season ends soon, and this is the last performance of *Romeo and Juliet*. I bet people have come from all over the world to see the show tonight."

The candles burned quickly, which was good because when the orchestra filed into their seats and the conductor took his place, applause swelled around them and Olivia wanted to clap too.

The conductor raised his hands.

The noise stopped instantly and the silence was as stunning as the sound.

Olivia held her breath. One note, a violin, pierced the air, and a throng of performers poured onto the stage, singing. The words were sung in Italian, but she knew

if Alessandro would stop and talk to the man. He hoped not. He didn't want anything to delay them. He was looking forward to going back to the villa and disappearing with Olivia until tomorrow morning. He shifted to ease the fit of his pants, then realized the problem wasn't arousal. He had set his new cell phone on vibrate and it was ringing in his pocket.

It was Russo. Damn it.

"Hello?" The crowd had carried them into the Piazza delle Erbe, and Sean stepped to the side to talk.

"I just got your text. What do you mean *think about coming to Italy*?"

"Your wife has said she won't contest the divorce if you agree to a two-week vacation in Italy. It's worth consideration."

"Did you give her the papers?"

"Yes." Sean pictured Mrs. Russo's devastated expression as she realized her husband had sent him. "But serving the papers is just the first step. She'll retain an attorney who will file answering papers and then we'll have to exchange financial information, go through discovery, and take depositions. We'll have to reach agreements on support, custody, and property, just to name a few. That will take a hell of a lot longer than two weeks. It will also cost more. At least this way, you get a vacation out of it." Oddly, Sean didn't feel a bit guilty as he waded into murky ethical territory.

He could almost hear Russo grinding his teeth. "How long will it take if she doesn't contest?" he asked.

"Best case scenario—two months." With Mrs. Russo's agreement, they could claim the marriage was irretrievably damaged and speed through the process.

"I'll let you know when to expect me." Russo ended the call.

Sean rejoined the group. "Sorry about that. Duty calls." He checked the time. It was late, but he suspected Mrs. Russo would want to know her husband was coming to Verona no matter what the hour. "I just need to make one more quick phone call before we go." It would only get later and he didn't want to be thinking about work when he got back to the villa.

Alessandro slung an arm around Olivia's shoulders and steered her toward a busy café. "No problem. We'll have a drink while we wait." Sean glared at his back as the Germans hurried to keep up with them.

Sean dug the Hotel Loggia Antica card out of his pocket, wishing just this once he could shrug off responsibility. The last thing he wanted to do was talk to Mrs. Russo, but the Villa Farfalla gang was already seated and ordering. The damage was done. He might as well finish the job.

---

Olivia looked away from Sean, pacing back and forth in front of a statue as he talked on his new cell phone, and eyed the shot of limoncello Alessandro placed in front of her. "Is it supposed to be bright yellow?" she asked. "It looks atomic."

"Take a sip," he urged.

She picked up the glass and sniffed. Next to lavender, lemon zest was her favorite scent and the Limoncello smelled like lemon zest in liquid form. She took an eager sip.

Lemon fire hit her nose, then her throat. "Oh my God," she croaked. "That's fabulous."

"And potent," Alessandro warned, downing his shot in a gulp.

Her second sip went down smoothly—probably because her throat muscles were paralyzed. The alcohol hit her immediately, making her feel giddy. She would limit herself to one drink and hope the heat in Sean's kiss had meant what she thought it did. Oh God, what if it didn't? What if attending to business was his way of letting her down gracefully? Maybe she had imagined the regret in his eyes as he walked away. Maybe it had been relief instead.

Alessandro signaled for another round, and she noticed Mr. and Mrs. Schmidt were keeping up with him. "Just water for me," she said, resisting the urge to drown her doubts in citrus vodka.

When the next round arrived, Alessandro tossed it back and ordered a third.

"Rough day, Chef?" she asked.

He shrugged. "No rougher than the rest of them."

Olivia nodded. She knew that feeling well. The happy bustle of the café made her feel isolated, especially when the Germans excused themselves and joined a spirited discussion of *terroir* at the next table, leaving her alone with Alessandro.

"I'm not really a chef, you know." Alessandro's low whisper carried across the table.

Had the Limoncello pickled her brain cells already? "Pardon me?"

His grin was full of mischief. "I'm a waiter. I thought I should tell you the truth before the cooking class tomorrow. We don't want a catastrophe," he said cheerfully and snagged his new drink right out of the server's hand. "*Salute!*" He tipped the glass.

"But what about all that glorious food? The osso buco? The ice cream? That perfect white beef stock?"

"Marco does most of the cooking with ideas I find on the Internet."

"No way!" Internet recipes were notoriously unreliable, and no one could make food that good with luck. "But you've been at Villa Farfalla for almost a year, right? How on earth did you fool my mother for that long?"

"She is so busy, she doesn't notice who is cooking as long as dinner is ready on time."

"You're kidding me."

He shook his head. "Why would I lie?"

Now that she thought about it, it made sense. She'd never actually seen Alessandro cook anything and Marco had been a huge help to her today. "Why does he help you? Why doesn't he demand to be the chef?"

Alessandro raised his hand, trying to catch the eye of their server again. "We have an understanding."

Olivia assumed that meant he was paying him. A zillion questions hit her at once so she started firing them at him. "Who made the lasagna?"

"Me. All fifty pounds of it."

She chuckled. "Lasagna is like that. It never looks like enough and then the noodles multiply. What about the gnocchi?"

His eyes darkened. "My grandmother's recipe."

She sat up straight in her chair and put her hands on her hips, remembering her indignation. "You put me to work chopping herbs that first day!"

He held up his hands. "I didn't know what else to tell you to do."

She slumped as she realized she'd had so little faith in herself that she had allowed him to intimidate her. "What about that list you made for Marco? You didn't have any trouble telling him what to do."

Alessandro looked sheepish. "That's easy. He made the list himself. I wouldn't know where to begin."

That struck a chord. Having run her own kitchen for two years, she knew exactly how hard it was to keep other people busy. The boss had to organize, inspire, and keep everyone moving. That's probably why she'd been so happy in the kitchen today—she had only been in charge of herself. The cooking class tomorrow would be another matter entirely. A kitchen full of amateurs attempting to cook an untried menu was a recipe for disaster. She winced as she realized those recipes had probably been cribbed off the Internet too. Maybe she should have another drink.

She tilted her head to the side. "Why are you telling me now? Why not keep your secret?"

Alessandro grimaced. "It wouldn't be a secret for very much longer. You've barely left the kitchen since you got here."

Ironic, since she had come to Verona to escape a kitchen.

He continued, "Plus, I've never made *bollito misto* in my life. Or *la peara*. Or a cake."

She groaned and buried her head in her hands. "Tell me Marco has."

"I hope so. The menu was his idea," he said.

That was something, at least. She took a deep breath and lifted her head. It was easier than she had expected to make the shift from being the person following directions to being the person giving them. The class was truly her responsibility now. Hers and Marco's.

Alessandro finally caught the attention of the waitress, but when she arrived with his shot, Olivia said, "He'd like a glass of water, please." She pointed at the complimentary snack mix on the table. "And eat up, Chef Alessandro. I expect you to be useful tomorrow."

His glazed eyes met hers. "Are you going to tell your parents?"

She shook her head. "Then I'd never get out of the kitchen."

"But isn't that what you want? To cook at Villa Farfalla?" His voice held an accusation and his dark eyes flashed with challenge. "Your mother has talked of nothing else for months. *My daughter can cook anything. She wouldn't burn the sauce. I wish Olivia were here.*"

She snorted. "It's only fair to tell you she's been saying the same things to me. *My new chef is amazing. His pesto is perfetto!* I was sick of you before I even got here. Trust me, the last thing I want is your job, but I won't have you making me feel like an intruder in the kitchen either. You keep doing your thing, and I'll do mine."

Alessandro looked wary as he gazed across the table at her. She was fiercely glad he felt threatened by her, even though she had no intention of staying at the villa. God, she couldn't imagine anything worse than being directly under her mother's thumb again. "Do *we* have an understanding?" she asked.

He nodded slowly.

"Good." She reached across the table and picked up his shot. "*Salute*," she said, watching Sean walk toward them.

# Chapter 13

OLIVIA PUSHED HER CHAIR AWAY FROM THE TABLE AND stood up. It was time to go. They'd lost enough time already. The look on Sean's face could only be described as hungry, and he was looking at her.

Mrs. and Mr. Schmidt said goodbye to their new friends, and Sean led the way to the car. She was relieved when he gestured for Alessandro to climb into the back of the vehicle.

The chef laughed. "Nonsense, it will be an adventure if I drive."

"Your driving is enough of an adventure when you're sober. Humor me." Sean held out his hand for the keys.

With a philosophical shrug, Alessandro handed them over and crawled into the car. Olivia sat in front.

"Where can I take you?" Sean asked, when everyone was inside. "I'm happy to pick you up for work in the morning."

"Don't trouble yourself," the chef mumbled. "I can get a ride out to the villa tomorrow no problem."

"What did you do to him?" Sean whispered as Alessandro began to sing something in Italian that had the Germans crying with laughter.

"Don't blame me. I cut him off at three drinks. Lightweight."

In between verses, Alessandro called out directions to Sean, leading them on a circuitous route through the city streets. Finally, Alessandro called "*Alt!*" also apparently the punch line to the joke he was telling.

Sean pulled to the curb in front of a small house that looked like it had been divided into apartments. Alessandro got out of the car.

"Are you sure you'll be okay?" she asked.

The chef laughed. "Never better." He leaned in the window to kiss her hand. "*Grazie.*"

Sean cleared his throat loudly and Alessandro let go of her hand, chuckling.

Sean pulled away from the curb before Alessandro reached the house. The rest of the drive was silent. The Germans seemed to have finally run out of energy, and Olivia was floating in a happy bubble of quiet anticipation.

As soon as they had reached the villa and bid the Germans good night, Sean pressed close behind her and wrapped one arm around her waist. His beard stubble rasped her neck. She turned to face him.

"Olivia, I'm sorry I had to make that call—"

She reached up and pressed her fingers to his lips. "I don't want to hear any apologies right now." She felt brave and desirable, and she didn't want the feeling to disappear again. The words would get in the way.

This was her moment. She knew it even before she took it. Suddenly it was easier to breathe, easier to be. "Do you want me, Sean? Do you want to make love to me tonight? Because if it's too late or you're tired or you have work to do, tell me now. Rejection feels like failure, and I've had enough of that lately."

His eyes blazed and his arms tightened around her. "I want you."

She savored the raw thrill that shot through her as he dropped a kiss on her lips. Her heart began to pound. Heat and gratitude filled her with euphoria. She turned toward the stairs and held one hand back to him. They climbed the stairs hand in hand, not speaking. His thumb played over her knuckles, stroking heat into her body, filling her with melting desire.

She unlocked her door and stepped through, hearing the lock click as Sean shut the door behind them. She turned around. Sean drew her to the bed. His fingers were nimble on the buttons on the front of her dress. "In a hurry to live out your high school fantasies, counselor?"

He pushed the material over her shoulders and the fabric fell from her body into a pool on the floor, leaving her clad in her bra and panties. His rough chuckle sounded strained. "Aren't you?"

She laughed, hoping it didn't sound as weak to him as it did to her.

His hands cupped breasts encased in thin satin, skimmed her bare waist, lingered on her hips. "I have to be honest. My high school fantasies never got much past this point." He pulled her body forward into his and found the perfect way to fit them together.

"What about all the things you said in the restaurant in New York?"

His eyes flashed silver. "I've had a lot of time to refine my plans since then." He reached forward to pop the front clasp of her bra, making a low sound as her breasts spilled into his hands. He cupped them, rolling her nipples under his thumbs until her breath came fast in her throat and her knees felt weak. Pleasure shot in a direct arc between his thumbs and her sex and she moaned softly when he took her mouth. His clothes felt rough against her sensitized skin, yet she pressed closer.

His lips drifted down her neck, pausing to lick warmth across the top swell of each breast. He kissed each tender nipple. She sank down to sit on the bed. His fingers caught the fabric of her panties and tugged them over her hips. "You don't need these."

He pressed her down to the bed. She felt very naked, lying beneath him while he was fully dressed. "Aren't you forgetting something?"

"Hmm?" he asked, shifting his weight to the side and trailing a hand over her breasts, down her belly. His finger dipped into her belly button.

"You still have your clothes on." She was glad she had finished her sentence before his fingers reached her freshly waxed bikini line. The appreciative sound he made as he traced the smooth skin chased every coherent thought from her head.

"Not for long." He sat up and slowly pulled his shirt over his head.

His unhurried movements as he kicked his shoes to the side and unbuttoned his pants made her want to shriek. "Take your time," she said tightly.

He grinned and shoved his pants and boxers off his hips and kicked them to the floor. He stripped off his socks. Again, he stretched out beside her, but this time the long, warm length of his body was completely naked. Sudden, unwelcome panic made her throat feel tight. *You want this. You just begged for it. Demanded it. You can't wimp out now.*

He rolled on top of her, keeping his weight on his elbows. His hairy legs felt rough against her smooth ones. She could feel his erection touch her belly. She reached between their bodies. She'd be more comfortable once he was inside her.

Sean caught her hand. "Not so fast." He chuckled softly and brought her hand to his mouth and kissed it. "My fantasy, remember? Yours can be next." He shifted so he was kneeling between her thighs.

She bit her lip, trying to take a deep breath without looking like she was nervous. It wasn't like she'd never done this before, for God's sake. She'd been married for two years. *To a guy whose idea of foreplay was taking off his pants*. Sean looked like he might spend the rest of the damn night making love to her, and she had no idea what to do.

"Relax," he said, reading her mind. His hands stroked slowly down the length of her thighs and back up to her waist. She shivered and it felt like every inch of skin under his hands missed his touch when it was gone. "I've been picturing you like this all week, naked, spread out on a bed with yes in your eyes."

She swallowed hard. "Do I have yes in my eyes?"

His smile was tender. "Not exactly, but I know you want to be here. I know you want me." He hooked his hands beneath her thighs and pulled her into a more yielding position. "I know the last man you had sex with was an asshole."

There it was. He'd said it. "I'm trying not to think of him."

"I promise you won't be thinking of him for very much longer." She loved his grin, the one that challenged her to be as brave as he was. She felt a smile tremble across her lips. This was Sean. She'd known him almost forever. He'd never hurt her.

"Welcome back." He bent to kiss her, a soft kiss that turned searching. She closed her eyes, didn't flinch when the hand he tangled in her hair slid down to cup her breast. He pinched the tip and she gasped under his mouth. His groan was rough and exciting.

She opened her mouth to deepen their kiss. When their tongues touched, Sean's hips jerked forward in a response that thrilled her. She wrapped her legs around him, shifting her hips to embrace him.

He lifted his head to whisper. "I knew I would love being naked with you." She was disappointed when he broke the perfect mesh of their hips and slid down her body. She grabbed his shoulders and tried to pull him back to her.

"You're doing it again. My fantasy." His words were muffled against her breast. He lingered there. She had to listen hard to catch his words, spoken between nibbles. "I mean, sure, we could just go right at it, but I don't want to rush you."

"It's okay, rush me." She gasped as his lips closed around her nipple.

She felt his tongue, his teeth. Strangely, she felt it in her breast and her groin, as if they were somehow connected. Sean moved to the other breast and cool air hit her flesh. She gasped, feeling it everywhere. She moved her hips, trying to ease the growing ache, feeling liquid and languid, as if his touch, his hands on her body removed the necessity for thought.

Sean shifted his weight lower. His hand moved from

her breast, down her belly, lower. His fingers were gentle and warm. He groaned and stopped.

"What? Is something wrong?" she asked.

His chuckle was weak. "Not a thing. You're ready for me."

She felt a blush start on her cheeks and spread quickly. She tried to ease away from his hand, but he slid a finger inside her, making her writhe against his hand. "That's a good thing, Olivia. But I'm hard as a rock and fighting against the urge to nail you to the bed right now. I want this to be good for you."

Honesty demanded honesty. "Sean, it's already better than it's ever been before."

"Really?" He moved his finger. She blushed hotter.

His eyes glowed and his sexy half smile made her shiver. His hand moved faster. She looked away, feeling herself respond but not knowing what she should do. What did he expect from her?

"Stop thinking," he whispered.

"Can't."

"Can't think or not think?" he asked.

He was laughing at her, damn it. She twisted under his hand, trying to roll away from him. He caught her shoulder and flipped her onto her back again, mastering her attempt to escape by throwing his leg over her hip. He straddled her hips and forced her hands above her head.

He kissed her stiff lips. "Give it up, Olivia. Why don't you just enjoy it?"

"I don't know how." She was not whining. She was not. "I don't know what to do."

"You do. Trust me."

"Trust you? I wouldn't be in this position if I didn't trust you."

"I know." He kissed her cheek. His eyes were dark, all mischief gone. "Let me do everything for you." He glanced at the clock on the bedside table, a wicked grin lighting his silver eyes. "Give me fifteen minutes to do anything I want."

His suggestion shocked a giggle from her throat. "You weren't kidding about high school fantasies, were you, counselor? You want to play seven minutes in the closet with me? But naked? And on a bed?"

"And with double the time limit." He released her hands. "I figure we can kill two birds with one stone this way—you won't be thinking about what you should be doing, and you won't try to escape."

She crossed her arms over her naked breasts. "You've given some thought to this."

His nod was slow and definite. "Say yes, Olivia."

Her pulse beat heavily in her ears, her throat, her sex. Sean waited for her answer. His hands skated over her skin, caressing her arms and shoulders, the tops of her breasts. He pressed his lips to her throat, making it impossible to think logically.

"Say yes," he urged in a rough whisper.

She didn't have to do anything but lie here? All the pressure was on him? She cleared her throat. "Is this is kinky or silly? I can't decide."

He raised his head. "Quit stalling." There was tension in his voice. The bones of his face stood out beneath his skin, and his jaw was clenched. His arms trembled and it wasn't from the effort of holding his weight.

She lifted one hand to his cheek. What was the worst

that could happen? Whatever happened between them tonight, she knew she could trust him. "Yes."

He rolled his hips against her, forcing her thighs apart and settling himself firmly into the soft space between them.

She gasped.

His smile was the furthest thing from safe she'd ever seen.

He pressed forward. "It's all I can do not to bury myself inside you. I can feel you, so close, so hot. You're killing me."

"Go ahead," she encouraged.

He reached for the bedside clock and turned it toward the bed. "Nope. You gave me fifteen minutes, and I'm not going to rush a single second." His body slid along her skin, moving downward. He licked her nipple and her body roared to life again, aching, making a demand.

"I hope you plan on sleeping in tomorrow." He licked her belly button. Oh my God, he was going to…was his mouth headed for …Oh God. *Thank heaven for the bikini wax*.

Sean urged her knees apart to make room for his broad shoulders. Her thighs trembled. A thousand doubts crowded into her head.

No thinking, she remembered.

She wasn't supposed to do anything but hold still. She looked at the clock. 1:14 AM.

One way or another, this would end at 1:29.

She stared down the slope of her belly. Sean smiled up at her, then bent his head. She closed her eyes. His tongue felt warm and wide as it moved slowly through her folds. She bit back a whimper.

His lips closed around her and she bucked her hips, unable to stop herself from pushing closer to him. Sharp pleasure rippled through her. It took her a second to realize she was moaning. She pressed her lips together and held her breath, trying to stay quiet.

Sean lifted his head. "Make all the noise you want, sweetheart. The walls are thick and the door is made of solid wood." He began to tease her again. New sensations bombarded her until she could no longer keep track of what he was doing with his hands and his mouth. He settled into a steady rhythm that made her pant and claw the bed.

Higher, tighter, he drove her, until she no longer had coherent thoughts except *yes* and *more*. It seemed like any second, she was going to explode. She wanted to explode. She rode his hand, his mouth, his tongue, desperately straining, eyes squeezed tight, hips thrusting in time to his swirling motions.

*How much time did she have?* The thought stole into her head. She looked at the clock. 1:24. Ten minutes had passed in a heartbeat. Was five more minutes enough to make it happen?

*Probably not.*

The thought hit her like a bucket of ice water. Her hips stopped moving. Now she really was going to scream. And maybe cry.

"Olivia?"

"I can't do this," she whispered.

"Yes, you can." Sean's voice held utter certainty. "Open your eyes." Reluctantly, she met the intense heat of his gaze. He didn't look angry at all.

"What was I doing wrong?" He wiped his mouth.

She winced. "Nothing. You were fine. I just can't. I don't—" Olivia twisted to maneuver her leg around his body, so she didn't feel so exposed.

"No way, sweetheart. You want this." His fingers brushed her thighs, striking sparks. She felt her core clench. "See?" he said.

Her head fell back against the pillows, and she closed her eyes. "Time's up," she muttered.

"Not quite." His hands touched her hips, stroking down the length of her thighs. Back up again and down, breasts to belly, never losing contact with her skin. She risked a peek.

He caught her looking. "Eyes open, sweetheart. I want you to watch." His fingers dipped between her legs. She gritted her teeth but kept her eyes on his hand.

Olivia tried to relax, but every muscle was clenched tight. It took effort to breathe without making noise. What was he going to do when he realized he was wasting his time? She was going to hate seeing pity in his eyes. She turned her face to the clock.

Out of time.

Sean reached across and swept the clock off the nightstand.

"Hey! Not fair."

"It was a stupid idea. I forgot you spend half your day trying to get orders done on time."

She took a sharp breath, realizing he was right.

He leaned down to kiss her. "I don't care how long it takes. You're mine tonight." He stretched out beside her as if they had all the time in the world.

"Sean, it's late," she began.

He nestled one leg between hers and cupped her

breast. She could feel his hardness against her hip. "You going to turn into a pumpkin?"

Olivia tried again. "Maybe you should just...you know." She raised her hands and wiggled her fingers in a *bring it on* motion.

He raised an eyebrow. "Maybe I should use your body to get myself off?" He shook his head. "Not my idea of a good time."

"What is your idea of a good time? Because this isn't working for me." She crossed her arms. *There*. That should fix his little red wagon.

He chuckled, looking completely unoffended. "Nice try." His hand moved from her breast to between her legs, and his fingers slid inside her with absolutely no resistance. Breath rushed out of her lungs.

"Turn your brain off, Olivia. Stop making comparisons. There's nothing wrong with you, trust me."

She did trust him. It was herself she wasn't sure about.

The ramifications of that pathetic fact began crashing around her head. She didn't trust herself to be a good lover. Or chef. Or best friend. She'd abandoned her husband, her restaurant, and Marlene. Now she was abandoning Sean before she gave him a chance.

"I'm sorry," she whispered.

"Don't be sorry. Be here. With me, right now. Just you and me."

She bit her lip and he nibbled at the corners of her mouth until she opened to him. His hand moved between her legs again, slowly.

"Please?" he asked, after a spate of teasing kisses.

"I can do that." *I can at least try*.

She felt him smile against her lips.

She couldn't hide her reactions from him, and it both aroused and disturbed her. Like now, she stirred beneath his touch and he moved closer, stroked deeper, somehow knowing what to do to make her respond. She thrust against his hand, feeling closer than before. Damn, the man had clever fingers. If he kept doing that, exactly that and didn't stop, maybe she could...

Not.

His hand stopped moving.

"Noooooo!" she groaned, a strangled sound that was not in the least bit sexy.

"Hang on." Sean reached over the side of the bed and grabbed his pants. A condom appeared in his hand. She watched him roll it down his length, and she opened her thighs, trying not to be disappointed. A man could only be expected to have so much patience after all, and he had no way of knowing she never came during intercourse. Unless she told him. And she wasn't going to do that.

He positioned himself between her legs and she raised her knees to accommodate him more easily. He slid inside, shuddered. Sweat beaded on his forehead as he thrust in and out of her body.

Olivia settled in for the ride, determined to hide her frustration. For a minute there, she'd actually thought it was going to happen. She closed her eyes tightly. No way was she going to cry.

She forced her thoughts away from the shame and focused on something useful. Had wines been paired with the cooking class menus yet? It was a great opportunity to showcase Farfalla wines. She made room for Sean's hand as he wedged it in between their bodies, still wondering if the Valpolicella would be too heavy for the *misto*.

She jumped, abruptly catapulted back into the present. "What are you doing?"

He moved his hand faster. "Looking for a way to drive you crazy."

"Sean, it's fine. Go ahead. It's not a big deal—"

"Please, woman." His implacable expression banished all thoughts of food from her mind. She arched beneath him, suddenly filled with heat and possibility. Sharp pleasure built under his touch.

*Clever fingers*, she chanted. *Clever fingers. Clever fingers.* "Ohh!" she cried, so full of longing and panic that she couldn't keep her mouth shut. Helplessly she met his thrusts, seeking his touch.

"Come for me, Olivia." Sean continued the motion of his hips and his hand, holding her eyes with his sharp, silver stare. His other hand tangled in her hair and his lips met hers in a kiss so hard and resolute, so full of strength and longing that she couldn't help herself.

She screamed.

Pleasure made her wild beneath him. She raced toward the edge and she no longer had any desire to stop. She ground her body against him, lifting herself, giving everything to him. He wrapped his arms around her shoulders, clasping her so tightly she could barely breathe. His hips slammed into her, pushing her higher, farther, until she fell off the edge.

Sean caught her next scream in his throat and carried it with him as he fell too.

# Chapter 14

SEAN OPENED HIS EYES SLOWLY, EXPECTING TO SEE Olivia sleeping beside him, but he was alone. She had escaped again. He wasn't completely surprised. She had fought him every step of the way last night. Well, not exactly fought him, more like she'd had zero faith in herself and by association, zero faith in him, but he had thought they'd made some progress.

He sat up in bed and saw a note propped on the bedside table. *Late for kitchen duty. Come find me.* He chuckled. Maybe they'd made more progress than he'd thought.

He rolled out of bed and picked up his pants. The weight of his cell phone in his pocket reminded him of the eternity he had spent on the phone with Mrs. Russo in the piazza last night. It had been less than half an hour, but it felt like much longer as he had watched Olivia and Alessandro talk and laugh.

His cell phone vibrated, alerting him to a new message. An unfamiliar number popped up on the screen. *I will join you at Villa Farfalla this afternoon. Marilyn Russo.* Speak of the devil. Mrs. Russo was coming here and her husband was on his way to Italy. For the moment, his work was done.

He checked his inbox, just to make sure he hadn't missed a message from Colin or his mother. Empty. He assumed no news was good news and Colin's silence meant he was enjoying having the house to himself.

He finished dressing, allowing his thoughts to return to Olivia. His work was not finished with her, not even close. Her hesitant response to his caresses had filled him with the determination not to fail her last night, and the fact that she'd slipped out of bed this morning told him he needed to try harder. He was looking forward to doing just that as soon as possible.

---

It had taken her ten minutes to wriggle out from underneath Sean's arm without waking him up. His warm body had been spooned behind her, their perfect fit an unsettling reminder of last night. She had never woken up with Keith in that position, not even in the early days of their marriage. Her ex-husband had preferred his own space, and she had gotten used to snuggling with her pillow.

The desire to roll over and embrace Sean had gotten her up and out of bed. She had slipped into the bathroom to dress and stolen out of her room as silently as possible, afraid he would wake up any minute. She didn't want to face him until she'd had time to think about what had happened. What did one say the morning after the only good sex of one's life? Thanks? Oops? What was Sean going to expect from her now?

She slipped past the guests in the dining room and into the kitchen where she sat down at the trestle table and rested her head on her arms, jerking upright as the door opened. Rosa and her daughter entered the kitchen with Gia right behind them, looking fresh as a daisy and perfect, as always.

Olivia groaned and put her head back down.

"Can we have two cappuccinos, please, Rosa? It looks like our Olivia has worn herself out sleeping."

The women giggled.

"That obvious, huh?" Olivia asked.

"What happened last night?" Her cousin sat down beside her. "You don't look like a girl who played Juliet all night."

Olivia weighed her options. Share her confusion or keep it to herself? Given her cousin's experience level, she might have some insight to offer. "I ran away."

"Before, during, or after?"

"This morning, before he woke up."

Gia's understanding nod made her feel a little better. "I've done that."

"You have?"

"Who hasn't?" Rosa set down two steaming cappuccinos and a tray of pastries.

"*Grazie*, Rosa." Gia dragged her finger through the foam on the top of her cup. "Was Sean the first since the divorce?'

Olivia nodded.

"Well, no wonder, poor thing."

It was the exact response Olivia needed to tell her the rest of the story. The floodgate opened. "I know it's hard to believe in this day and age, but Keith was the only other man I've ever slept with…" Her cousin's mouth fell open. "Just wait—it gets worse. I'd never…um, well…hmm." She forced herself to say it. "I never had an orgasm during sex until last night."

Gia's dark eyes flew wide and she began to splutter.

"I know, I know, don't say it. Just tell me what I should do because when I woke up this morning I was terrified."

"Terrified of what?" Her cousin blinked several times, long lashes fluttering.

Olivia thought about that. "I'm not sure." Thank God Rosa and Elena were in the dining room and not hearing any of this. "Gia, I don't want to run Chameleon anymore. I have no idea what I'm going to do with the rest of my life, but I know I shouldn't be distracted by..." She paused.

"Orgasms?"

"Maybe." Olivia grabbed a chocolate croissant from the tray and jammed it in her mouth. She chewed, swallowed. "This past year sucked. My marriage fell apart. I almost lost Chameleon." Her cousin raised both eyebrows. "Long story." She continued, "My two best friends back home are doing a better job running my restaurant than I ever did, so I put my house on the market and came to Italy to tell Mamma and Papà that I want to sell Chameleon. Only instead of taking responsibility for my actions and making a plan, I'm having an affair. I'm going from bad to worse."

"You are not bad." Gia rolled her eyes. "I never knew how you did it anyway."

"Did what?"

"Olivia, my God, you've been working since you could walk! I spent summers with your family, remember? It was fun, but we worked our butts off at that restaurant. I haven't been to Norton in twenty years but I can't imagine it got any easier for you when you became the owner." Gia sipped her cappuccino. "Is the restaurant in good hands? Making money?"

Olivia nodded slowly.

"Then who cares? Don't you think you deserve to

have some fun after what you've been through this year? Sean's a great guy and he's obviously crazy about you. Enjoy it. Give yourself a break, huh?"

"Is that what you're doing?"

Her cousin shook her head. "You and I are on opposite ends of the spectrum. You need to shake off your roots, and I need to find some."

"What do you mean? Your roots are here."

"No, *your* roots are here. My roots are somewhere in Asia, I think. Or they were the last time I heard from them. I envy you for having Zia Anna Maria and Zio Paolo. At least they care."

"Your parents care, Gia. They just…" There was no good way to end that sentence and they both knew it.

"It's okay. I've learned to place my own value on my life because they are never around. It's very freeing. You should try it."

Could she really shuck off the weight of her parents' expectations and choose to do whatever she pleased? What would that feel like? Selfish, she decided. Irresponsible. Guilty. "I'll think about it."

Her cousin reached over to squeeze her hand. "Can I say one more thing?"

Olivia nodded.

Gia's eyes were bright. "When you mentioned Joe and Marlene and Chameleon, I noticed you said back home. It's always good to know where home is, don't you think?"

"Hmm." Olivia took another bite of pastry. Did she consider Norton home? How would she feel if she never went back to New York? She couldn't decide if the ache she felt was homesickness or relief, so she changed the subject. "Enough about me. How was *your* night last night?"

Gia looked at her watch and stood up. "Amazing. I'd tell you all about it, but I have a massage client in fifteen minutes." She crammed the rest of the pastry in her mouth and darted away from the table. Halfway to the door, she turned around, swallowed, and said, "You sure you aren't going back to Norton?"

Olivia nodded. *Pretty sure. Almost sure.* Her heart ached again.

"Sean is?"

She nodded again, more slowly.

Gia's eyes gleamed. "If you take my advice about nothing else, I hope you have the good sense to enjoy the rest of the week together…naked." She walked out of the kitchen.

Olivia sipped her cappuccino and watched Rosa and Elena move between the kitchen and the dining room. They didn't seem to need her help replenishing the simple breakfast buffet, so she stayed where she was and indulged in another pastry. She looked at the cappuccino and croissants on the table in front of her, thinking of Sean and wishing she'd had the sense to stay in bed this morning.

It was too late to go upstairs and crawl back in bed with him, but she wouldn't make the same mistake tomorrow morning. If she had the good fortune to wake up with Sean tomorrow, warm and naked, she was going to stay in bed all day. Her heart began to beat faster. Her body heated with anticipation, and she closed her eyes to savor her favorite moments from last night. The silvery flash of his eyes. His dangerous grin. The way he had looked into her eyes as her world fell apart. Heat flashed in her center. Oh yes, she was definitely staying in bed next time.

She drained her cup and stood. She had a lot of work to do first. Alessandro and Marco would be here soon. She lined tasks up in her mind. Divide and conquer.

Were there copies of the recipes somewhere? She walked over to the desk and started looking for papers. Surely Alessandro had copies somewhere. She pulled a thick sheaf of invoices out of a cubby and glanced through them. All bills. She looked closer, noticing they were past due. It wasn't like her mother to get behind on payments. It also wasn't like her to jam papers into cubbies and forget about them.

Olivia tucked the bills back into the desk, making a mental note to mention it to her mother later. She checked the next cubby and found photocopies of the recipes. She sighed. None of them had been scaled to size, and they were all in metric. It was going to take an hour to do the math. Maybe it was a good thing she'd gotten out of bed, after all. She opened the desk drawer, found a calculator, and got to work.

———

After a quick shower in his room, Sean found Olivia sitting at the trestle table in the kitchen, hunched over a pile of books and papers.

"Good morning." He sat down next to her, giving her no chance of escape. "I missed you when I woke up this morning. We only worked our way through half the things on my list last night, you know."

Her cheeks turned pink. "Back to your list, huh? I

thought we had a deal, counselor. Isn't it my turn for a fantasy?"

Her words made him release a breath he hadn't known he was holding. He wrapped his arms around her. She wasn't on the run. She was simply busy. He bent to kiss her and she met him halfway with a sigh of surrender that made him want to lay her out on the kitchen table. His imagination caught fire trying to guess her fantasy. "Definitely. Let's go back to bed right now," he murmured against her lips.

"I've got too much work to do," she sighed and pulled away. "Later, though, I promise."

"I'm going to hold you to that." He resisted the urge to corner her for another kiss. Instead, he asked, "Do you need any help in the kitchen?"

"Can you cook?" she asked.

"Nope, but I follow directions really well."

A teasing smile played around the edges of her mouth. "I'll keep that in mind for later."

Desire surged through him, keeping him in his seat. "You are killing me."

Her smile widened. "Not what I had in mind, although I do think the French have a rather curious expression for…"

He held up a hand. "If you keep talking dirty, I won't be able to walk into the dining room." Her wicked laugh delighted him. "I'm going to get some breakfast. After that I'm going to tour the vineyard with the rest of the guests. Then I'll come back here and take great pleasure in following orders from you for the rest of the day…and night." He dropped one last too-quick kiss on her lips before he stood up.

"Have you seen Alessandro?" she asked.

"Just saw him arrive with Marco."

"Thank goodness." She nodded and picked up her calculator again.

Sean walked back to the dining room where the other guests were milling around a buffet table of fresh fruit and rich-looking pastries. He poured himself a cup of coffee and grabbed a croissant.

As he took his first bite, Mr. Marconi appeared at the door. "*Buongiorno*, everyone. Are you ready to tour the vineyard?"

The guests cheered and began to trickle into the foyer. Sean brought up the rear, carrying his breakfast with him. When everyone was gathered, Mr. Marconi led them out the front door and around the side of the villa.

It was already warm outside, but a light breeze stirred the air. Sean followed the dozen guests down the path toward the vineyard, admiring how the sun lit the tops of the trellises with green-gold light. Mr. Marconi pointed out the red and pink roses that bloomed around the perimeter of the vineyard, explaining that the flowers were susceptible to the same diseases that struck the vines. By watching the roses they could anticipate when the vines needed pesticide treatments. Mr. Marconi led them down a row, explaining the trellising system and how it was perfectly suited to the weather in Verona, the needs of the grapes, and the characteristics of the wines they would eventually become.

He stopped at the end of a row. "At Villa Farfalla, the first grapes picked will become Amarone. Only certain bunches can be used because they must be unbruised, skins intact, grapes loosely packed to allow air circulation within the bunch. *Amarone* grapes are dried for four months before they are pressed. This technique is called *appassimento* and has been used in Verona for thirty-five hundred years."

Mr. Marconi led them through each section of the vineyard, explaining what each traditional grape varietal, the Corvina, Rondinella, and Molinara, contributed to Valpolicella and Amarone. Sean forced himself to focus on the grape lesson even though he hadn't had enough coffee and the warm sun was making him sleepy. He followed the small crowd through a short break in the rows to the farthest section of the vineyard. Mr. Marconi waited for them to gather around him. "In Verona we love tradition, but we are also a practical people. The laws that govern winemaking honor tradition and quality; however, our wines will not survive if we cannot sell them. Winemaking laws must protect our industry, thus the five to ten percent of Molinara grapes usually used in Amarone can now be replaced with darker, more powerful varietals that have a more fashionable color."

He frowned, looking down the row of pinkish Molinara, then began walking again. "I disagree with fashion. At Villa Farfalla, the woman who sells us cheese walks up a mountain to get the best goats' milk. The man who grinds our rice uses the same stones his grandfather used. What is the saying? 'If it ain't broke, don't fix it'? The Molinara is an elegant grape that lends acidity to the blend. It holds its own and keeps things lively. Last year Amarone was granted DOCG status, the highest recognition of quality among Italian wines. It is our goal at Villa Farfalla to use this honor to propel our Amarone to the top of the market—by honoring traditional grapes. One day we hope to equal the success of our legendary wine La Farfalla."

Sean finished his croissant and followed the group across the vineyard to the barn-like building that sat below the tasting room. Mr. Marconi raised his arm. "This is the *fruttaio*, where we dry the grapes. If the weather holds and the grapes continue to sweeten, the harvest for the Amarone will begin at the end of the month." He opened the door to the *fruttaio*. "When we bring the grapes in here, we open all the doors and windows to allow the air to circulate. The perfume of drying grapes is indescribable—intoxicating. After four months, we crush the grapes, press them, and age the wine for at least two years."

Sean cleared his throat. "Didn't you say you only pick the best grapes for Amarone? What do you do with the rest of them?"

"We make the Valpolicella. Although the remaining grapes are not chosen for the Amarone, they are by no means inferior. A picking crew sweeps through the vineyard to pick the rest of the grapes. They are crushed immediately. If Amarone is the heart of Villa Farfalla, then Valpolicella Classico is its lifeblood. Valpolicella is meant to be drunk young, so we have a quicker return on our investment." His grin was a sharp flash of white in his swarthy face.

They filed into the *fruttaio*, where Sean saw neat rows of racks stacked ceiling high. Mr. Marconi gestured at the racks. "Although many wineries have switched to plastic or wooden racks for practical reasons, Villa Farfalla uses the traditional river reeds, which allow for better air circulation." There were no grapes in evidence but the air smelled sweet, as if the souls of millions of dried grapes surrounded them in the wide room.

The crowd was silent, eyes wide, as if they too could feel the presence of history and tradition. "It is my goal to produce the best wines in Italy and bring the legend of La Farfalla back to life," Mr. Marconi vowed.

"Will we get to taste La Farfalla?" Mrs. Schmidt asked.

"The old bottles are very valuable. Each one costs almost as much as a week at the villa, so no, I'm sorry, we won't taste La Farfalla." Mr. Marconi gave her a warm grin. "But I will show you the remaining bottles of the vintage. Last year we began exporting our Valpolicella Classico and just this summer our first vintage of Amarone became available in the world market. I hope you'll like our wines enough to look for them in your local stores when you get back home. Like La Farfalla, all our wines bear a butterfly on the label, making them easy to recognize."

He opened the door again and gestured outside. "Let's take a quick trip through the wine cellar and the barrel tunnel before we go to lunch and taste the other wines—always the favorite part of the tour."

Sean stayed toward the back of the crowd as they moved toward the tasting room.

The winemaking process was unbelievably complicated. With so many variables—weather, soil, varietals, sugar, and aging—it seemed impossible to believe that anyone could recreate a vintage. How many years would it take to recreate La Farfalla? A lifetime?

Giovanna greeted them with a wave as they entered the tasting room. He waved back and followed the crowd into the back hallway. They passed the offices and the small kitchen. Mr. Marconi used a key to unlock the door at the end of the hall, the door Sean had discovered the day they arrived. He reached into the darkness and flipped a switch.

They shuffled forward into a low room now filled with dim light. Mr. Marconi shut the door behind them.

Racks of wine bottles filled the mouth of the tunnel. Farther down, he could see barrels lining each side of the long tunnel. The smell of oak made Sean feel woozy, as if he were recovering from a weeklong bourbon bender. Mr. Marconi began explaining about the wines in the racks, stopping to display a dusty bottle or two. He walked farther down the tunnel and stopped in front of a large cabinet built into the wall. He pulled a set of keys out of his pocket and unlocked the cabinet.

There was a collective gasp as he opened the doors.

Five wine bottles sat nestled in red velvet. "The legend lives on," Mr. Marconi said, caressing the hand-drawn butterfly on the label with one gentle fingertip. Sean noticed there was room for one more bottle in the rack and wondered if it had once held six.

Mr. Marconi closed the cabinet and locked it, urging them to continue down the aisle. On the right, small barrels were stacked three high, to the ceiling. On the left, fatter barrels were lined up single file. Each barrel sat on its side and had a fat cork wedged in the top. Mr. Marconi launched into a detailed explanation of what was in each barrel and how long it would stay there, but Sean tuned him out and wandered toward the end of the row. His brain had already acquired about as much wine knowledge as he could handle today.

His phone buzzed in his pocket, so he stepped behind
a barrel to check his text messages.

*Arriving Valerio Catullo eleven thirty pm. Pick me up.*

Dare he suggest Russo take a taxi? Before he could
hit reply, another text came through.

*I need to talk to you.*

He sighed. The sound was loud and he noticed Mr.
Marconi was no longer talking. He stepped back into
the aisle. When he saw the others were already near
the mouth of the tunnel, he hurried to catch up with
them. Mr. Marconi led the crowd through the tasting
room and out the door, but Sean hung back. What could
Russo need to get off his chest before he reached Villa
Farfalla? A mistress? An offshore account?

*I'll be there.* He hit send.

From the wine bar, Gia held up a glass and raised
her eyebrow.

"Wine before lunch?" he asked as she poured two
samples.

"Wine before everything. You're in Italy, remember?
Did you enjoy the tour of the vineyard?"

He nodded and pointed at the bottle. "Let me
guess—Valpolicella?"

"Absolutely." He heard the bell on the front door
tinkle. She sighed. "No wine for the weary. I'll be
right back."

He nodded and took a sip. He was no connoisseur but
he would describe this wine as fruity. It wasn't sweet but
he tasted cherries—or was that the power of suggestion
from his recent wine lesson? Whatever its properties, it
made him hungry. His stomach growled and his mouth
began to water as he thought of the cold cuts that had

been served as appetizers when they arrived at the villa. He craved olive oil, bread, and more wine. And cheese. If Olivia didn't have to cook today, he would have loved to take her on a picnic.

Sean finished his wine and leaned over the counter to place his wineglass in the dish rack, waiting for Gia to return so he could ask her how to get to the airport.

# Chapter 15

OLIVIA GLANCED AT THE CLOCK. ANY MINUTE THE guests would stream into the kitchen for the cooking class. They were actually in pretty good shape as far as prep work, but she had butterflies in her stomach anyway.

She went over her checklist one last time. All the tools were gathered, all the ingredients within easy reach. She had multiplied all of the recipes by five and made copies for everyone. She had even kept copies of the original recipes in case anyone wanted to make a smaller batch for their family once they got back home. They had plenty of aprons, towels, and tasting spoons, but she still felt like they were missing something.

The door swung open and the guests poured into the kitchen. *Showtime*, as Marlene would say. Olivia began to hand out aprons and direct them to their stations. When everyone was settled, she still had one apron in her hand. Where was Sean? Skipping class? Disappointment struck low in her belly as she realized she'd been waiting all day to see him again. She ignored the sinking feeling and divided the guests into teams and explained the menu.

As everyone got busy, the noise level rose and her nerves sharpened. Everyone had a question for her to answer and she couldn't take a step without needing to say, "Excuse me," and gently nudge someone out of her path. She wanted to say, "Behind you!" which was kitchen slang for "Get the hell out of my way," but she controlled the impulse. Instead, she took a deep breath and focused on putting out fires, cleaning up spills, and making sure everyone was handling their knives correctly.

The kitchen congestion eased as the guests settled into their tasks, but half an hour passed with no progress. The simple menu, which had seemed brilliant yesterday, now seemed impossibly complex, even with much of the prep work already done. At this rate, they wouldn't eat until midnight.

She heard Marco singing in the dish room and dashed up the stairs. "Have you seen my mother?" she asked, hoping for some reinforcement since Marco was still finishing the lunch dishes and Alessandro was flitting around the kitchen being charming but useless.

Marco broke off in the middle of his aria. "She'll be back in time for dinner. She said she had to bribe a banker."

Olivia frowned. "Really?"

He laughed. "With your mother, it's hard to tell. She also asked me to tell you that someone named Marlene called for you."

Olivia blew a breath out through puffed cheeks. "Thanks. I'll call her back later when I don't have to be in four places at once, trying to get dinner on the table."

Marco dried his hands on a towel. "The dishes are done. What can I do to help?"

"Honestly? I have no idea." She began to laugh.

The fact that she was laughing instead of screaming or crying made her laugh harder. Last week, this situation would have been the last straw. The sheer impossibility of producing a decent meal for twenty people with at least twelve of them standing directly in her way would have sent her around the bend. Today, she felt only mild irritation coupled with the urge to order takeout Italian for twenty and drag Sean upstairs. A week ago, calling for takeout food wouldn't even have occurred to her. What had changed?

She felt her cheeks heat. No way. She refused to believe that all she had needed to regain perspective on her life was good sex. Sean was good, but not that good. Actually, he might be that good. How would she know?

"Olivia?" Marco waved a hand in front of her eyes. "Can I help you cook?"

"Right. Sorry." She pressed her hands to her hot cheeks. No time to think about sex, especially since Sean wasn't even here. She would focus on the food, the job, the challenge of the moment, and would handle this in her tried and true fashion.

One plate at a time.

She grinned, remembering Alessandro had said this was Marco's menu. "Marco, my friend, you're in charge of the entrée."

---

Olivia stood on the kitchen stairs looking out over her students. She released a sigh of relief. Everything was going much more smoothly now that Marco was working on the *bollito misto* with three of the four chatty American couples. The selection of boiled meats, beef, veal, and a local smoked sausage would be served as the entrée with *la peara*, a special Veronese bread sauce, and Marco had assured her it would be *perfetto*.

The Australian couple had recovered from their jet

lag and had the appetizers well in hand. *Primo piatto*, an easy risotto with pumpkin and walnuts, was being tended by the Germans, and the fourth American couple had the *dolci* under construction. Jury was still out on whether they could handle the *torta sabbiosa*, a cake made with polenta flour, but so far, so good.

The door opened and Sean walked into the kitchen. Her heart did a happy dance and she walked to meet him, half expecting a kiss, but stopped short when he beckoned to a stunning redhead standing in the dining room with her father.

"Sorry I'm late," Sean said. "My client's wife is now staying at the villa." The woman shook her father's hand and walked toward them. "Mrs. Russo, this is my friend Olivia. Olivia, meet Marilyn Russo."

Olivia held out her hand. "Nice to meet you, Mrs. Russo."

"Thank you. Please call me Marilyn."

This was the woman Sean had called last night? Was it too late to be jealous? Reluctantly, she offered, "The villa guests are making dinner tonight. Would you like to join us in the kitchen for the class today?"

Mrs. Russo stifled a yawn. "I think I'll nap instead. I was too excited to sleep last night."

Sean and Marilyn smiled at each other and Olivia felt another flash of uncertainty. "Please excuse me. There's chaos in the kitchen at the moment, but I hope you'll join us for dinner. I have a feeling it's going to be an adventure."

"Thank you. I will." Mrs. Russo walked toward the stairs.

Sean followed Olivia back through the dish room. "Chaos, huh? Everybody certainly looks happy."

She glanced down at the lower kitchen. The guests were smiling and laughter rose above the noise of the hoods. "Happy? Happy won't get food on the table, but I'll take it." She walked to the stairs, feeling the need to get everyone moving faster.

Where should she start? Marco was directing traffic at the stove and Alessandro was leaning on a table, watching the Australians spoon tomatoes onto grilled bread, a job that should have been done at the last minute. The bread would be a soggy mess by dinnertime. Why wasn't he stopping them? If every task had to be done twice, they'd never eat tonight. She felt her muscles cord and her jaw clench.

Sean put a hand on her arm. "Relax, Olivia. Nobody is here to become a chef. They're here to have a good time."

She paused, hand on the rail, foot poised to descend the stairs. She'd never thought about it like that. Was her job done if everyone was smiling at the dinner table, even if the food was terrible? Understanding bloomed, giving her an idea. "You are a genius."

She hurried down the stairs. "Alessandro!" she called. "Would you get us some wine, please?" Then she turned to the Australians and said, "Your bruschetta looks so good, I think we should eat it now. What do you think?"

The Australians beamed with pride and Alessandro and Sean headed out the back door to the tasting room for wine. Olivia relaxed and reached for an appetizer. She cupped a hand beneath her chin to catch any falling tomatoes and bit into the crunchy bread. It tasted like sunshine. The late summer tomatoes and basil had been tossed with olive oil, sea salt, garlic, and fresh-cracked pepper, and the bread had been kissed with more olive oil before it had been marked on the grill. It was amazing how something so simple could be so intensely satisfying.

She pretended to swoon and popped the other half into her mouth. The guests crowded around the platter and she faded back toward the stove to keep an eye on dinner.

~~~

Sean followed Alessandro out the back door and up the small slope to the tasting room. The chef selected several bottles from the rack on the wall and Sean helped him carry them back to the kitchen, where the guests had abandoned their tasks and were clustered around a platter of hors d'oeuvres. Sean snagged one while Alessandro gathered glasses in the upstairs wine bar.

Olivia was busy at the stove, stirring, then bending to peer into the ovens. He watched her buzz around the room, talking and laughing as she gathered dirty dishes and rearranged the tools and ingredients at each station. She might have her doubts, but to him, she looked utterly capable and completely in command. There was no question in his mind she belonged in the kitchen.

His stomach hollowed out, and he looked at the hors d'oeuvre in his hand, no longer hungry. Leaving Norton, he'd had every intention of making sure she returned home with him, but as he watched her work he couldn't deny she was in her element in a way she hadn't been in the Chameleon kitchen. He watched her dice an onion, feeling just as wistful as he had in high school, sneaking peeks at her in study hall.

Abruptly, he wondered what was going on at home. Colin's hearing was coming up, and although no news was good news, he should probably check in. He sent a quick text to Colin and his mother. *How's it going?* He dropped the phone in his pocket as Alessandro came down the stairs, easily balancing a full tray of wineglasses.

As the guests converged on the tray, Sean steeled himself to ask, "Would it be possible for me to borrow your car tonight? I need to pick up a friend at the airport."

"Not a problem," Alessandro said. "Marco can take me home."

"*Grazie*. I'll fill up your tank."

Alessandro nodded and handed him the last two glasses from the tray. The chef was a mystery, alternately infuriating and accommodating. Sean was never sure what to expect from him, but he was glad Alessandro was in a helpful mood at this moment. "*Grazie*," he said again.

Sean joined Olivia at the stove.

She arched an eyebrow. "Ready to take orders?"

His pensive mood vanished and he returned her smile with a wink. "Ready and willing."

---

Eventually all of the food was finished and they were seated at the trestle table. Each team served the course they had been responsible for and told how it was made, accompanied by giggling over the mistakes. The atmosphere was relaxed and celebratory. There were smiles on all the faces around the table. Even her mother looked content.

Alessandro had been charming and suave all afternoon, pretending to learn the recipes right along with the guests, which put everyone at ease. Of course, he wasn't pretending, but she and Marco were the only ones who knew that. Marco had come through like a champion with the *bollito misto*, and the bread sauce was melt-in-the-mouth perfection.

Marco had retreated to the dish room as soon as everything was on the table, declining her invitation to join them. The guests had pitched in to scrub pots, so she didn't feel guilty leaving the rest of the cleanup to him, but he deserved to celebrate a job well done. All day, he had moved around the kitchen with the ease of one born to cook. It was a shame that he seemed most comfortable cleaning. Before the end of the week, she and her mother were going to have a talk about kitchen organization. She didn't care how comfortable he was in the dish room, he should be offered a promotion—if for no other reason than because the villa needed all of his talents at its disposal.

The wine continued to flow, but Olivia only sipped at hers. Now that the stress of teaching the class was over, she was looking forward to dessert, and not the moist, buttery polenta cake that sat in front of her either. As the food had cooked, her private fantasy had simmered in the back of her mind all afternoon.

Sean took her hand under the table and she blushed, sure he must have sensed the direction of her thoughts. She looked up at him and he winked.

"Think anyone will notice if we skip dessert?" he whispered.

She looked around the table. The Germans were regaling the Americans with their summer wine adventures, her parents were chatting with Gia and the

Australians, and Alessandro was pouring more wine for Mrs. Russo. No one was paying attention to them, but she couldn't bring herself to leave the table just yet.

She moved closer to him and put her mouth by his ear. "Everyone will notice if we skip dessert."

He laughed and put his arm around her. She had loved spending the day in the kitchen with him. He hadn't been kidding—he really couldn't cook, but she had enjoyed showing him the proper way to hold a French knife, the most efficient way to dice an onion, and how to skim a sauce. Most of all she had loved the way he had appreciated her skill without somehow making it a competition, like her ex-husband would have.

She leaned into him, inhaling. Even though he had spent most of the day in the garlic- and onion-scented kitchen, she could still smell clean soap on his skin. Desire rolled through her, tempting her, setting her on fire. She knew what she wanted—to be the one in charge. She wanted to take pleasure from him, to give pleasure to him the way he had pleased her last night. It was her turn for a fantasy—if she dared. How long until they could sneak away?

Sean faked a dramatic yawn and she pinched his leg under the table, trying not to giggle.

Across the table Mrs. Schmidt yawned too. "I think our late night is catching up with me." Her husband stood and took her hand, drawing her away from the table amidst a flurry of good nights. The Americans picked up their wineglasses and moved toward the dining room, bickering good-naturedly about which card game to play tonight. The Australians looked like they might sit and talk to her parents all night, but Olivia no longer felt awkward leaving the table.

She seized the moment and stood up.

Sean rose casually beside her and they eased toward the dish room.

"Your room or mine?" she whispered over her shoulder when they reached the stairs.

"Mine." He took her hand at the top of the steps and pulled her down the hall to his room, swiftly unlocking the door. He swept her off her feet and she clutched his shoulders, laughing as he kicked the door shut behind them.

"Shower?" she asked.

"Later." He carried her to the bed and laid her down on the mattress, immediately following her with his hard body. Arousal was instant and reassuring.

Yes, she dared.

"Oh, no you don't, counselor. It's my turn for a fantasy, remember?"

# Chapter 16

Sean looked down at Olivia. Her cheeks were flushed and her eyes were bright. His blood pounded in his ears. The air grew thick and heavy between them, but he resisted the urge to kiss her. He rolled to the side and lifted her body up and over his. "Be my guest," he said, now gazing up at her.

She leaned down to kiss him. Her hair tickled his cheek and her lips brushed against his with the delicacy of a butterfly's wings. There was no hesitancy or fear in her kiss, and the transformation was breathtaking. Last night he'd had to haul her kicking and screaming through her doubts, all but forcing her to orgasm, but tonight she was seducing him with a sweet heat that made him ache.

He remained silent and still, letting her have her way with him. Her tongue touched his, and he closed his eyes, focusing on the connection between them. *Vivi nel presente.* They fit, just as he had always known they would.

He opened his eyes when she sat up to unbutton his shirt. Her hands stroked his chest, his stomach, making him shiver. He buried his hands in her silken hair as she bent to nibble the path her hands had just followed. The soft feel of her breath was luxurious, exhilarating. She spent long minutes tracing the planes of his body with her lips, then her tongue. Her hair trailed over his chest like a sash of spun gold as she moved downward.

She paused, staring at his belt. Her eyes darkened to the color of moss. He felt her hand tremble on his stomach and watched her take a few slow breaths.

Sean pushed up onto his elbows, shrugged out of his shirt. He kicked off his shoes. Gently, he moved her to the side so he could unfasten his belt and his pants and push them over his hips. He tossed his pants and his boxers onto the floor. He stripped off his socks and lay back on the bed to wait. He could take control, make it easy for her by taking the choices away, but Olivia wasn't a coward. This was her fantasy, and he wanted to give it to her, whatever it was.

He met her uncertain gaze with a calm smile. "I'm all yours. What do you want, Olivia? Tell me. Or show me."

⁓

He took her breath away. So confident, so comfortable. So…naked.

She kept her eyes on his familiar face, considering, fighting against the urge to chicken out, to ask him to decide, to lift the burden of her desire and therefore potential failure from her shoulders. The idea of living out her fantasy had lit a fuse inside her and it had burned all day, but now that the moment had arrived, she felt locked in place, unsure of how to begin. What if it didn't turn him on? Oh God, what if it didn't turn *her* on?

Olivia laid her hand on his chest. "Why don't you tell me how to please you, and I'll start there."

He smiled and stretched out on his side, facing her. "This isn't about me. It's all about you tonight." He reached forward to tuck her hair behind her ear, making her realize she was hiding behind it. "You have so many

people depending on you every single day. Your em-
ployees. Your customers. Your friends and family. So
many people expecting you to succeed, so many people
to please. Don't think about them. Be selfish, Olivia.
Embrace your own needs and desires. I'm just happy
to be here, and whatever your fantasy is—I know I'm
going to love it."

His words encouraged her—actually, they dared her.
He wasn't going to give her an out. How could he understand her so well? Her gaze skittered to the balcony. No
escape there. Well, she could hide behind the curtain,
but he wasn't going anywhere. He looked willing to lie
there all night, just looking at her with those watchful
gray eyes, waiting for her to make a move.

A wicked idea struck her. She stood up and walked
across the room to release the curtain on one side of the
balcony door. She brought the tie that held it back to the
bed with her. There was always more than one way to
get a job done. She could hide in plain sight.

She wrapped the sash around his eyes and tied it.

He smiled, a quick flash of teeth. "Spoilsport."

"You said I could do anything," she reminded him.

Freed of his gaze, her self-consciousness evaporated.
She pulled her shirt over her head and dropped it. When
it hit the floor, it made a noise, and he groaned. She
stepped out of her shoes, her jeans, her panties, making
sure each article of clothing made a sound when it hit
the floor too. She unhooked her bra and shucked it from
her shoulders. Now they were both naked.

She sat down next to him again and looked her
fill. Sean's body was beautiful, lean and taut, biceps
and triceps smooth bulges of flesh. His abdomen was

ridged and tense, his thighs relaxed. She reached out with one finger to trace a line from his shoulders to his wrist, then from his collarbone down the taut muscles of his chest, over his ribs to his navel. He sighed, moving just the slightest bit toward her. She flattened her palm to caress the warm, silken skin covering his hard abdominal muscles. He moaned and jerked, flexed toward her palm as if asking for more touch. Power surged through her, giving her the courage to take him in her hand.

They gasped at the same time. He was hot and hard, groaning softly as she explored his length, his arms and legs straight and straining, heels dug into the mattress, telling her he was enjoying her caress. She was enjoying him too, loving the way the slightest movement of her fingers provoked a corresponding movement of his body. He rose to meet her when she moved down, fell away when she moved up, giving her wordless praise.

She released him and moved to straddle his body, bracing her hands on his chest. It wasn't close enough, so she stretched out on top of him, settling herself against his warm skin, loving the clasp of his strong arms around her.

She bent to kiss him. Heat flared. His mouth opened under hers and she felt the freedom of possibility expand between them. Tentatively, she widened her lips and caressed his upper lip with the tip of her tongue.

He moaned, deepening the kiss. "You feel incredible," he whispered.

Satisfaction surged through her.

From the way his jaw was clenched and his head moved restlessly back and forth, she could tell it wasn't easy for him to remain passive, but clearly, he was having a good time. A man could not fake an erection like that, and his was impressive—at least by her previous standards. *Do not think of Keith*, she warned herself, but it was too late. She sighed.

"You're thinking again, aren't you?" Sean murmured, caressing her bare back.

Olivia cleared her throat, trying to banish the sudden thickness brought on by her stupid memory. "How did you know?"

"I don't have to be able to see you to feel your brain waves pounding against me. Smart women are sexy, but trust me, what we have going on at the moment doesn't require thought. Don't think, Olivia. Just feel. Do whatever feels good to you, for whatever reason. You have my full permission to do anything you like."

She narrowed her eyes, forgot he couldn't see her. "You make it sound so easy."

"Isn't it?" He shrugged, looking so relaxed beneath his blindfold that she almost believed him.

"In that case, I think I've put the blindfold on the wrong person."

Olivia untied his blindfold and drew it away. His eyes glowed silver as they adjusted to the return of light, then flared with hunger as he saw her nakedness. His fiery regard brought her arousal back to life, unfamiliar and scary, but welcome. Resolutely, she closed her eyes, wrapped the sash around her head, and tied it.

It suddenly became more difficult to breathe, but not because of fear. Not being able to see increased the slick need stealing through her. She felt his hardness against her as she leaned forward to find his face, clasp it between her hands. "I'm going to stop thinking now," she warned.

He settled her hips over his. "I'm looking forward to it."

With that, she kissed him. When his mouth opened beneath hers, she met his tongue with her own, gliding, exploring. She shifted above him, seeking more connection. Was she doing this right? *Stop thinking*. With his permission to do whatever she wanted, and all of his reactions blocked by the curtain tie around her eyes, it was just possible to stifle her thoughts.

His thrusting tongue in her mouth made her want to spread her legs, so she did. She shifted against him. It felt so good she pressed forward, down. She reached between them, drawing a deep groan from his chest. "One second," he said. He stretched away from her.

She froze, fearing she had done something wrong.

"Condom," he explained.

She breathed again, waiting, eyes shut tight, hanging on to her courage. She heard a drawer open, shut. A tearing sound.

He relaxed beneath her. She felt his hand over hers as he drew her forward again. Her fingers found him, now covered, and he gasped, one tight inhale. He felt huge in her hand. She leaned over him, lifted, forced her mind away from what he must be seeing as she settled her body onto his.

His low moan drove her on. Was he doing it on purpose? To reassure her? *Stop thinking*.

She began to move, slow, tight rubs that made her skin itch. She flexed her thighs to move higher and she felt her breast brush his cheek, felt his tongue on her nipple. She held still and let him draw her breast into his hot, wet mouth. His seeking tongue built urgency inside her. She thrust her hips, caught a bounce from the bed, and found a rhythm that made lights flash behind her closed lids.

How could she have been married for two years and never...*Stop thinking*. Sean sucked and tormented her with his strong tongue, wringing a wild cry from her throat. She felt his touch in other, deeper places and ground against him rubbing, arching, needing satisfaction.

His thighs pressed against her buttocks and she realized he had bent his knees, effectively making a seat for her with his body, urging her forward, toward his mouth as he levered his hips up into her in a hard caress. He sucked harder, making her move faster, and suddenly something burst inside her, chasing every thought from her head. She reached up to drag the blindfold from her eyes, wanting to see him, no longer afraid.

"You are so beautiful," he whispered.

Olivia's heart soared. She moved faster, urgency building within her. Mindless above him, she chased her peak, desperate to bring him up with her. She held fast to his shoulders, driving him now, forcing him to meet her frantic pace.

His face tightened. His muscles tensed. Fierce joy exploded inside her as he grasped her hips and they flew over the peak together.

---

Slowly, Sean came back to himself. Olivia was collapsed on his chest, a warm weight. He twisted his head to the side to see the clock and groaned. Russo.

Olivia slipped to the side and entwined one leg with his. Her arm stole over his chest and she pressed a sleepy kiss to the side of his neck. The last thing Sean wanted to do was get out of bed, but he'd made a promise.

He brought her hand to his mouth and kissed it before disentangling their bodies. He got out of bed, gathering his clothes on the way to the bathroom. When he returned to the side of the bed, she was sleeping. In the hustle and bustle of the cooking class, he'd forgotten to tell her about his trip to the airport, and during dinner, he hadn't wanted to mention it in front of Mrs. Russo. Should he wake her to explain why he was leaving? He tucked his room key into his pocket instead. He would collect Russo, hear what he had to say, and be back in bed with Olivia before she realized he was gone.

He grabbed a jacket and shut the door silently behind him. He checked to make sure he still had Alessandro's car keys in his pocket, grateful that the chef hadn't minded loaning him his car. It had saved him the expense of a taxi or the awkwardness of asking Mr. Marconi for another favor.

The directions Gia had given him were simple enough and he reached the airport without any trouble. Russo was standing at the curb, bag slung over his shoulder, arms crossed, face set. Sean glanced at his phone. Two missed calls. Patience was not Russo's strong suit.

Sean pulled up to the curb and rolled down the window. "Hello, Mr. Russo, how was your trip?" he said, wondering if the man had slept at all on the flight. He looked exhausted. After throwing his bag into the back, Russo sank into the passenger seat with a loud groan.

"Wretched." Russo closed his eyes.

"Well, you'll be settled in at Villa Farfalla in no time." And Sean would be back in bed with Olivia.

"No!" Russo's eyes popped open. He ran both hands through his salt and pepper hair, making the silver wings at his temples stick out to the sides.

"What do you mean, no? You're here to vacation with your wife, right? So you can divorce her?" Sean didn't intend the scathing tone, but there it was.

"I need a drink," Russo said, looking out the window. "Pull in there."

Russo pointed at a bar up ahead and Sean pulled over, more out of grudging admiration for the man's audacity than a desire to please his client. Russo had demanded a pick-up at midnight and now he wanted a nightcap? The guy had nerve.

Russo was out of the car before Sean could put it in park, leaving him no option but to follow. He made a bet with himself as he locked the car and was rewarded to see Russo already had a drink in front of him when Sean arrived at the bar beside him.

Sean ordered coffee. The strange car, unfamiliar route, and unpredictable client made him want to stay sharp. He watched Russo take a long drink of whiskey.

"What?" Russo asked. "Why are you staring at me?"

"I thought you had something you needed to discuss."

Russo's eyes shifted to his drink.

"No?" Sean asked. "Then let's go. It's midnight. Your wife is waiting for you."

"It's not midnight to me. It's dinnertime." Sean had forgotten about the time change. "And as for Marilyn, she deserves to wait, don't you think? After all, she abandoned me. Did you tell her you were coming to pick me up?"

Sean shook his head.

Russo pulled out his cell phone and began texting. "I'll take care of that."

He stared at the cell phone in Russo's hand. "How did you get that? When I got here, my phone couldn't get a signal."

"My new secretary picked it up at the mall for me." He shrugged and set the phone on the bar.

Russo raised his hand for a refill and when the bartender arrived, Sean said, "Make that two." The coffee was intensifying his urge to grab Russo by the scruff of his neck, stuff him into the Fiat, and deliver him to his wife. Sean had gotten out of a warm bed with a naked Olivia for this? His drink arrived and he took a slow sip.

Russo gazed around the busy bar with interest. "So, where are we going for dinner? Have you had time to scope out the local restaurants?"

"Mr. Russo, I doubt any restaurants are open at this hour. I assumed you were coming to Italy to spend two weeks with your wife, as per her stipulation."

Russo's jaw dropped and his eyes went wide with mock surprise. "According to your text, Marilyn wants me to take a two week vacation. You didn't say it had to be with her."

"Don't play stupid with me. Of course you have to spend it with her. Otherwise, she's going to contest the divorce, which could drag the process out for months, maybe even years. With her full agreement, we can claim the marriage is irretrievably damaged and everything will be much simpler for you."

Russo picked up the bar menu.

Sean snatched it out of his hand. "Villa Farfalla has food. Let's go."

"What's your hurry? According to you, it's my last night of freedom, after all. I'd like to enjoy it."

"You'll have all the freedom you can handle in a couple months." Russo's cell phone signaled a text. "Your wife is waiting," he said again.

Russo stared down at the phone with an unreadable expression. He picked it up. For a moment, Sean thought his hopes had been answered. Then Russo dropped the phone in his pocket and picked up another menu. "Let her wait."

# Chapter 17

OLIVIA WOKE UP WITH A SMILE ON HER FACE AND reached for Sean. Her hand met nothing but a cold pillow. She opened her eyes. The absolute silence in the room told her she was alone. Where had he gone?

There was no note on the bedside table. She looked around the room. The clothes he had shed last night were gone too. So much for her fantasy of sleeping in with him today.

She scrambled out of bed and dressed, not wanting to be there when he got back. She had spent too many mornings exactly like this, wondering if her ex would bother stopping at home before he went in to work. She doubted Sean was with another woman but his absence aroused the same empty feeling in her center. It was better to get up and get busy. Staying in bed would only underline the fact that he had left her alone.

This was a fling, she reminded herself, a vacation. Sean was leaving at the end of the week and unless she went with him, she'd be waking up alone every day. A glance out the curtains told her dawn was approaching, and Alessandro's black car was making its way up the driveway. Since he was early for work today, maybe they could do something special for the guests' breakfast. She hurried back to her room for a quick shower.

Just as she emerged from the bathroom, she heard

a light knock on her door. She tightened her robe and opened the door an inch.

"Thank God," Sean said, pushing the door open just as she decided to shut it in his face. He stumbled into the room and sprawled on her bed.

She shut the door and went over to him. "Are you drunk?" she asked.

"Hung over," he replied. "Is it possible to be hung over from three drinks?"

"Depends. What were they?"

"Whiskey, prosecco, and grappa, I think. I wasn't paying attention. I was just keeping up with Russo until I decided one of us needed to sober up to drive home."

Betrayal knocked the breath out of her. "What the hell were you doing with Mrs. Russo?" she gasped, furious.

"Not Mrs. Russo. Her husband. Shhh, my head is killing me."

He looked like his head was killing him. His face was gray and his eyes were shut tight. His shirt was untucked and he had one fist pressed against his forehead.

Mr. Russo was in Italy now too? She lowered her voice, somewhat mollified. "Why weren't you in your room when I woke up?" Wincing at the whine in her voice, she quickly asked, "Where did you go?"

"I had to go get Russo. I forgot to tell you. You looked so pretty asleep in my bed. I didn't want to wake you. Sorry," he mumbled, and rolled over, scrubbing his face into a pillow.

She grabbed his shoulder and hauled him onto his back. "Hold on a minute. I'm not done with you yet. Sit up." She went into the bathroom and rifled through the drawer, sure she had seen a first aid kit in there. When she found it, she grabbed a pack of ibuprofen and ran a glass of water from the tap.

She returned to the bedroom. Sean was sitting up, but his head had fallen back against the headboard. He groaned when she touched his shoulder. "Here." She handed him the glass of water and the pills.

"Now, what's going on with the Russos?" she asked when he had finished drinking.

He groaned again and collapsed sideways in the bed. "Who knows? Mr. Russo wants a divorce and Mrs. Russo will only play nice after her vacation." His voice was muffled by the pillow. "I can't imagine how those two stayed married for almost thirty years. Can you keep an eye on them while I get some sleep?"

"Where's Mr. Russo?" she asked, covering him up with a blanket.

"I gave him my room."

Sean caught her hand and tried to draw her into bed with him. "Not a chance, pal. I want coffee." And some time to think about the fact that she had been way too disappointed when she woke up alone for this to be a simple fling for her. "Sleep it off. I'll watch the Russos." She pushed his hand away and left the room, shutting the door quietly behind her.

Why did she find it so disturbing that Sean had left her in bed to carouse with a client? She had often run into Sean at Johnny's bar late at night and on weekends, and it was hypocritical to be upset about him facilitating the breakup of a marriage. He was her divorce lawyer, after all. It was his business to break up marriages. Still, it hurt. She wanted to mean more to him than a week of good memories.

*Not good. So not good.* Apparently she was incapable of having a decent breakdown and having a proper affair. It would be funny if it weren't so damn tragic. She shoved the kitchen door with more force than necessary and gasped when Mrs. Russo jumped out of the way.

"I was just...I wanted—" Mrs. Russo began.

"I'm sorry!" Olivia exclaimed at the same time. "I know better than to open a door that fast." She frowned, taking in the other woman's tear-streaked face.

Mrs. Russo dropped her eyes. She hovered in the doorway, seeming to be uncertain of whether she should stay or flee.

"Can I make you a cappuccino?" Olivia asked. "I don't know about you, but I can't function without coffee in the morning. What brings you into the kitchen so early?"

"I wanted coffee too," Mrs. Russo admitted. "But I can't work the machine."

"It's not as complicated as it looks." Olivia began assembling the ingredients. The kitchen was empty, so the black car must have been Sean and Mr. Russo returning to the villa. "I hear your husband has arrived."

Mrs. Russo flinched.

Olivia paused. She set the milk on the counter, unable to ignore Mrs. Russo's distress any longer. "Listen, I have no idea what is going on with your marriage but is there anything I can do to help?"

Mrs. Russo shook her head. "My husband wants a divorce."

"And you don't?"

A sad smile curved the older woman's lips followed by a melodic sigh. "I want my husband back."

"Well, he's here. You must have done something right."

"Have you ever seen one of those fishing shows on TV? The ones where they catch a huge marlin, and it fights and fights, and by the time it's on the boat everyone is exhausted and at least one person is bleeding?"

Olivia nodded.

"That's us. Tony is the fish, but I'm not tired of fighting him yet."

"So what are you going to do when you catch him? Throw him back, like they do on the fishing shows?"

"I'm not sure. If both of us survive this, I might jump back in the water with him."

"I never would have thought of that," Olivia said, taking a deep breath. Was that the answer to her problem too? Did it have to be a fling? The spark of an idea began to glow, but it was too early for heavy planning. She needed caffeine to clear the cobwebs from her head.

Olivia flipped the switch and the nozzle began to steam and hiss. Over its roar, she asked, "Would you like a frittata? I'm in the mood to cook breakfast."

———

Sean blasted his lingering headache with a hot shower and went down to the kitchen, sure he would find Olivia there. It wasn't quite lunch time and he hoped to lure her away with another fantasy—a picnic.

Most of the guests were in the game room and the kitchen was quiet. Olivia, Alessandro, Marco, and, strangely, Mrs. Russo were working in the lower kitchen.

"Good morning," Olivia greeted him with a gleam in her eyes. "How's your head?"

"Fine." He glanced at Mrs. Russo. "Has—"

"He's still hiding." Mrs. Russo put her hands on her

hips. "As well he should be. What was the meaning of sending me a text if he wasn't planning on coming to the villa? I was up all night waiting for him."

Sean winced, feeling lucky that he'd managed to get Russo to Villa Farfalla at all. "Sorry about that. He's—"

"Impossible?" she supplied. "Ornery? A pain in the behind?"

"Still sleeping, I guess," Sean finished with a bland grin. "I'm sure he'll be down directly."

Mrs. Russo snorted and went back to chopping onions. He hoped her red eyes could be attributed to the vegetable and not her husband, but he wouldn't count on it. "What's on the schedule?" he asked Olivia. "Any chance we can sneak away for a picnic in the vineyard?" After listening to Russo talk about his wife last night, he wasn't sure he wanted to witness their reunion.

Olivia frowned, looking around the kitchen. "The guests are going into the village for lunch and a walking tour, but there's a lot to be done for dinner…"

"Which can all be done after your picnic," Marco piped up from the stove. "An excellent idea. I'll pack it myself."

Olivia looked torn.

"Fantastic." Sean smiled his thanks at Marco, then turned to Olivia. "Go get changed and meet me on the back patio." She looked reluctant to leave the kitchen, but she went.

Sean was waiting with a blanket and a basket when she arrived on the patio fifteen minutes later. He'd never seen anyone pull a lunch together as fast as Marco and Alessandro, and he was grateful. He was still annoyed with his client for keeping him out of bed last night.

Nothing sounded better than spending the next hour or two stretched out on the soft blanket with her.

They found a little clearing not too far into the woods behind the villa and chose a shady spot on the edge for the blanket. Sean felt the last of his hangover disappear as Olivia smiled at him. He loved seeing her like this, carefree and happy. They lounged in the sun-dappled shade, eating fruit, cheese, and thin sandwiches made on flat bread. Across the clearing, a stream trickled into the deeper part of the forest, providing tranquil background music. She unearthed a packet of cookies with a grin of delight. "Still hungry, are you?" he asked.

"Nope, just feeling indulgent." She sank down onto the blanket and stretched. He rolled over and looked down at her, noticing that her forehead no longer showed a hint of the lines she had worn in New York. Her mouth was soft, her jaw relaxed. Her clear green eyes held nothing but drowsy pleasure and contentment. "Why so solemn, counselor?" she asked, curving a hand around his neck and pulling him down for a kiss.

He licked a crumb off her lip. "Just thinking about how much I love being here with you."

She smiled. "I love it too. I can't remember the last time I felt this relaxed. I'm not sure I ever have."

He bent to kiss her. "Italy certainly agrees with you." Her mouth opened sweetly and hot need replaced the sinking feeling in his stomach. How could he ask her to go back to New York with him, back to all the things that had carved lines in her face and filled her eyes with fear and doubt?

She mumbled something against his lips, and he drew back. "What was that, darling?"

Her sigh puffed against his lips. "I wish I didn't have to make dinner tonight. I'd love to go into town and do some sightseeing. We could stuff ourselves silly, drink until we're senseless, and…" She trailed off.

"Make love until we pass out?"

She bit her lip and her cheeks got pink, but she nodded.

"So why can't we? Why do you have to cook dinner? Isn't that Alessandro's job?"

"Technically, yes. But he can't cook."

"What?"

"While you were talking to Mrs. Russo after the opera, Alessandro confessed he's really a waiter—he can't cook at all."

"Then why did he take a job as a chef?"

"I didn't ask. I was scrambling to figure out how to handle the cooking class and wondering whether or not we were going to…"

He pressed a kiss to her lips. She wrapped her arms around his neck and he forgot they'd been having a conversation. When he came up for air, he remembered to ask, "So who has been doing the cooking?"

"Marco."

"So let Marco cook tonight."

She laughed.

"I'm serious. Let's go into town—or to Venice. The villa was doing just fine before you got here." Except he knew that wasn't true. Mrs. Marconi had actually almost smiled at him when he had introduced her to Marilyn Russo and explained she wanted to book a two-week stay. And hadn't Gia told him the villa was having money trouble?

He felt like a traitor for not wanting Olivia to become

more firmly entrenched in the everyday operations of the villa, especially when it was clear she was so valuable. The cooking class yesterday had been an enormous success. In fact, he'd overheard the guests asking when the next class was scheduled. He also knew the grape harvest was approaching, and that there was a big party planned for the weekend. That meant Olivia would definitely be needed in the kitchen. He should be glad that she had found happiness here, and yet all he wanted to do was spirit her back to New York where he couldn't lose her again.

Her hand stroked his back. "I would if I could—"

"But you can't," he finished for her.

She shook her head and even though his heart ached, he was proud of her.

He looked down at her. Her lips were swollen from his kisses and her hair was spread out on the blanket. "At least we still have a few hours." And the rest of the week. It wouldn't be enough, but he wasn't going to waste a minute of their time together.

---

Olivia sat up and yawned. "What time is it?" She hadn't meant to drift to sleep but her full stomach, the warm sun, and Sean's fingers stroking her hair had relaxed her to the point of unconsciousness.

"Two thirty," he said. "I was going to wake you up at three."

"Time to get moving," she said, yawning again. "You've been keeping me up too late."

"Complaining?" he asked. "If I remember correctly, you were the one keeping me up last night."

Their eyes caught, held. She traced his playful smile with a fingertip and laughed. "A technicality." She rolled off the blanket and got to her feet, stretching the kinks out of her back and watching Sean repack the basket and fold the thin blanket.

"Thank you for the picnic. It was lovely," she said. It was also another first for her. The more time she spent with Sean, the more she realized how much her marriage had lacked in the romance department. Her ex-husband had never taken her on a picnic. He'd never held her while she slept and stayed awake to make sure she wasn't late for work. For once, thoughts like that didn't make her feel bitter. She wasn't going to waste her energy being angry with Keith anymore. She would just love Sean instead.

A dull roar filled her ears and she missed the words coming out of his mouth. "What did you say?" she asked.

"I said it was my pleasure." He took a step toward the path, looking back at her when she didn't follow. She turned her back, pretending to take one last look around the clearing to make sure they hadn't forgotten anything. There was no point in denying it anymore, at least to herself. She loved him.

On some level she had always hoped to rekindle their high school connection. Was that what had prompted her to take her restaurant business to a divorce lawyer? Was that why she had turned to him when her marriage failed? She had certainly jumped at the idea of spending the week with him. She swallowed hard, feeling sick as she remembered Sean hadn't argued the night she told him she might not return to New York. He hadn't brought it up since then either. For all she knew, he was enjoying a vacation fling with her. Period.

"Olivia? Are you coming?"

She squared her shoulders and turned around, pasting a smile on her face. A few slow steps brought her back to his side and she took his hand and held it. He quirked an eyebrow at her, but she shook her head. She didn't want to talk about it. It was too new, too fragile, and possibly all in her imagination. She wasn't going to be the one to turn this week into something it wasn't. That would ruin the fantasy for both of them.

"Let's go," she said and led the way back to the villa.

When they reached the back patio, Sean followed her into the kitchen. "Hey, chefs, what's cooking?" she asked Alessandro and Marco, who were peering into a stockpot. They broke apart.

"Minestrone," Marco said with a wink, grinning back at her. "Then shrimp with grilled polenta."

"*Antipasto?*" she asked.

Marco held up a hand and crossed to the cooler. After a moment, he declared, "Cheese. A few perfect vegetables." His dark eyes lit up. "And I found some fresh white figs in the market today." He held up a piece of prosciutto and gave her a triumphant grin.

She was still full from their picnic, but the menu sounded perfect. "Sounds great. What can I do?"

"*Dolci?*" he said hopefully.

She groaned. She was much better at the savory side of the kitchen. Marlene had always handled desserts at Chameleon. She felt a pang of guilt as she remembered she had forgotten to return her call yesterday — and why. She glanced up at the clock. Marlene was just beginning her work day now and probably wouldn't welcome an interruption. "Dessert, huh? All right."

Marco pulled a tub of mascarpone out of the cooler. "Tiramisu?"

She shook her head. "Needs to set overnight and unless you have ladyfingers, I'd have to make them."

He looked so disappointed that she relented. "Fine, I'll make it for tomorrow. But for tonight, something simple." What, she had no idea, but she'd figure it out. "Give me something small to do while I think."

Marco tossed her a bucket of broad beans. She nodded and grabbed a cutting board, showing Sean what to do with the beans. They worked in silence for a minute. "Any of that lavender ice cream left?" she asked Alessandro.

"About a gallon."

"Perfect." She had just enough time to make pastry dough and put together a couple of *tarte tatins*. They could bake during dinner, and the lavender sorbet would be exquisite, melting over the hot flaky crust and harmonizing with the floral notes in the caramelized apples. "I'm going to need some room on the stove," she warned the boys.

They shrugged and began consolidating pots and pans. She left Sean with the beans and did a sweep of the kitchen to gather ingredients and consult a cookbook from the shelf on the desk. She quickly tossed the right ratio of flour, salt, and sugar into a bowl and grabbed a pound of butter from the reach-in. She plugged in the food processor next to Sean. A few minutes later, her dough was wrapped and chilling and she was peeling apples.

She could feel Sean's eyes on her as she worked. She moved faster, showing off a little. She hoped they could find another small task for him to do so he would stay in the kitchen and keep her company.

"Olivia! There you are."

She turned to see her mother on the stairs. "*Ciao*, Mamma."

Her mother caught sight of Sean and frowned.

Olivia smothered a giggle. Her mom would really glower at him if she knew they had spent the day making out on a picnic blanket. "Do you need me for something?" Olivia asked.

Her mother nodded. "I need to talk to you."

Olivia set her knife down on the cutting board and followed her mother up the stairs. "What's going on, Mamma?"

Her mother led her through the dish room and into the empty dining room. She stopped next to the table and crossed her arms. "I need you in the kitchen," she said flatly.

"Didn't you just find me in the kitchen?" Olivia asked, stung.

"Hours and hours after I started looking for you. We have a lot to do for *la Sagra dell'Uva* and I can't afford to hire more kitchen staff because that damn tractor keeps breaking down. And for some reason, our creditors have lowered our limit to a ridiculous level. I need working capital. The only reason I'm making payroll this month is because I bribed the banker with a bottle of La Farfalla."

Olivia gasped. Those bottles were her father's pride and joy. Shame made her cheeks feel hot. "I'm sorry, Mamma. Of course I'll help." Her cheeks felt stiff as she smiled. Resentment burned a hollow in her middle.

*Of course I'll go to culinary school, business school, run Chameleon, work in your villa.* If her parents needed help, she would help. She turned her thoughts away from how it made her feel and focused on solving the problem. That was easier. "Do you have reservations for the coming months? Is there any money coming in?"

"We're half booked," her mother said.

"At least you have some deposits to work with." That was something, at least.

"We don't take deposits. Guests pay in full when they arrive."

"What?" Olivia asked, aghast. "What about cancellations? That's a terrible policy."

Her mother's face tightened. "I'm not going to take money for a service we don't provide."

"But you can't provide a service at all without working capital," she argued.

Her mother grunted. "I'll figure something out. It is a very good thing the Russos arrived when they did. Thank you for helping in the kitchen, *cara*. You're a good girl." She turned her back and walked toward the staircase, leaving Olivia to stare after her. Her mother had done it again, neatly put her in place without making her part of the larger puzzle. She could do more to help at the villa than chop herbs and vegetables.

Every restaurant struggled with labor costs, but there were always ways to scale back without sacrificing quality. Labor was the single largest expense in any hospitality business, and it couldn't be helping Villa Farfalla to have a chef in the kitchen who wasn't doing the work. Should she tell her mother about Alessandro? Probably, but now that he wasn't trying to intimidate her, she actually liked the guy. He had talent and he shadowed Marco's every move, clearly showing his commitment to learning how to cook. The fact that he had confessed his ignorance to her instead of botching the cooking class told her he cared about the reputation of the villa. Chef or not, he was an asset in the long run.

She heard footsteps and ducked out of sight as Mr. and Mrs. Russo came down the stairs.

"They serve dinner here, don't they?" Mr. Russo sounded as grim as Sean had looked this morning.

"Yes, but I saw the loveliest *osteria* yesterday. We're going to have dinner there." Mrs. Russo's voice was cheerful and calm. Olivia pressed her back against the wall and grinned, picturing Mrs. Russo with a sturdy fishing pole in her hand.

"I'm not."

"Fine. Stay here. I'll go without you. There's my taxi now."

"You can't go alone!" Mr. Russo's voice exploded in the foyer.

"What's one more night alone, Tony? Can you remember the last time we went out to dinner together?" There was a harsh taunt in her voice that told Olivia it had taken two people to damage this marriage. She knew that truth intimately.

The front door shut behind them and Olivia walked over to the window to watch the Russos get into the taxi together. The poor guy was hooked. He just didn't know it yet.

Sean was gone when she returned to her cutting board. Oh well, she'd see him later. Her mother didn't expect her to sleep in the kitchen. She picked up her knife and dug into the apples again. A smile curved her lips as she thought about the ice cream and remembered Sean liked lavender too. When she saw him again, she'd bait her hook with a very seductive *tarte tatin*—and another fantasy.

# Chapter 18

SEAN SAVORED THE LAST BITE OF THE BEST APPLE TART he'd ever had in his life. "Outstanding," he said to Olivia. Dessert had been served on the back patio and the guests were clustered at the wrought-iron tables. Alessandro and even Marco had joined them tonight.

"Where's Gia?" he wondered aloud, realizing he hadn't seen her since last night at dinner.

"With Vincenzo." Olivia rolled her eyes.

Alessandro's espresso cup clattered as he set the cup in its saucer. "*Mi scusi.*" He pushed away from the table. "I think I left something in the oven."

Marco glanced from him to Olivia, then stood to gather their plates, apparently deciding three was a crowd. "*Buonanotte.*" He winked and headed for the kitchen.

Sean felt a hand on his thigh and glanced over at Olivia. She beckoned to him and he bent to hear her whisper, "Do you still have all those towels in your bathroom? And a Jacuzzi?"

He nodded, feeling a grin spread across his face. Their eyes met. As one, they stood. He didn't look back to see if anyone was watching them and neither did she. When they walked through the kitchen, Alessandro and Marco were nowhere in sight, and he was glad. He didn't want to have to make any more small talk while visions of Olivia naked and slippery were floating through his head.

Olivia took the lead as they climbed the stairs. Her steps were swift. He unlocked his door and held it open for her, following her into the room. As soon as the door shut behind them, he turned her around and flattened her against the wood. She melted into his arms, all lean strength and softness. Her lips were sweet and he couldn't wait to taste more of her.

"Get naked," he said. "I'll go run the bath." He pushed away from her body and went into the bathroom.

It didn't take long for the water to reach the perfect temperature, but it was going to take a while to fill the huge tub. He hardened, thinking of all the things they could do while they were waiting. He placed a folded towel on the wide edge of the tub. Thinking for a minute, he placed another folded towel on the bottom of the tub to cushion his knees. Yes, that would do nicely. He dug a condom out of his travel bag and tossed it next to the tub. Then he placed a few more towels on the floor to catch the drips. He stripped and was ready for her when she walked into the bathroom, wearing one of his Oxford shirts.

"Hey, what happened to naked?"

She bit her lip. "It just seemed a little...bare."

"Really? Hmm...okay." He noticed she hadn't buttoned the shirt, so he reached forward and stroked the back of his hand across her flat belly. She inhaled sharply. He moved his hand up, across the hard peaks of her breasts. She swayed toward him and he opened the lapels of the shirt, so that her breasts made contact with his chest. He slid one hand into her hair and tipped her face. Their lips met, opened, tongues stroked.

He reached down to clasp her thighs and lifted her

body. She wrapped her legs around his waist. Slowly, carefully, he walked to the marble counter. She hissed a little as he set her down, moving to sit on the tail of the shirt.

"Cold?" he asked.

"Freezing."

"I'll get another towel," he said, easing her off the counter.

"I have a better idea." She took his hand and led him to the tub. She sank down onto the towel, looking adorable sitting on the edge of the half full tub, wearing his shirt and a very naughty smile. She reached forward.

He groaned as her hand closed around him. He was unable to take a single breath as her lips touched his shaft. His eyes slid shut, but with nothing to focus on but the slick heat of her mouth around him, his control shredded. He gasped, eyes popping open, but it didn't help. The many mirrors in the room gave him view after view of them.

Need spiraled through him, filling him with urgency. He had been planning playful Jacuzzi time, but if she kept doing that exact thing with her tongue, playtime would be over.

He put his hand on her head and she eased back, looking at him with a question in her eyes. He stepped into the water and knelt, placing his hands on her thighs to keep her sitting. "Feet in the water, please."

She turned to face him.

"My turn," he said, putting his hands on her knees and easing them apart. He smoothed his hands over her thighs and bent his head, inhaling her addictive scent. She quivered as he touched her with his tongue and her low moan rose above the sound of the water. He looked up, glorying in the way her head was thrown back and her breasts were peeking out of the shirt.

She braced her hands on the edge of the tub and thrust her hips forward, opening to him. His tongue slid through her folds, meeting wetness. She whimpered and pressed toward him, so he focused on that spot, teasing it with his tongue while his fingers traced a path into her body. She felt so tight around his fingers that it was hard to resist the urge to rise up out of the water, carry her into the bedroom, and lever himself inside her body, over and over again.

Her fingers clutched his skull, pulling his hair. With one hand, he held her still for his tongue while he explored her core with the other. He felt her swell to meet him, so he crooked his fingers and rubbed harder, flicking her with his tongue.

Her hips thrust in time with his fingers and he caught her first few pulses against his tongue. He kept his fingers inside her, pushing deep, and pressed his other palm against her belly. She jerked under his hands and rippled against his fingers again. Satisfaction surged through him as he eased his hands away from her body.

Her eyes fluttered open. She shrugged his shirt to the floor and sagged forward into the water, making him chuckle.

"Ready for some action?" he asked, finger poised over the button that would start the jets.

Her giggle was weak and breathless as she nodded. He hit the button, bringing the jets to life, and reached behind them to turn off the taps. Her body floated in front of him, and he reached out to wrap his arms around her. The jets pummeled his back and he pondered the logistics of having actual sex in the tub. He might have made a tactical error. He should have let her finish him.

She peeled his arms from around her waist and turned to face him in the tub, wrapping her long legs around him. He felt her heels press against his lower back as she scooted forward. The softest part of her bumped up against the hardest part of him and he groaned, embracing her.

He reached over the side of the tub, groping until his fingers touched the condom. Having sex in the tub was bound to be a little awkward, possibly uncomfortable, and it might cause a minor flood in the bathroom, but what the hell. If he didn't get inside her in the next two minutes it was going to be embarrassing anyway. "Hang on."

He unlocked her legs from around his waist and kneeled to roll the condom onto his cock. When he sat back down with a splash, she climbed back onto his lap and gripped his shoulders while she forced her buoyant body onto his. Her breasts were at mouth level and he took advantage of that happy coincidence, entertaining himself with her sweet pink nipples while she experimented above him. He remembered from past tub encounters that the problem usually lay with lubrication. That didn't seem to be a problem at the moment.

She shifted and ground into him, using her knees to support her body as she searched for the perfect fit. Her maneuvers left his hands free to slide between their bodies, reminding him of last night when she'd been doing a similar move on the bed. Struck by inspiration, he gripped her knees and lifted her legs around his waist again.

"No traction," she complained.

"Just wait." He wrapped his arms underneath her buttocks to support her weight and began moving her body up and down over him. The water swirled and roiled around them. Color rose in her cheeks. Her teeth sank into her lower lip and her eyes fell half shut. Her fingers dug into his shoulders and the little pain put a sharp edge on his pleasure.

The friction was just perfect, the drag and sweep of the water caressing his skin in a constant arousing wave of pleasure. She dropped one hand between their bodies and he felt her searching fingers brush against the spot where their bodies joined. The depth of her newly discovered sensuality astounded him, and when she opened her eyes and gazed down at him with a knowing half smile on her lips, he held her tighter and moved her faster.

Her walls quickened around him, squeezing, pulling him deeper into her body.

"Olivia," he sighed, burying his head in her breasts as wave after wave of pleasure blinded him to everything but the taste of water on her skin and the heat of her body pulsing around him.

Her head fell forward onto his shoulder and he slowly became aware of the fact that his fingers were clutching her hips in a bruising grip. He blew a harsh breath and loosened his hold. "Sorry," he said, reaching beneath the water. She floated in the tub as he heaved himself to his feet and took care of the condom.

"I think I've had enough action." She hit the button to stop the jets and dipped below the surface of the water. She emerged dripping and reached for the shampoo.

"Let me," he said, stepping back into the tub.

He situated himself behind her again and poured shampoo into his palm. He worked it through her hair and carefully rinsed the suds from her scalp. When her hair was clean, he soaped his hands and began to rub her shoulders.

Her head dropped forward. "Feel free to do that forever," she mumbled.

He rinsed off the soap and kissed the back of her neck. "Why don't we move to the bed and I will?"

"Done." She rose and stepped out of the tub. He followed her, grabbing a towel and using it to dry every inch of her body. She smiled as she stretched up to give him a kiss, then padded out of the bathroom naked. He heard her sigh as she sprawled on the bed. *God, I love that woman*.

His heart slammed in his chest.

*Oh my God.*

He glanced into the bathroom mirror and noticed he didn't look surprised.

---

*This is what marriage should have felt like.*

Olivia rolled onto her stomach and groaned as Sean smoothed lotion over her back. His hands were magic, pure magic. His fingers sought out all her tight spots. For once her stress had not been born in the kitchen. She had sliced apples, rolled dough, and piped ladyfingers at warp speed. Her *tarte tatins* had turned out great and the tiramisu chilling in the cooler was bittersweet bliss. Nope, spending the afternoon in the kitchen with Marco and Alessandro had been fun. Her newly identified feelings for Sean weren't making her anxious either, although they probably should have been. Every time her thoughts spiraled into doubt, she heard him telling her not to think. So far it was working.

She had enjoyed cooking today, but her anxiety kicked up every time she thought about her promise to her mother. She didn't want to be pressed into service every waking minute. If she spent all her time in the kitchen she wouldn't have a chance to explore her feelings for Sean. She couldn't be sure she actually wanted to go…home.

Not home to the restaurant—to New York. The past year felt like a bad dream now, something she could shake off, not something that was going to ruin the rest of her life. She wished she could take full credit for getting her head back on straight and regaining perspective, but she knew she owed her renewed lease on life to the man who was currently digging his thumbs into her butt.

"I don't think you're going to find any tension there," she chided.

"You'd be surprised." His thumbs dipped lower, into a hollow. Her back arched and she yelped. "See?" He soothed her zinging nerves with long, smooth strokes of his fingers.

His hands drifted to the back of her thighs, slipped between them. She muffled her moan in the pillow as her body came to life under his hands. He wasn't even doing anything, just smoothing lotion over her legs, slowly, patiently, allowing her thirsty skin to drink up his lavish attention. She had been thirsty for a long time.

Two months ago, she had turned to him for comfort and been rejected. That seemed like a bad dream too.

Her throat tightened and she felt tears well in her eyes. Even then she'd known he was a safe anchor.

A muffled trill sounded from the bathroom.

She rolled over. "Is that your cell phone?"

He nodded. "I'll get it in a minute." He reached forward and wiped a tear from her cheek, frowning. "Are you okay?"

Her smile made another tear fall. He caught that one too, raising his finger to his lips.

"Never better. I didn't know I could be this happy," she said softly.

His eyes gleamed silver, in a look she recognized and welcomed. He grasped her hips and moved her to the middle of the bed, centering her head on a pillow and sheathing himself before he settled over her. "Let me see if I can make you just a little bit happier."

His chest and thighs were warm as he pressed her into the bed. She wrapped her arms around him as he took her mouth in slow, soft, drugging kisses. They shared a breath as he moved inside her, their union no longer in question. He lifted his head and his intense gaze demanded surrender. She gave it to him, body, heart, and soul, trusting him to keep her safe, going with him as he led her higher, no longer fearing she might fall.

# Chapter 19

SEAN WOKE, UNSURE WHAT HAD DISTURBED HIM. Olivia was tucked into the curve of his hips and his arm encircled her waist. Her hair tickled his nose and he smiled, inhaling her flowery scent. She felt so right beside him. He never wanted to leave this bed, never wanted to leave her side, never wanted to go home to New York without her, but he couldn't deny she belonged here—and he didn't. Dread stole through him, making him feel cold.

After their picnic yesterday, she had slipped on a chef coat, put her hair in a ponytail, and begun peeling apples like she'd been looking forward to it all day. He had stayed to watch her work, admiring the way she could carry on a conversation with Marco, half in Italian, half in English without once stopping the motion of her knife. When she had left the kitchen to talk to her mother, he had watched Marco and Alessandro cook, trading spaces at the stove and shifting to give each other more room when necessary. In contrast, Sean had moved farther out of the fray until he could no longer deny that he was in the way.

A muffled trill from the chair next to the bed made him realize what had awakened him. The phone sounded again and he sat up. He had rescued their clothes from the swamp in the bathroom last night but had forgotten to check his messages.

He slid his phone out of his pants pocket. Four texts? He tapped the screen. One from his mother and three from Colin. This couldn't be good.

He checked Colin's first. *No matter what Mom says, do not come home. I didn't do it and it's going to be fine.*

Panic spread through him. He had lived in fear of this moment for years, worrying every time the phone rang that it was Colin, calling from a bar, a party, the emergency room at the hospital.

His mother's message read: *I think Colin got arrested. Call me ASAP.*

His brother's other messages were variations on the first, but Sean didn't believe him. Even if Colin hadn't actually been charged, any little thing could jeopardize his release from probation. Even this late in the game, he could still be sent to jail.

God, what day was it? Tuesday already? The hearing was tomorrow. Shame chilled him as he realized how little he had thought of his brother since he'd been gone. He rolled to the side of the bed and punched Colin's number into his phone.

"Is everything okay?" Olivia's sleepy voice sounded worried.

"I don't know." He evaded her hand, reaching for his leg and went into the bathroom, closing the door. The phone rang and rang. What was he going to say when it went to voice mail? He didn't have to decide because voice mail never picked up. He switched to texting and paused. What did he want to know? *Are you OK?* That was a good start.

He called his mother, but she didn't answer either. Selfish. He'd been selfish to leave New York before

Colin's hearing. He should have known the kid couldn't hold it together without him. He strode back into the bedroom and grabbed his clothes from the chair. Even if he got on a plane immediately, he was at least sixteen hours away from New York. Could he get home in time to help Colin? Damned if he wasn't going to try. He found his leather attaché case next to the desk, swiftly repacking it with necessities. He didn't want to waste time booking a flight and dealing with the language barrier. He'd just go to the airport and take the first and fastest flight back home.

Olivia rose from the bed. "What are you doing?"

"Colin's in trouble. I have to go home."

She reached his side and wrapped her arms around him. "I'll go with you."

He looked down at her. She was willing to go back to Norton, to all the things that had made her miserable, just to support him? Now he really loved her.

He brushed her bangs out of her eyes and dropped a grateful kiss on her lips. She truly was the most amazing woman, but he couldn't allow her to come back to New York with him. He wasn't that selfish. He'd known it when he woke up this morning. She belonged here in Verona with her family. She'd come here to build a new life and she had blossomed, cooking great food and entertaining the guests with the cooking classes. Her happiness was a beautiful thing to see, and he would never forgive himself if he ruined her fresh start by dragging her back to Norton into misery and troubles. Selfishness had led him to leave Norton when Colin needed him most. He wouldn't compound his sins by ripping Olivia away from Villa Farfalla just when she was settling in.

He hugged her tight, returning her embrace, savoring the feel of her sleep-warm skin against his own. He bent to inhale the flowers in her hair one last time and press his lips against the smooth skin where her neck met her shoulder. His arms tightened convulsively around her and his body hardened. She pressed closer, caressing him from shoulder to thigh in long strokes that made him long to be inside her again. He closed his eyes, embracing the fantasy of making her his forever.

Then he let it go.

He stepped back, putting necessary distance between them, and shook his head. "There's no need for you to come with me. There's probably nothing I can do, but I have to go. You should stay here."

She looked at him in bewilderment. "And what? You'll see me later?"

He didn't say anything.

"Sean? I thought—"

He saw doubt in her eyes and felt like he'd been punched in the gut. He forced himself to continue packing. "It's not your problem, Olivia. Stay here with your family." He heard her take a sharp breath and then silence. He risked a glance to the side and saw that she was picking up her clothes.

When she was dressed, she raised her face to his. Her eyes were a dangerous green, darker than he'd ever seen them. "I understand you need to help your brother, Sean, I really do. Of course he's important to you. Your protective instinct is part of what I love about you, but I'm not getting an *I'll call you when I get home* or *I'll come back as soon as I can* vibe from you."

Sean said nothing, helplessly watching her come to

her own conclusion. Her expression gave nothing away, but he knew from the tense set of her shoulders and the clench of her jaw that he had hurt her. "You're not going to call me when you get home, are you?"

"I think it's better if I don't." Better for her to start her new life unencumbered.

Her cheeks flooded with color. "I feel like such an idiot. You felt sorry for me, didn't you? Poor, frigid Olivia needs some good loving to fix her right up."

"No." At least in this he could be honest. "I'm just a selfish bastard. I wanted you. I've wanted you for years, Olivia."

"And now that you've had me, you're done. Wasn't good enough for you, huh? Couldn't hold your interest for more than a week? The story of my life. I just wish you hadn't pretended to enjoy yourself so much."

The bitterness in her voice froze him to the core. He couldn't leave her thinking that. Some good had to come out of this sacrifice. "You are incredible." He grasped her arms. "You exceeded my wildest fantasies."

"Don't mention fantasies to me." She shrugged his hands away from her body and bent to pick up her shoes. "We've known each other for too long to play that game any longer. It was never just a fantasy for me. Now that I see how easy it is for you to leave, I'm sorry I thought it could be anything more. God, you're the cold one, Sean." He saw tears rise in her eyes, but she blinked them away. "I hope you can help your brother. I wish…" She paused. "Never mind. The number for the taxi service is printed on the phone. Good luck."

The door shut quietly behind her. He didn't blame her for making *good luck* sound like *fuck you*, but it took him a minute to shake off his grief. He'd done the right thing. Colin needed him and Olivia didn't, but he still felt like he was making a mistake as he reached for the telephone.

# Chapter 20

OLIVIA IGNORED THE KNOCK AT HER DOOR AND THE voices calling her name. She stayed in bed, glad her door was locked. She wasn't ready for kitchen duty yet. Her food would probably kill someone à la *Like Water for Chocolate*.

Sean was gone. Thinking about last night felt like fingering a bad bruise, sharp pain and then a sick, drifting sense in her middle. He had never wanted a relationship, just a quick fling, easily abandoned. She sighed and heaved herself out of bed, feeling heavy inside, as if someone had carved out her chest and replaced it with rocks. She stood under scalding water in the shower for a long time.

Getting dressed seemed to take forever. Finally, she made it to the stairs but she couldn't force herself to go into the kitchen. She looped around the staircase and walked out the back door toward the vineyard. The guests were going in to the village again today, shopping and having lunch at a *trattoria*. This afternoon, they would tour a cheese shop and learn how the local varieties were made. When they left, then she would go to the kitchen and begin prep for *la Sagra*. The thought made her want to go back to bed.

She sat down on the soft ground cover in between two rows of vines. Looking up at the fat grapes, she thought her father must be pleased, although she knew size and sugar content didn't always equate. She would have to ask him when the harvest would begin. Now that was something she could handle. Mindlessly picking grapes for hours on end was just her speed. She'd beg for a spot on the crew. She shivered, but the chill in the morning air wasn't enough to drive her back inside. She wrapped her arms around herself and raised her face to the sun.

A shadow passed over her eyelids. "Your mother is looking for you." Her father's voice was amused.

"What else is new? Do you think she'll find me?"

"Not out here. You're safe."

"Good." She shaded her eyes and looked up at him. "Sean is gone," she ventured slowly.

He nodded and thankfully said nothing.

"I don't want to go back to Norton."

Her father shrugged and plopped down next to her. "So don't."

"But Mamma is going to kill me. I don't want to run the restaurant anymore. Now that Joe and Marlene are both there, there is nothing for me to do. My day is a joke. I'm useless."

"That's my favorite girl you are talking about," he chided her. His eyebrows rose, two sharp arcs. "Did I ever tell you why we left New York so suddenly after your wedding?"

"Nonna wanted to come to Verona?"

He shook his head. "Your mother was lost without the restaurant."

"But she insisted on giving it to me!"

"She wanted you to have it, but it had been her life for so long, she didn't know what to do. She was so proud of you, so happy you loved the work, but she felt useless too."

Olivia scowled at him.

He grinned. "How else could she feel when you came home from that fancy cooking school and started telling her how to make pasta? When you insisted we needed to change the menu to keep up with the times? When you were right? Your mamma couldn't get away fast enough, but she was so proud of you. She just needed to find her place again. Just like you. We came to Verona at Nonna's insistence, but your mamma was the one who needed to find a new home, a new passion."

Olivia's heart began to beat faster. Her throat felt thick with the beginning of understanding. "I want to sell the restaurant to Marlene and Joe."

He shrugged. "So do it."

It wasn't that simple. It couldn't be…could it?

He chuckled. "Ah, my girls. So much alike. Stubborn to the core, the both of you."

Olivia felt a void yawn wide inside her. "It can't be as easy as you make it sound."

He smiled kindly. "No, probably not, but you should talk to your mamma. Ask her about how she felt when she left Norton. She's probably recovered enough to talk about it by now. Possibly."

Olivia shook her head. "No way."

"Talk to her, *cara*. Give her a chance to understand. Tell her how you feel."

"I can't, Papà. She doesn't get it. She just tells me what to do, and she doesn't ever listen. And then I do what she wants because I hate to disappoint her."

"You don't disappoint her, *cara*. She thinks the sun

rises and sets on her girl. You should hear her in the market. My daughter this, Chameleon that—"

"That's just what I mean, Papà. I can't run Chameleon and now she expects me to help at the villa too. I can't do it anymore. I don't want to do it, and I don't know how to tell her."

He shrugged philosophically. "Well, you didn't come here not to tell her, did you?"

He had her there.

She rested her head against his shoulder. "Can I work in the vineyard instead of the kitchen?"

He put his arm around her. "You're going to have to face her sometime."

"I know. I will, but not yet. I need a plan first."

"You and your plans. Ever since you were a little girl you never took a step unless you were sure of how your foot would land." He leaned over to kiss her forehead. "Of course you can work in the vineyard."

He pushed himself to his feet. "There's a lot we need to do to get ready for the harvest. I'm off to pick up some barrels this morning, but I can keep you busy this afternoon."

"The busier the better." She wanted to work until she couldn't think.

Her father's grin was a sharp slash across his tan face. "This is the year, *cara*. This is the year of the next La Farfalla."

"I hope there is something good about this year."

He pulled her to her feet and hugged her tightly. "I'm sorry about your man, *cara*. I was starting to like him."

She nodded, feeling the prick of tears again. She eased out of his arms and headed toward the villa, deciding she would cook after all. She needed something to keep her mind off Sean until her father got back. She pulled open the door of the lower kitchen.

Hearing raised voices, she climbed the stairs.

Alessandro stood near the dish room with two men she didn't recognize and one she did—Vincenzo.

"Am I interrupting something?" she asked.

"No." Alessandro's smile was strained. "They were just leaving."

Olivia held out her hand to Vincenzo. "I'm Olivia Marconi."

He tucked an envelope into his jacket pocket before he shook her hand. "Vincenzo Ferrari." The press of his palm against hers was cool and brief. The other two men stepped back slightly as if they didn't want or expect to be introduced. All three men were dressed in the sharp fashion Italian men had perfected. Olivia barely controlled a shudder. Vincenzo was definitely a player. He might be ten or fifteen years older than her ex-husband, but he had the same slick charm, the same air of entitlement, and the same atrocious effect on her nerves. Why did her wonderful cousin have such terrible taste in men?

"Are you here to see Gia?" she asked.

He nodded casually. "We have a brunch date, but I thought I would say hello to my old friend Alessandro Bellin first."

"I didn't realize you were acquainted." The back of her neck prickled.

The door from the dining room swung open and Gia entered the kitchen, making a beeline for Vincenzo. "I thought that was your car. You're early!" She leaned up to kiss his cheek.

Vincenzo put his arm around Gia. "It was nice to meet you, Olivia. I'm looking forward to *la Sagra dell'Uva.* Villa Farfalla's hospitality is legendary."

She forced herself to return his smile. Of course Gia had invited him. Everyone in the village would be at the party. "Nice to meet you too," she said.

Her cousin hung back as Vincenzo moved toward the door, trailed by his silent entourage.

"Olivia!" Her cousin's sharp whisper drew her attention away from the door. Gia clapped a hand to her chest. "I'm so thoughtless to desert you when your heart must be broken. I just heard about Sean. I'm so sorry."

"What happened to Sean?" Alessandro asked.

Gia smacked his arm.

Olivia felt her cheeks burn. "Nothing. I do not want to talk about it. I don't even want to think about it." She faced Alessandro. "Let's just cook." Anything was better than thinking. Pain pricked her memory.

Marco poked his head around the divider. "I'll put you to work, Chef Olivia," he said. "And you too, Bella Giovanna." He'd been so quiet she hadn't realized he was in the dish room.

Gia groaned. "Zia already roped me into kitchen duty for the rest of the week. There goes my manicure."

Olivia gave her a gentle push toward the door. "Go while you can, then. I'll see you tomorrow." She didn't want her cousin forcing sympathy on her right now.

Alessandro followed Gia out of the kitchen, probably to get the scoop on Olivia and Sean. Gossip traveled fast along the grapevines in Verona.

She gave Marco a warning look. "Just give me a list."

---

Sean stared at the woman behind the airport counter. "What?"

"I'm sorry, sir, but your credit card has been declined. Do you have another one?"

He shook his head. No, he didn't have another one. He had just brought the one, thinking it would be easier to keep track of his expenses. Now he saw the flaw in that logic. "I used this card to purchase my ticket and I have identification." He kept his voice calm and reasonable. "I don't want to buy a new ticket. I just want to make some changes to my itinerary. Can you call my credit card company? The number is right here on the card."

"Sir, I'm sorry, but I need a valid card to make the changes." Her voice was firm. She glanced over his shoulder at the next customer in the line.

He stepped sideways into her line of vision. "This is a valid card. It's mine and I pay the bill in full every month. A simple phone call, please. There must be some mistake. I need to get home as quickly as possible." Desperation bled into his voice.

She reached for the telephone and dialed, either moved by his plea or deciding it was the quickest way to get rid of him. Sean didn't care as long as it got him on the second flight. There were only two flights that would get him out of here in time to make Colin's hearing, and he'd already missed the earlier one. He watched her punch numbers into the phone and waited.

After a few moments, she nodded and relief made him take a deep breath. "You see, it was all a mistake," he said as she hung up the telephone.

"No mistake. This card is expired." She opened a drawer and pulled out a pair of scissors.

Sean snatched the card out of her hand. He pointed at the expiration date. "It doesn't expire for two weeks!"

"According to your credit card company, this card has been deactivated. Did you get a new one recently and forget to destroy the old one?"

"I've been using this credit card for years." He put the card in his wallet and backed away from the desk, hoping she wouldn't call security. He walked down the concourse until he felt calm enough to call his credit card company himself. They gave him the same information, plus more. Yes, he did have a new card. It had been activated from his home phone, and there was no way for him to use his old card. At least they offered to overnight a card to Verona, but that would be too late. Sean was determined to find a way out of Verona on the ten thirty flight, so he could get home and kill the only person who could be responsible for the mix-up. Colin.

He ended the call and stared at his phone for a moment, refusing to allow rage and frustration to overpower logic. He didn't need a credit card. He needed money, but every person he knew in Italy was at Villa Farfalla and probably hated him by now. He closed his eyes, trying to think, but all he could see was Olivia's face as she blinked away tears. Her eyes had held disappointment but not surprise, reminding him of the way Mrs. Russo had looked when he appeared in her hotel with the divorce papers. He had done the right thing for Olivia, so why did it sting so much? He felt himself sink a little lower as he realized there was one person at the villa who might help him.

He called up the contacts in his phone, selected Russo, and dialed.

# Chapter 21

THE SUN WAS MERCILESS AND THE BUGS WERE BITING. Her father hadn't been kidding about the amount of work that needed to get done. She felt like she'd peered beneath every leaf in the vineyard, looking for mold, signs of bugs or anything that might damage the vines. She brushed her hair out of her eyes and examined a bunch of purple-black Corvina grapes.

Her father dropped another box of sparkly ribbon at her feet. She picked up a trailing strand and tied it to the trellis to scare the birds away. He watched her work for a minute, nodding his approval. When she glanced over at him, his eyes were serious. "Do you know why we dry the grapes for Amarone?" he asked.

Olivia stopped working and frowned. "No, actually. I never thought about it."

He nodded. "Part of the reason is to concentrate the sugar, but there is something special about the Corvina. Dehydration stresses the grapes and brings out flavors and aromas that are found in no other varietals." He touched her shoulder. "Like you, *figlia*. Your stress has made you strong. Unique. Valuable."

She turned back to the vine. She didn't know what to say.

He patted her shoulder again and headed back down the row to the tractor. Her brain buzzed with the heat, the mosquitoes, her father's words. She wanted to believe him, but she didn't feel strong.

She felt used, worn out, and broken. How could Sean have left her here—just like that? How could she have been so wrong about what was happening between them? He'd wanted a week, and she had wanted…more. Given another few days, she might have been thinking in terms of marriage and babies and building a life together. She had already begun planning her return to New York. She grasped a post, afraid this last failure might take her down to her knees again, and if it did, she wouldn't be able to find the strength to get up this time.

Hadn't she learned anything from her marriage? She had nearly run Chameleon into the ground by allowing her ex-husband to make decisions she didn't feel capable of making herself. She sucked in a harsh breath as she realized she had wanted Sean to guide her too. God, she was such a weakling, hoping for a man to ride in with answers, waiting for Romeo, sad sack that he was, to rescue her.

The blame wasn't entirely hers this time; she hadn't asked Sean to come to Italy with her. However, she had certainly allowed him to take charge of her state of mind once they got here. Well, not anymore. Now he was gone and she could go back to figuring out what she wanted to do with the rest of her life. She had felt strong, secure, and capable with him, and she refused to believe he had taken her strength with him when he left.

*You let him go*, the voice that had been getting louder over the last few weeks declared.

She grabbed more ribbon and tied it, taking stock of her life. Her marriage was over. Joe and Marlene had Chameleon covered. Sean was gone. What was left for her?

Her heart throbbed. She missed him. How was that even possible? Tears ran down her face. She lifted her shoulder to wipe the moisture out of her eyes and continued to move through the vineyard, examining the vines one leaf at a time.

—⁓—

Sean stood as he spotted Russo striding into the airport. "Thank you for meeting me here," he said as his client stopped in front of him.

"Not a problem," Russo replied. "I was glad to get away from Marilyn. She planned to drag me to Venice today." The older man led the way to the ticket counter where the same woman was waiting. "Let's make the changes to your ticket, and then I'll give you some traveling money."

Sean handed his passport across the counter with a smile. "Let's try his card now."

She tapped numbers into her keyboard. "I'm sorry, sir, but the ten thirty is full. I can get you on the seven o'clock flight tomorrow morning."

Too late for Colin. Damn it. "Are there any other options?" he asked, trying to hold his patience.

"I could check flights leaving Venice." She looked hopeful, probably wishing to avoid the scene he was about to cause. He nodded, not trusting himself to speak.

"There's a direct flight to New York City leaving Venice at ten o'clock tonight, and from there you can take a connection that arrives at eleven thirty tomorrow morning."

"I'll take it," Sean said. "What's the quickest way to Venice?"

"The train," she began, pointing toward a sign.

"Nonsense," Russo interrupted. "We'll get a taxi and I'll go with you."

"I thought you didn't want to go to Venice."

"Not with Marilyn. I can't go to the most romantic city in the world with my wife." He shuddered and leaned against the counter.

Sean stared at him for a moment before he shrugged, figuring it didn't matter how he got there or with whom as long as he got on that plane tonight. A few minutes later the woman handed him an updated itinerary and Russo signed for the charges. "Thank you very much for your help," he said before he followed Russo toward the airport exit.

Russo had already caught the attention of a taxi driver and was opening the door. Sean climbed into the back with him, fastening his seat belt as Russo leaned into the front seat and said, "Take us to Venice."

Sean checked his phone for messages and sent Colin another text. Why the hell wasn't his brother contacting him? He tried his mother again. No answer. Again. God, what if Colin was already in jail?

"How are things going with your wife?" Sean asked, trying to distract himself.

"Fine." Russo's voice was curt.

Sean looked out the window, doubting that Russo was telling the truth but reluctant to pry. Beautiful scenery passed at a fast clip, and after about an hour, the driver dropped them off at a curving bridge.

"Let's see what Venice has to offer," Russo said with an almost manic gleam in his eye.

Sean followed him over the bridge to a narrow footpath, watching Russo check his phone again, as he had every few minutes during the ride. The last time Russo had been avoiding his wife, she had called or texted every few minutes. Mrs. Russo must have changed her tactic. Grudging admiration made him wonder again if he was on the wrong side of this battle.

Russo bought pastries for them and continued to walk, dodging an aggressive street vendor intent on selling him an elaborate gold watch. "No *grazie*."

Russo seemed lost in thought and that suited Sean perfectly. They made a damn fine pair tramping all over Venice, glaring at their cell phones and making polite comments about churches and architecture. After about two hours, they paused to rest in a square that housed an enormous clock with a bell on top. "Gondola?" Russo asked.

Sean nodded and they were off again. As they traveled down the Grand Canal in a gondola draped with Persian rugs, all Sean could think about was the night he and Olivia had eaten at Trio. *There aren't any gondolas in Verona. The canals are in Venice.* He wished she was here with him now.

Russo looked as morose as Sean felt as he called to the gondolier to take them to shore. After paying their fare, they headed toward one of the many restaurants that lined the canal. Russo looked in at the display of fresh crab in the window and cursed. "No matter what I do, I can't escape her."

Sean raised an eyebrow.

"Marilyn loves fresh crab." Russo scowled.

Sean followed him inside, offering no comment as they were seated and allowing Russo to order for both of them. He sipped his wine and tried to reach Colin again, unsurprised when a great mound of chopped crabmeat piled high in its shell arrived at the table. He picked up his fork and dug in, frowning when the smell of fresh herbs made him think of Olivia.

"You left her, huh?" Russo shoved his plate away and wiped his mouth with the back of his hand. He refilled their wineglasses. His eyes, when he met Sean's gaze, were fierce. "Better now than in thirty years when it's too late."

"We wouldn't be sitting here now if it were too late. You'll get your divorce." He couldn't keep the rancor out of his tone.

Russo shook his head and glowered. "It's no use."

Sean crossed his arms, glaring back at him.

"My wife is demanding. What do they call it these days? High maintenance? Everything has to be done a certain way, at home and at work, or there's hell to pay. She insists we drive to work every morning, even if I have to wait for her to get ready, sitting in the car, fuming. She stays up late at night, reading, although she knows I hate the light in my eyes. She's everywhere—at her desk every time I leave my office, in the kitchen every time I want a snack, in bed before me every night, and now…" He trailed off, staring into his glass.

"Now?" Sean prompted.

"Now that she's gone, I'm confused when I come out of my office and she's not at her desk. I can't sleep without her reading light shining in my eyes." He sighed, seeming to shrink a bit in his chair before he gained steam again. "I sat in the car for fifteen goddamn minutes the other morning, waiting for her to come out of the house. I do things my way now, at home and at work, but when I do, I think of her, every time, with every change, and I don't feel the satisfaction I thought I would. She's still driving me crazy every single day." He downed the rest of his wine and gave Sean a belligerent look. "Her absence is driving me crazy. All these years I wanted to get rid of her but now that she's gone I've discovered something horrible. I love her more than I loathe her. Go figure." Russo's mocking chuckle turned into a sob and he clapped a hand over his mouth.

Sean looked away, giving the man a moment to compose himself. The gilded gondolas gleamed in the light of the setting sun. When he turned back, Russo's eyes were watery and his expression was haggard. There was defeat in the sag of his shoulders beneath his expensive suit.

Russo spoke softly, as if he were talking to himself. "All day, I thought of her. In the taxi. On the bridge. In the gondola. I think of her every time I take a step, every time I take a breath. I can't stop thinking about her…"

Sean cleared his throat. "Then what the hell are you doing with me?"

"Because I've ruined everything!" Russo grabbed his temples, making his thick hair stick out in sharp tufts.

Sean shook his head. "No, you haven't. The woman loves you, God knows why. Don't waste it. Go back to Verona and tell her how you feel."

"I can't."

"You have to."

"What am I going to say? 'Sorry, darling, I forgot I loved you'? 'I'm sorry I've been such a bastard for, oh, twenty years'? She must hate me. Can't you tell her for me?"

"Coward."

Russo gave him another imperious scowl. "Don't forget, you work for me."

"Not anymore." It was way past time to step out of the middle. "I quit."

---

The sun was beginning to set when her father patted her on the shoulder and said, "*Finito*." The day had passed in a blur of sun, sweat, grapes, and tears. Her fingers felt sticky. Her shoulders ached from raising her arms to tie the shiny ribbons. She had taken no breaks except to help her father get the bins out of storage.

She was grateful for the exhaustion that made her mind as leaden as her muscles. She washed her hands and sat down with the guests in the dining room, ate her dinner without tasting it or hearing a word that was spoken around her until her father kissed her cheek.

"Get some rest, *cara*," he said.

She nodded and watched the guests leave the table, noticing that Mr. Russo was absent. She thought about calling out to Mrs. Russo, who looked a little lost herself, but remained silent, not sure she could take any more misery.

She pushed away her untouched tiramisu and pillowed her chin in her hands, mustering the strength to climb the stairs in an upright position. Her arms had done most of the work today, but she had also spent time stooping and bending. Could her legs support the weight of her upper body? Or should she go sleep on a lounge chair on the patio?

As the thought crossed her mind, she knew she was in trouble. The last time she had considered such a thing, Sean had been here. She had been happy. They had kissed, almost made love, and she had fallen asleep in his arms. She swallowed thickly, feeling her mother's eyes on her as she rose, hoping to get to the stairs before the tears began again. The vines could not comment on her emotional state, but her mother would have no compunction.

"When is Nonna arriving?" her mother asked.

Olivia shrugged.

Her mother consulted her watch. "I'll call her."

Remembering Nonna's injunction about needing a break too, she said, "I'll do it."

"We need her help in the kitchen as soon as possible. The guests will spend part of every day cooking traditional festival foods. Alessandro will have his hands full, and I'm not sure you…"

Olivia appreciated her mother not saying what she was thinking for once. Her mother must have realized the fact that liberal doses of wine and low standards had made the first cooking class a success. She probably had doubts that Olivia could pull off food preparations for the entire extended villa family. All of Verona, the grape pickers, their families and friends, the cheese man, the rice man, the mailman, absolutely everyone who was anyone was invited. "I'll tell her, Mamma."

Her mother still looked concerned, but she allowed her husband to draw her back to the head of the table.

"Wait." Olivia walked to stand in front of her parents. She'd been thinking about it all day, rehearsing what she was going to say until the words no longer took effort. The growing grapes had been an excellent audience.

"I know I've disappointed you." Her mother frowned, so she rushed to explain. "I married Keith and I let the restaurant fall apart. If it weren't for Marlene, I don't know what would have happened to Chameleon. She and Joe are the best people to run the business, and I want to sell it to them. I'm not going back to Norton. I came to Italy to tell you that I am finished."

Her father put his arm around her.

Olivia was surprised that she felt none of the emotions she had expected to feel when she finally told her mother she wanted to quit. No guilt, no shame, no desire to apologize. She just felt empty. She waited for her mother's response. Maybe then she would feel something.

Her mother clapped her hands together. "*Perfetto!*"

Of all the responses she had anticipated—fury, disappointment, scorn—delight hadn't even entered her mind. There was no other word for it. Her mother looked joyous. "You will stay here and I won't have to pay someone to help Alessandro."

She stared at her mother in confusion. "You don't care that I want to sell the restaurant?"

"To Marlene? Of course not. She's like family."

"But I failed, Mamma. I couldn't do the job."

Her mother's smile was rueful. "I think we are learning the same thing at the same time. Sometimes you can't do the job yourself and you must find the right person to do the job for you. I think it is called management."

Her father chuckled. "You did a wonderful job in the vineyard today, *cara*."

"And a magnificent job in the kitchen too." Her mother poured three glasses of wine and handed one to her. "*Cincin*. To your future at Villa Farfalla."

Olivia's heart felt like a butterfly trapped in her chest. She drank to dull the panic.

She hadn't actually said yes, but her mother had

taken her assent for granted. She had been pulled back into the fold, unable to resist the pull of her mother's expectations. It was better than she deserved. So what if she felt trapped? She could be happy here. She stood woodenly in their embrace, locked in place by the vision of her future taking shape before her, filled with family, tradition, security…and no Sean.

Her mother set her empty glass on the table. "Is that why Marlene called? To talk about the details?"

Olivia shook her head. She had completely forgotten about Marlene again.

"You should call her back and give her the news."

Her parents left the dining room and Olivia sank back down into her chair, refilling her wineglass. The door from the kitchen swung open and Alessandro entered. She swirled the red wine in her glass and watched the thick legs of the viscous liquid cling to the sides. She inhaled. It was peppery, unique to the *terroir* of Verona. The first sip bloomed on her tongue, bright with the essence of cherries. Surely a lifetime spent making wine like this would be satisfying.

"Good, is it not?" Alessandro said.

Olivia nodded and took another sip. Actually, it was a gulp. She rested her elbows on the table.

He took the seat next to her. She glanced over at him, surprised.

"Your Sean is gone?" he asked in a low voice.

"He's not my Sean," she growled.

Alessandro cleared his throat. "I am sorry for your sadness, but I have a proposition for you."

She raised her head and sighed, lifting an eyebrow to encourage him to go on.

He clasped his hands in front of him. "I couldn't help but overhear your conversation with your parents. You don't want to return home and I don't want to lose my job. Together, we could make Villa Farfalla the greatest hotel in all of Verona." His face was earnest, his words even more so. Oh God, she hoped this wasn't going where it sounded like it was going.

Silence stretched between them. She heard her heartbeat in her ears, a slow, deliberate thud. What was she supposed to say? "Okay"? "Go team"?

Alessandro dropped to one knee next to her chair. A tiny bubble of hysteria welled up in her throat. *No, he couldn't possibly be going to…there was no way he would…*

"Olivia, will you marry me?" he asked.

A laugh escaped, even though she didn't want to be cruel. "What on earth for?"

"I have loved this villa and the vineyard my entire life—"

"You have? Didn't you just get here six months ago?"

He took her hand. "We share the same goals, Olivia. Let's work together and save Villa Farfalla. We can make it great again," he insisted.

"Just stop it. You know damn well Marco has been doing the work for both of us." It was just too much. "I can't do this."

His brow furrowed. "Of course you can. Isn't that why you came? To help your family?"

Caught, she said, "No…Yes, but—"

"It is natural that you should want to take over the kitchen. I am proposing a partnership. I don't expect you to have feelings for me, but it is inevitable that you will be the mistress of Villa Farfalla. It is what your parents want for you, and it is your duty to carry out their wishes."

She'd been thinking along those same lines, but somehow having him spell it out in black and white like that made her bristle. "It's the twenty-first century, not the fourteenth, Alessandro. My parents are perfectly happy to live their own lives and let me live mine. I don't have to carry out their wishes."

His glance was astute. "But you will."

He was right. She remembered the anticipation with which her mother had introduced them. Her mother would probably think this was a fantastic idea. *Perfetto*. A brilliant business decision. She could see how much work there was to do at the villa, and her parents were getting older. She'd already agreed to stay to help...but marriage?

"Alessandro, I'm perfectly happy to work with you without tying our lives together."

"I want you to know I'm not going anywhere. I want you to know that whatever happens, I will not leave you or the villa." His gaze was fierce now, proud.

She felt the walls close around her. She shook her head.

Alessandro held up his hand. "I won't take no for an answer just yet. Sleep on it. There are many benefits to a partnership between us. Let me help you, Olivia."

Hurriedly, she slid out of her seat. "Good night."

"*Buonanotte*," he returned. She felt his eyes on her back as she escaped to the hall and found her mother and Mrs. Russo sitting on the stairs. Clearly, they had heard every word.

Her mother stood. "*Cara!* How wonderful!" she exclaimed and reached to embrace her.

Olivia stepped around them and began to climb the stairs. *No way. Not happening. Not discussing it. Not even thinking about it.* Exhaustion returned full force when she reached her room. All she wanted to do was crawl under the covers and fall into oblivion but she forced herself to pick up the phone and dial her grandmother's number instead.

"*Pronto?*" her grandmother answered.

"Nonna? How are you?"

"*Cara!* It is so good to hear your voice!"

"It's good to hear your voice too, Nonna. Mamma wants to know when you will arrive for *la Sagra*." Damn it, her voice broke.

"We're just leaving now. What's wrong, *cara*?"

"Nothing," she squeaked.

"I have known you forever, *mia cara ragazza*. Tell me your troubles."

There was no point in lying, so she told her grandmother everything, starting in the restaurant in New York and ending with Alessandro's proposal and her mother's reaction.

Her grandmother was silent.

"Nonna? Don't you think it's bizarre that Alessandro proposed?"

"Actually, I don't find that strange at all. Who wouldn't want to marry the future mistress of Villa Farfalla? I'm still thinking about Sean. I really thought he cared for you, and I'm going to have to have a little talk with him the next time I see him."

"Nonna! Don't you dare! I'm already humiliated."

"Bah! He's the one who should be embarrassed. He promised his intentions were honorable or I wouldn't have given him your flight information before you left Norton. I feel like this is partly my fault. I let my romantic streak get the best of me. Maybe I'll have Benito talk with him." Her grandmother sounded thoughtful.

Olivia groaned. "Nonna, I'm begging you. Leave it alone. Or pick on Gia instead. I'm pretty sure she's dating a thug." *Maybe he and Big Daddy can bond*, she didn't add.

"Oh? Who is she seeing now?"

"Vincenzo Ferrari."

"Your cousin is dating Vincenzo?" Her grandmother sounded alarmed.

"Yup. What a creep." She sent a silent apology to Gia for the smokescreen.

She could almost hear her grandmother nod. "Tell your mother Benito and I will arrive tomorrow afternoon. Everything will be fine. We'll get there as soon as we can. Keep an eye on your cousin and take care of yourself. *A presto*, darling."

Her grandmother hung up.

Olivia set the phone in its base and sat down on the bed, realizing she had been pacing back and forth across the room. She dropped her face into her hands. Her grandmother wanted to sic her mobster boyfriend on Sean? This was a new low. Laugh or cry? She couldn't decide.

A chuckle bubbled up in her chest, so she released it. Then a tear slid down her cheek. Perfect—hysterics. Maybe she was capable of a meltdown after all.

A knock sounded on her door. With the way her day was going, it was probably her mother with a dozen *Brides* magazines and a wedding coordinator in tow. She opened the door. Close. It was Alessandro with a bottle of Prosecco and a plate full of chocolate-covered strawberries.

"I noticed you didn't touch your tiramisu at dinner," he said.

Clearly, he couldn't take a hint.

"I can't eat—" she began and then paused. The thought of discussing marriage made her want to break out in hives, but eating a strawberry would actually make it happen. Judging from her past experiences with strawberries, a rash would quickly spread over her face, chest, and arms. It would itch like hell and last for about a day. Triggering her allergy was a dramatic way to get rid of Alessandro, but it would have an added benefit. She wouldn't have to spend the day in the kitchen with him tomorrow either. Her mother wouldn't let her near food if she couldn't stop scratching. She wouldn't have to socialize with the guests either. It was the perfect escape—simple, poetic, Shakespearean even. She'd pull a Juliet until Nonna got to Verona. Her mom wouldn't care about Olivia's love life once Nonna showed up with her mobster.

She held the door open. "Come in."

He entered her room set the wine and berries on the desk. He faced her, looking as if he were about to plead his case again. "Why don't you open the wine?" she suggested, picking up the plate of berries and heading for the balcony.

The sun had set.

She hadn't actually eaten a strawberry for years. She grabbed one by its long green stem, ignoring the tingling in her fingers. She sniffed it. The sweet smell beneath the dark chocolate made her want to gag, but she forced herself to take a bite. She chewed quickly, swallowed. She took another bite, then one more.

Her tongue began to tingle. Her lips and face began to burn and her throat tightened. She clutched her throat, turning back toward the bedroom. Panic made her head spin and she couldn't focus on Alessandro as he came out onto the balcony. She couldn't breathe, couldn't speak. She began to fall.

"*Mio Dio!*" He caught her before she hit the marble. Her vision turned black and the last sound she heard was shattering glass.

# Chapter 22

RUSSO SCOWLED AND SIGNALED FOR ANOTHER BOTTLE of wine.

Sean held his hand over his glass. "None for me. I still have to find the airport."

It was difficult to ignore the chasm of panic opening wider with every hour that passed. This much silence from Colin could only mean one thing. Jail. He glanced at his phone and saw it was later than he thought. "I should get going."

A sudden sharp ring had them both clutching their phones. Sean glanced at his display and felt dizzy with disappointment. "It's your wife," he said.

Russo's eyes flew wide.

"Hello?" Sean answered.

Mrs. Russo's voice was nearly unintelligible.

"Slow down. I can't understand you. What?" Sean asked.

She took a long shuddering breath. "Olivia ate strawberries. The paramedics are on their way. I thought you would want to know."

Her words hit him like a brick to the head. "What happened? Is she okay? What's going on?"

"Her mother had an EpiPen in her room, and she seems to be breathing now," Mrs. Russo sobbed, "but she looks terrible. Where are you?"

"I'm in Venice." He glanced across the table and added, "With your husband."

She sobbed harder. "Tell him to stay there." Her voice was loud enough to be heard across the table.

"Tell her I will," Russo burst out.

"Both of you shut up." He needed to think.

He would miss his plane if he went back to Verona, but he couldn't leave Italy with Olivia in danger. How had he ever thought he could leave her at all? "Stupid, stupid, stupid," he muttered, forgetting Mrs. Russo was listening. "Sorry. We're on our way." He put the phone back in his pocket.

"You." Sean pointed at Russo. "Pay for dinner."

Russo threw a wad of bills on the table. "Done."

He led the way out the door. "Olivia had a bad allergic reaction. We're going back to the villa." Thank God they were close to where they had entered the city. It was full dark now, but as they jogged over the bridge he saw the lights of a few taxis. He knocked on the window of the first one he reached. "Verona? Villa Farfalla? *Immediatamente?*" He'd learned the word from Gia and hoped it got his point across.

The driver nodded and they climbed into the back, barely getting the door shut before the car sped off down the road. Sean stared out into the dark, his heart twisting with grief. Taking care of Colin had been his focus for so long it was a reflex. It had been years since he could truly protect his brother from anything, especially his own choices—but it hadn't stopped him from trying. Why couldn't love be easy? Sean took a long, slow breath and pushed the guilt away.

The glare of Russo's cell phone lit the back of the cab. "What are you doing?" he asked.

"I'm telling my wife I love her, of course."

"In a text?" Sean asked, appalled.

"Why not?" Russo's grin was a quick flash. "That's how she's been telling me."

———〜〜〜———

The sound of Olivia's breathing was loud in the quiet room. Her lips were swollen and red. Her eyes were puffy. A raised rash covered her face, neck, and arms. She was out cold.

"Is she all right?" Sean's voice was uneven.

Mrs. Marconi nodded. "Alessandro shouted loud enough to bring the house down as soon as it happened. I keep an EpiPen in every first-aid kit, just in case…" She cleared her throat. "The paramedics said she'll be fine. No need to go to the hospital, thank God. Steroids and Benadryl. She'll sleep for hours."

Sean nodded and sat down beside the bed, taking Olivia's too-warm hand in his. "What happened? Why did she eat the strawberries?"

Mrs. Marconi shook her head back and forth. "I don't know." Her voice broke on the last word, but she mastered her tears quickly. "I'd like you to leave before she wakes up."

Of course she blamed him for leaving. "I had to make sure she was okay."

"She'll be fine. I'm sure it was an accident, a mistake. Now that Olivia is going to stay in Verona, we'll stop ordering strawberries." Mrs. Marconi continued, ignoring his shock, "I hate to be the one to tell you, but Alessandro proposed marriage to my daughter tonight. I think they'll be very happy together, don't you?"

Sean blinked, feeling numb. The chef had moved in that fast? He glanced at Olivia and then back at her mother. "If her current condition is any indicator, I wouldn't be so sure."

Mrs. Marconi's face darkened. "Don't make this more difficult than it has to be, Mr. Kindred. I want what is best for my daughter."

So did he. That's why he had left her.

A shout from the hall made them both jump. Damn it, could Russo not do anything quietly? "I'll take care of this," he said.

Mrs. Marconi stepped out into the hall with him but turned toward the stairs.

Sean walked the other way, to where Russo was standing outside his wife's room. "Open the damn door!" Russo shouted again.

"Be quiet. Olivia's sleeping," Sean said. "Why don't you try a more subtle approach? Start with *I'm sorry* and tell her you love her again."

Mrs. Russo opened the door. Her eyes were red, but she smiled at him. "Are you going to take your own advice?" Her impish grin faded when she looked at her husband. "Get in here."

She gave Sean a sly wink and shut the door. He shook his head in amazement. Those two were baffling.

"Mr. Kindred?" Olivia's mother was coming back down the hall with a frown on her face. "There's someone here to see you." An unmistakable mop of shaggy blond hair appeared above her shoulder.

"Colin?" he gasped. "What are you doing here?"

His brother grinned. "Celebrating my freedom."

Joy and fury fought within him as he embraced his

brother. "Please tell me you didn't skip out on the last day of your probation."

"Hell no. Hearing got moved to yesterday morning. I'm free, bro. I thought it would be fun to tell you in person."

"So you bought a ticket to Italy?" Sean said slowly. "Just out of curiosity, how did you pay for that ticket?' he asked.

"With your new credit card. I'll pay you back, I promise."

Fury, definitely fury. "Credit card fraud is a felony, you know. And as soon as you activated the new card, I couldn't use the old one."

"I didn't think about that last part, sorry." It was typical of Colin not to consider the consequences. "And it's only fraud if you prosecute."

"It would serve you right if I did. You realize I thought you were in jail, right? Why didn't you return any of my texts?"

Colin dug his phone out of his pocket and held it up. "No signal."

Sean pressed a hand against the wall to combat the disorienting rush of déjà vu. A disapproving sniff from Mrs. Marconi reminded him of her presence, and Sean gestured down the hall toward his old room. "Do you think we could…"

She narrowed her eyes.

"Just for a little while? My brother and I have a lot to discuss."

Mrs. Marconi led them down the hall without saying a word.

"Thank you very much," he said, truly grateful when she opened the door.

Colin turned on the light and flopped on the bed. "I sent you a bunch of texts before I left. Didn't you get them?"

"I did…"

"But you didn't believe me." Colin raised himself up on one arm.

Silence hung heavy between them before Sean said, "I'm sorry, Colin." Suddenly, he was exhausted. He sank into the desk chair.

"It's all right." His brother gave him a cautious look. "Are you okay, bro? You look like shit."

"It's been a rough day," he admitted. "I was worried about you." *And I'm an idiot*.

"Seriously—did you think I would do anything the last week of probation? Jesus, I'm not that stupid. I was in the wrong place at the wrong time when the cops raided Johnny's bar downtown. Mom saw me on the news and freaked out."

"What were you doing at Johnny's?"

"Absolutely nothing illegal, not that it's any of your business. And Mom left on a cruise with Dave yesterday, which should tell you exactly how concerned she was about the situation."

And it also explained why he hadn't been able to reach her. Sean slumped in his chair. "She was supposed to be keeping an eye on you."

"You're the only one who still thinks I need a keeper." His brother snorted and cocked an eyebrow. "So how's it going with Olivia Marconi?"

Sean sat up straight in his chair. "How do you know about Olivia?"

"I ran into Marlene and Joe at Wegmans last weekend.

It didn't take us long to put it together when I told them you were at Villa Farfalla. Haven't you been hot for her for, like, a decade?"

Sean groaned. "Let me get this straight. You didn't get arrested. You're not in jail. You aren't on probation anymore, and you want to talk about my love life?" His adrenaline high was fading, making him even more aware of his exhaustion.

"I thought I'd find the two of you drinking wine and feeding each other grapes. Where is she?" Colin asked.

Sean told him, starting with the strawberries and working his way back.

When he explained his reason for leaving Olivia in Verona, Colin burst out laughing. "That's fucking priceless, bro."

"Shut up."

His brother lay back on the bed and clasped his hands behind his head. Colin stared at him for long enough that Sean felt compelled to say, "What? Stop looking at me."

"I can't…it's just…you usually aren't such an idiot."

"Stop being an asshole, Colin. I'm sorry I told you."

Colin shook his head. "You went off to Italy chasing after Olivia Marconi—"

"I had business," Sean reminded him.

"Whatever. An excuse to hook up with Olivia, I bet. And then you decide to run home because you get one stupid text from Mom that makes you think I need your help?"

"Some people would appreciate that I cared." Sean spoke through gritted teeth.

"And some people would be insulted. Why did you

really leave her? It wasn't for me. It couldn't be for me. You aren't that dumb."

Sean slammed his hands down on the desk and stood. "Olivia went to Italy to build a new life. I couldn't ask her to come back to Norton. She was miserable there." He stalked across the room to glare down at his brother on the bed.

"Oh." Colin looked sympathetic. "So you asked her? She said no?"

"No, I didn't ask her. I didn't have to. She left Chameleon. She's selling her house. Her parents have the perfect job for her here at the villa. She's really happy."

His brother smirked. "Obviously. Happy people do self-destructive things all the time—I should know. God, bro, you're such a fucking martyr."

Rage shot through Sean, making his vision blur. Colin sat up just as Sean grabbed the front of his shirt and dragged him off the bed. He gave Colin a shove that sent him spinning into the armchair by the window.

"You ungrateful little son of a bitch." Sean moved in to backhand him, but Colin ducked under his hand and hit him with an uppercut that felt like thunder.

He pushed his little brother away with a sharp jab to the stomach and caught him on the side of the head with one fist and then another. Colin tackled his legs, and they were down on the rug, then the wood floor, rolling until Sean landed on top, panting.

He planted his fist in Colin's face—not hard enough to break his nose, but good enough to give him a whale of a black eye. "I have been taking care of you your entire life. Of course I wanted to help you. The least you could do is show some gratitude."

"Gratitude for what? Treating me like a child?" Colin's voice was winded but droll.

Sean drew his fist back to hit him again.

"Enough!" Colin covered his face with his arms. "You're a good guy, Sean, a great big brother. I'm lucky to have you. But you need to get over yourself, man. You're not perfect, and it's annoying as hell that you try to be. I don't need a keeper anymore. You need to get a life, bro, because Mom and Dave have each other and I'm all grown up now. If you don't let anyone else get close to you, you are going to be alone. Trust me." His blue eyes were hard but not cold.

Sean's heart felt like a fist in his chest. His anger deserted him so suddenly he felt dizzy. He lowered his arm. "You know I love you, right?"

"Back at you, big brother." Colin thumped his heart twice with his fist in the gesture of affection they had used when they were kids, making Sean's eyes sting.

He levered himself to his feet and hauled Colin off the floor.

"Ouch." Colin raised a hand to his eye, which was already beginning to swell.

"You had that coming. Give me my credit card." Sean held out his hand.

Colin chuckled and handed it over on his way into the bathroom.

Sean sat on the bed, rubbing his sore jaw, his brother's words ringing in his ears. Why had he left Olivia? *To help Colin. To leave her free to build a new life in Verona.* Faced with the gaping hole in his chest that felt like it was getting bigger every minute, those reasons didn't feel valid anymore. His brother was right. He hadn't asked Olivia what she wanted. He'd made the decision for her.

Dread stole through him, choking him, the same feeling he'd had when he woke up next to her this morning. Dread of what? There was absolutely nothing standing between him and a future with Olivia—not his family obligations, not her marriage. Hell, she wasn't his client anymore either. There was no obstacle to their happiness except...him.

Colin was right; he'd acted like a martyr, sacrificing happiness while telling himself it was the best thing for Olivia. He hadn't told her he loved her or given the feelings between them a chance to grow. Instead, he had reinforced every doubt she had about herself. He had left her, probably feeling like a failure, the thing she hated most in the world, and gone after Colin, who didn't need him anymore.

He fell back on the bed and stared at the ceiling.

"I'm starving," Colin said, coming out of the bathroom.

"Can't help you, buddy. I'm persona non grata around here now. You're on your own."

Colin shrugged and grabbed an apple from the fruit basket on the desk. Sean left him there and walked back down the hall to Olivia's room, hoping he wouldn't find her mother camped out by the bed. Would Mrs. Marconi actually throw him out of the villa? He shrugged and opened the door. Only one way to find out.

# Chapter 23

OLIVIA DRIFTED BACK DOWN INTO SLEEP. SHE FELT heavy, as if she were sinking, but something kept pulling her back up. She had been dreaming of Romeo and Juliet, but she itched.

She opened her eyes. They itched too. She tried to rub them but couldn't move her hand.

She looked at it and gasped. Sean was asleep with his head on the bed, his fingers clutching hers. She slid away from him, wondering why he wasn't in the bed with her. God, she was so tired. Maybe she'd go back to sleep. She rubbed her itchy eyes, then stared at her hand. What was wrong with it? It was all blotchy and red. She pressed both hands to her face, finding it swollen.

Strawberries. Alessandro. *Oh my God. Sean.* Her heart pounded as her sludgy brain tried to sort through what had happened. He'd come back?

The door opened.

"*Cara!* You're awake!" Nonna Lucia rushed to the bed. "How are you feeling?"

"I don't know," she croaked. If Nonna was here, how long had she been sleeping?

Sean lifted his head, blinking.

"What are you doing here?" she asked him, pulling the covers up to her chin. If her face looked anything like her hands, she wished she could cover that too.

He pried her hand away from the blanket and held it.

"Marilyn Russo called to tell me what had happened. I couldn't leave. I had to make sure you were all right."

So he was still leaving, then. Disappointment made her feel like an even bigger fool, but she hid her embarrassment with anger. "I'm perfectly fine. Don't let me hold up your travel plans." She yanked her hand out of his grasp. "I don't want your pity. You were right to leave. I'm staying in Verona, and everything is going to be fine." Oh God, just saying it made her skin itch like crazy. She clenched her hands into fists to keep from scratching. "Just go. I don't want you here." The last word ended in a wheeze. What the hell was wrong with her? It had to be the strawberries, but she'd never reacted this badly before.

Sean didn't budge. In fact, he moved closer, making her breath come even faster. She wanted to hit him. She wanted to throw herself into his arms. "Get out!" she sobbed.

Nonna opened the door. "I think you'd better go for now." Her sympathetic expression made Olivia feel like screaming again. Nonna was supposed to be on her side.

She turned her face away as Sean moved toward the door, waiting for it to close behind him before she lost it completely. She felt Nonna's hand stroking her hair. "What happened, *cara*?" her grandmother asked softly, when her sobs turned into whimpers. "You've always been so careful about strawberries."

She reached for a handful of tissues and mopped her face. "I've never gotten that sick. I thought a few hives would get Alessandro to leave me alone and buy me some time to hide out in my room for a while." Another tear slid down her cheek. So she'd tried to escape from her life again and had almost succeeded permanently. "Running from my troubles doesn't work out so well for me, Nonna."

"It didn't work out well for me either, *cara*." Her grandmother sighed. "I have a story to tell you."

Nonna helped her to sit up, then handed her a drink of water. She sipped, letting the cool drink soothe her throat and watching her grandmother pace slowly across the room.

"Benito and I met at *la Sagra dell'Uva* when we were children, only eighteen. Sofia Conti and I were best friends and the belles of the ball that year. There was an orchestra in the courtyard and people dancing everywhere. He saw me. And I saw him. That was it, for both of us. Love."

Nonna cleared her throat. "It was very romantic. We danced every dance together, spent every waking minute together after that night. My parents were horrified."

"Why didn't they like him?"

"It wasn't that they didn't like Benito, so much as they didn't like his father. Pasquale Capozzi had quite a reputation with the ladies and he was considered to be a little bit crazy. The more my parents disapproved, the more I rebelled, sneaking out, telling lies, until they were afraid I would run away with him, like our Juliet Capulet."

"Were you going to?"

"Of course, but my parents planned a vacation to America and insisted I accompany them. I kicked and screamed the whole way. I didn't make it easy for them. They were hoping that time and distance would cure me of my childish infatuation."

"And did it? Did you forget him?"

The stricken look on Nonna's face told her the story was going somewhere bad in a hurry. She braced herself. She already knew the ending. Now she knew the beginning. The middle was probably an absolute train wreck.

Nonna raised her chin. "No, he forgot me. While we were gone, my parents received word from Sofia's parents. She was going to marry Benito Capozzi and they hoped we could make it back for the wedding."

"Ouch."

"Sofia was pregnant, of course."

Olivia dropped her head into her hands. "Of course she was."

"She was my best friend. He was my first love. And I lost them both that day."

Olivia lifted her head. "But I thought Sofia never married."

The warmth that usually lingered in her grandmother's eyes was absent. They were flat and dull. "Benito left her at the altar. He and his father disappeared. Benito came after me, told me the child wasn't his, but I sent him away. He had made his bed, and I thought he should lie in it. Not too long after that I met your grandfather. He was a good man and I married him, even though I was still in love with Benito. Your grandfather always knew it, but he loved me anyway. On the day he died, I held his hand and I looked into his eyes. I knew I had wasted our time together, that I had thrown away a lifetime of love with a good man, a strong man, strong enough to love me without asking the same in return. Oh, I did love him eventually, but never quite enough, eh? Certainly not as much as he deserved."

"You're breaking my heart, Nonna. Where is the happy ending?" Her question drove the tears from her grandmother's eyes and she smiled.

"You are the happy ending, *cara*. My blood, my life, my family," she said simply. "You and Anna Maria and Paolo. Marlene and Joe too." Nonna leaned over to embrace her. The comforting smell of lemons wrapped itself around her. "I should warn you that your friends are in Verona too. Marlene found the power of attorney papers in the filing cabinet and she's fit to be tied. Did you really forget to return all her calls?"

Olivia looked away. "I've been having a little problem dealing with reality lately." She wasn't quite ready to face it now either. "But what about Benito? He betrayed you."

"It doesn't matter anymore. I still love him. Sofia's dead. We've lived a lifetime without each other. We were so young, and life almost doesn't seem real when you are just learning to live it. But it is. Your choices, good and bad, have more power than you could ever imagine. If I haven't learned to forgive by now, it's too late." Nonna's swollen knuckles patted her hand, and she shook her head slowly from side to side. "And I don't want it to be too late, *cara*. I want to forgive him, just as you should forgive your Sean."

"He doesn't care if I forgive him or not, Nonna. He left me."

"But he came back." Her grandmother's satisfied smile made her feel sick again.

"Not for long."

"How do you know? You didn't give him a chance to say anything," Nonna chided. "He's here now, isn't he?

Your mother said he spent all night by your bed. I think I was right. He cares about you."

Anticipation began to flutter in her chest. Could Nonna be right? She threw off the covers and went into the bathroom to change into loose pants and a long-sleeved T-shirt to cover up the rash on her arms, legs, and chest. She was afraid to look in the mirror, but the swelling on her face wasn't quite as bad as she feared. As long as she didn't scratch, she might look normal by tomorrow.

"Marlene and Joe are in the kitchen," Nonna warned, when she returned to the bedroom.

*Of course they are.* She would expect nothing else. Strangely, she felt no jealousy at all, just excitement. She took Nonna's hand and drew her out of the bedroom, down the stairs, through the dining room, and into the kitchen. She looked for Sean, but didn't find him.

Marlene looked up as Olivia reached the kitchen stairs and rushed to embrace her. "Oh, I'm so glad to see you! What were you thinking? You ate strawberries?"

"Temporary insanity."

Marlene let go of her and fished a crumpled, twice-folded manila envelope out of her back pocket. It was the same one Olivia had stuffed into the filing cabinet the day she left Norton. Marlene's eyes narrowed as she thrust the envelope into Olivia's hands. "What the hell is this?"

"Power of attorney papers. Sign them and you'll have everything you need to take care of the restaurant until we make other arrangements."

"It's not my restaurant."

"It could be. It should be. You and Joe don't need me around anymore. I just slow you down."

Olivia kept her eyes on the envelope in her hands

because she didn't want to see the recognition in Marlene's eyes. She also didn't want to watch her friend struggle to say the right thing, the nice thing.

"Oh boy," she heard Joe say. "Now you've done it."

"That's the biggest load of crap I've ever heard," Marlene said vehemently.

"No, it's not," Olivia replied firmly. "It's a small kitchen. There was nothing for me to do, so I left."

"No, you freaking ran away like a coward. You slunk out the back door without even saying goodbye. You barely left a note, and when I found those papers, it scared the heck out of me. Nonna told me you put your house on the market. I couldn't get you on your cell, and you wouldn't return my calls. What the hell is going on with you? Are you really getting married to that chef? What the hell happened with Sean? He barely even said hello to us before he took off out the back door."

Olivia ignored her questions. "Do you want to buy the restaurant or not? I already talked to Mamma."

"Yes, I want it." Marlene's voice was tight and there were tears in her eyes. "I've always wanted it. But not if it means you aren't coming back. Not if it means I lose my best friend." Tears began to slip down her face. "Olivia, I was so scared when I found the papers, and even more scared when I heard you were sick. I thought maybe you had tucked your last will and testament into the cabinet too."

Olivia gasped and gave her a hard hug. "Oh, Marlene! No! Never that. I just needed some time to think."

"But what about the strawberries? If your *fiancé* hadn't yelled so loud and if your mom hadn't had an EpiPen in the first-aid kit in your room, you'd be a goner."

"It was an accident. I swear. I'll never touch them again. And he's not my fiancé." She held Marlene at arm's length as a sudden thought occurred to her. "Hey, if you two are here, who's running Chameleon?"

"We closed it," Joe offered, with a wicked grin.

"What? You can't just lock the doors. We'll lose all our customers!"

Marlene crossed her arms. "Good help is hard to find." Clearly, she wasn't ready to forgive her completely.

Olivia let go of her. "You're not the help anymore. Now you're the owner." She felt a weight lift from her shoulders. Speaking of help, Olivia looked around the kitchen. "Where's Alessandro?" she asked. She needed to apologize and thank him for saving her life.

"I haven't seen anyone in the kitchen yet," Marlene replied.

Olivia turned to her friends. "You two feel like cooking dinner?"

"Hell no," Joe said. "We're on vacation."

Olivia widened her eyes. "You can't expect me to cook. I'm still recovering from poisoning my system."

He didn't look sympathetic. "Yeah, being stupid doesn't get you out of KP." He slung an arm around Marlene's waist and led her toward the back door.

"Nonna?" Olivia asked. "Would you like to help me make dinner?"

"It will be my pleasure, *cara*. Believe it or not, it will be the first time I've had the opportunity to cook for Benito." The misty expression on Nonna's face reminded her of the pleasure she had felt when cooking for Sean. Her heart clenched.

"Where is Big Daddy, anyway?"

"With your father. They get along like a house on fire. Benito has been a long time away from wine. He's missed it," she said.

Olivia wasn't sure she felt quite as forgiving as her grandmother. She was still a little peeved at Big Daddy for his behavior at the beginning of the summer and her grandmother's story hadn't improved her opinion of him, but for Nonna's sake, she would try. "Let's make him a welcome home dinner. I'll check the walk-in and see what we've got to work with." Olivia stepped into the cooler, wondering where Sean had gone. She was glad he had left out the back door and not through the front door with his suitcase.

She forced herself to turn her thoughts to dinner. As she stared at the shelves, she couldn't breathe. Her throat began to tighten. Was she still reacting to the strawberries? No, this felt different, more like how she had felt her last day at Chameleon and the way she had felt earlier in the bedroom.

She forced her mind to clear. She would think about a menu when the dizziness went away. Her anxiety spiked. Deliberately, she thought about cooking dinner for the villa guests. Her head began to spin.

What the hell was wrong with her? Marlene had agreed to buy Chameleon, and her mother was fine with it. She should be thrilled. She was finally free, or at least, she would have been free if she hadn't agreed to work at Villa Farfalla, an even larger and more complicated operation than Chameleon. She wheezed.

Oh God, she couldn't do this. She couldn't stay at Villa Farfalla.

She leaned her forehead against the cool shelf.

Leaving Norton, she had feared she'd lost her love of cooking, but the last week had proved otherwise. She had enjoyed making the fennel soup, the pumpkin crème brûlée and all the other foods. The cooking class had gotten off to a rocky start, but she'd pulled it off and been proud of her students and the results of their work. She still liked to cook, but she didn't want to cook at Chameleon, and clearly she didn't want to cook here.

For just a minute, she let it all fall away, the guilt, the responsibility, the disappointment, even her mother's expectations. If she could do anything she wanted, anywhere she wanted, what would she do? Where would she go?

*She would do this. In Norton. With Sean.*

The answer was as simple as it was impossible, but thinking about how to make it happen didn't fill her with anxiety; it filled her with determination.

She lifted her head. She could do this. She focused on the ingredients on the shelf in front of her, and as a menu took shape in her head, a plan took shape in her heart.

---

Olivia wasn't surprised when Marlene and Joe wandered back to the kitchen. She put them to work, although she assigned herself the most intricate tasks, hoping to keep her mind occupied with something other than Sean. It worked for a while. Unfortunately, making *cazunzièi* was like riding a bike and the ravioli flew from her fingers faster than they had when she was a child, which left her mind free to obsess.

She hungered for the sight of him.

Her mother joined her at the table, forcing Olivia's mind back to her work. They took turns filling and rolling the dough in companionable silence. The ravioli army on the table increased its ranks. Her father's question from earlier in the week floated back to her. *What's the worst thing that would happen if you disappointed her?* Her mother didn't mind selling Chameleon because Olivia had agreed to work at Villa Farfalla. How would she feel if Olivia told her she wanted to go back to Norton?

"Mamma—"

"*Cara*—" They spoke at the same time.

"You go first," her mother said.

Olivia nodded. "I've had a lot of time to think this week, Mamma. I know you want me to stay here in Italy and help you with the villa, but I want to go home to Norton. I'm excited by the idea of cooking again, and I want to find a job where I can be creative." Joy arced inside her.

"Creative?" Her mother gestured at the pasta on the table in front of them. "You can create anything you want here at the villa."

Olivia gazed steadily at her mother. "I appreciate everything you and Papà have given me, everything you have done for me, but this time, I need to do it myself. I need to know I can. I've always said yes to you, Mamma, always. I went to business school, culinary school, ran Chameleon—I saw it as my duty. So when you asked me to stay at Villa Farfalla, I said yes. But I can't do it. It makes me feel like I'm choking."

"Choking! You did that to yourself with the strawberries."

"After I agreed to stay and work at the villa."

Her mother gasped. "You risked your life to avoid staying here?"

Olivia rolled her eyes. "Now who's being dramatic? No, of course not. I was just…trying to run from my troubles again." They had never discussed her divorce, mostly because Olivia felt that was the biggest way she had disappointed her mother. It was time to get that out in the open too. "Being married to Keith was hell, Mamma. I lost my confidence, my faith in myself. It's a lot easier to follow than it is to lead. I need to do this. I need to make my own way now."

"I guess that means no Alessandro then." Her mother sighed. "I knew it was too good to be true."

"Definitely no Alessandro."

"And Sean?"

It was Olivia's turn to sigh. "That remains to be seen. I hope so."

"I guess I'll have to tell him he can stay, then." She heard a catch in her mother's voice and looked up to see tears rolling down her cheeks. She felt like the worst daughter ever. "Mamma! Please don't cry."

Her mother wiped her eyes with the back of her hand. "I'm crying because I'm proud of you."

"You are?" Olivia held her breath, afraid she had misunderstood.

"Of course I am!" Her mom enfolded her in a floury hug. "You are everything I ever wanted in a daughter."

"I am?" The words slipped out before she could stop them.

Her mother squeezed her harder. "Yes, of course. So much like me but better. You've been such a help this week and I'll miss you, but I know it's selfish to want you to stay. I can't blame you for wanting to spread your wings, *mia bella farfalla*. You can do anything. You never cease to amaze me." She clutched her mother, fighting tears. She had waited her entire life to hear those words and, better yet, believe them.

Her mother gave her another squeeze then turned her attention to the pasta again. Olivia began to fill the dough, amazed by the turn of events. Once again, she'd had too little faith in someone else, too little faith in herself.

When all of the pasta was filled, trayed and frozen, her mother took off her apron and held out her hand for Olivia's apron too. "Thank you, my darling daughter."

Olivia hugged her mother. "Glad to help," she said, meaning it.

Her mother handed her a bowl of olives and a platter of cheese. Together, they moved toward the dining room to serve the antipasto. From across the room, she heard her mother share the news with her father. His smile was sweet as he gave her a simple nod. She bit her lip and blinked away tears as Mrs. Russo handed her a glass of wine.

"I'm glad to see you are feeling better," she said.

Olivia nodded. "Much better, thank you."

Mrs. Russo cleared her throat. "I couldn't help but overhear your mother talking about your new plans, and I was wondering whether you might welcome a business partner. I love what your mother has done here at Villa Farfalla and I believe we could do something similar in Norton on the Niagara Wine Trail. A bed and breakfast, perhaps?"

Mr. Russo joined them. "Finding another way to spend my money?" His voice was gruff, but he took his wife's hand and gave her a tender smile.

"I don't know what to say," Olivia stammered.

"You would be full partner, of course, but I would handle all of the pesky business details. It's what I usually do for my husband, but I've decided I need a project of my own."

Mr. Russo's expression was mournful as he let loose a gusty sigh.

"Hush, dear. It will be good for you." His wife patted his hand. "Please think about my offer. Chameleon has always been my favorite restaurant, and I would love to work with you." Olivia watched them walk toward the table, still holding hands. She already knew what her answer would be.

Her nerves were on edge throughout the simple feast of prosciutto, late-summer melon, *cazunzièi* with radicchio, and mullet with sea salt and olive oil as she waited for Sean to return. By the time she left the table to get the hazelnut cookies for *dolci*, she was wound tight as a spring. She gave the kitchen door a shove and sailed into the dish room.

Alessandro and Marco broke apart, panting.

The door swung shut behind her.

Alessandro's cheeks were pink and his lips were swollen. Marco's hair was finger-mussed. She considered reversing course for the dining room and walking around the villa to get to the lower kitchen but decided to brazen it out. She might as well get the awkwardness over with. It wasn't like she could pretend she hadn't seen them making out.

She walked past them to the trestle table and grabbed the two trays of cookies she had prepared earlier. Marco winked at her as she paused next to them. Alessandro looked stricken. "Olivia—"

"Thank you for saving my life, Chef Alessandro," she said. "I'm glad you were there to rescue me from my stupidity."

"You're welcome." He nodded, looking uncertain.

"As you were, gentlemen." She continued into the dining room and placed one tray of cookies on the dining room table, where her father and Big Daddy were deep in discussion. She took the other tray into the salon where Marlene and Joe were organizing a poker game with the Americans. Gia had left halfway through dinner to get ready for her date with Vincenzo, and the other guests had gone into the village. Both of the Russos were absent now too.

"Texas Hold'em. You in?" Marlene asked.

Olivia shook her head and grabbed a handful of cookies. She walked out the front door to the porch and found Gia sitting on a lounge chair, drinking a glass of wine.

"You're all dressed up," Olivia observed.

"We're going to a club."

Olivia sat down in the chair next to her, pondering. "You could have told me Alessandro was gay, you know." He probably wouldn't mention marriage again, which was a relief. Homosexuality wasn't a deal breaker, but the fact that she was still in love with Sean was a problem.

"I would have told you before you married him." Gia shot her a sideways grin and sipped her wine. "I guess I should probably mention that Sean was hiding in the tasting room all afternoon."

"Do you know where he is now?"

A look of irritation crossed Gia's face. "He went into the village to have dinner with his brother."

"Colin?" Olivia exclaimed.

Gia nodded. "He arrived late last night after your… incident."

Which meant Colin wasn't in jail, thank God. "Are they coming back to the villa?"

Gia nodded again. "He said they would be back after dinner."

God, she hoped Nonna was right and that Sean had come back to Verona because he loved her too. She grew cold remembering what he had said about prioritizing work and family over personal relationships, but then she grew warm thinking of how right it had been between them. They fit together. They clicked. She wasn't looking for a Romeo to rescue her anymore. She was looking for a partner, someone to stand by her side facing the future, and this time, she wasn't going to let him go without a fight.

A taxi pulled into the driveway, and her heart began to race. She clutched Gia's hand and pulled her to her feet. They watched Sean climb out of the back, followed by a younger man who had to be Colin because he looked just like Sean with longer hair. When he got closer, she saw his eyes were blue, not gray, and one of them was slightly swollen. He gazed admiringly at Gia, who blatantly ignored him. Why was her usually friendly cousin being so rude?

Colin reached across Giovanna to hold out his hand. "Colin Kindred. Nice to meet you."

Barely able to stifle a laugh at the strangled expression on Gia's face and the way she looked frozen in place while Colin looked easy as a Sunday morning, Olivia shook his hand. "Nice to meet you too. I'm Olivia Marconi."

"I figured."

A black car pulled into the driveway and Gia handed Olivia her wineglass. "That's Vincenzo. Ciao!" Olivia nodded and watched her cousin go, amazed by her ability to walk so swiftly in high heels.

"She's just playing hard to get," Colin said, making Olivia laugh. She could definitely see why Sean thought his brother was worth saving. She looked from him to Sean, forcing herself to keep her head high, even as the gunmetal gray of his eyes and his sober expression reminded her of the way he had looked packing his bag to leave.

The sudden sound of sirens split the night. Olivia turned to look down the driveway and saw the flashing blue lights of several dark blue Italian police cars in the lane.

A door slammed. She heard her cousin scream. She turned her head and saw Vincenzo trying to force Gia into his car.

"Hey!" Olivia shouted and took off at a run with Sean and Colin close behind her.

# Chapter 24

"*ALT!*" BIG DADDY'S GRAVELLY VOICE BROKE THROUGH the bedlam.

Sean kept running. He had no clue what was going on, but Gia was not getting into that car. He grabbed Vincenzo by the shoulder and flipped him around, leaving his two goons to Colin and, hopefully, the police, who had surrounded them and were pouring out of their cars.

Vincenzo reached for his pocket, but two police officers stepped between them, bent him over the car, and cuffed his wrists.

"Vincenzo? What the hell is going on?" Gia took several furious steps toward him, but stopped when the *carabinieri* gave her a warning look. Sean felt a rush of sympathy. It looked like she had another bad boy to add to her list.

"Please get that scum out of here," Big Daddy said to the *carabinieri*, who had already cuffed the other men. They led them to three separate police cars and thrust them into the back.

The villa guests had rushed outside and lined the porch. Alessandro stood slightly in front of them, looking stunned. Olivia put her arm around her cousin, and Sean followed them back to the porch.

Big Daddy joined them when the last police car left the driveway. "Vincenzo Ferrari has caused enough trouble at Villa Farfalla." He nodded at Mr. and Mrs. Marconi. "Lucia told me you've been having trouble with your credit." Mrs. Marconi nodded. "Had any broken or missing equipment?" he asked, and she nodded again. "Your troubles are over now, I'm sure. Vincenzo has a lot to answer for in Verona. I did some digging and made sure the carabinieri were aware of every one of his illegal activities." He looked at Alessandro. "Nobody messes with a Capozzi, eh?"

"I'm not a Capozzi." The chef's voice was filled with scorn.

"Oh no?" Big Daddy asked. "Who are you, then?"

"I am Alessandro Conti."

Suddenly, it clicked. Sean looked at Alessandro. "You're the Conti grandson, aren't you? The one who ran away."

Alessandro looked down his thin nose. "I didn't run away. I was sent. My grandmother had no use for me." His words were sharp but the anger behind them was dull, as if years had blunted its edge. "I had been raised in the fields and my world revolved around the grapes. All I cared about was the Amarone," he said bitterly. "But my grandmother didn't want me. She never wanted me, and she didn't want me to have anything of hers either. As the last of the Contis, the only thing I bear is the name. She sold my birthright to the Marconis, and a job in the kitchen is as close as I can get to coming home."

"Why didn't you tell anyone who you were? Why keep it a secret?" Sean asked.

Alessandro shrugged. "I was afraid to be sent away again."

Olivia moved to join them. "Then why didn't you

do something to stop your grandmother from selling the villa before she died? Didn't she know you wanted it?" Sean knew the answer from Gia's story, but he kept silent, waiting to see what Alessandro would say

"I wasn't here." Alessandro's smile was bitter. "I lived in Greece, then in Rome. I worked in Paris for a year as a waiter in a café. As I told you, I am no chef. All the while I was away, I ached for Verona. I couldn't forget the vines, and I didn't want the name of Conti to be forgotten."

Nonna Lucia stepped forward. "I knew you, Alessandro Conti. I knew you from the minute you appeared at the door asking for a job in the kitchen." She raised her chin to look into his face, now mottled with color on his high cheekbones. "You are not the only one to hate your grandmother. I swore I would not return to Verona unless it was over Sofia's dead body."

Sean was shocked by the cold, uncompromising tone of Nonna's voice. Next to him, Olivia sucked in a sharp breath. Big Daddy flinched too.

"Oh, child, I hated Sofia Conti until the last breath left her body. Almost." Nonna dropped her head, and when she raised it, she looked at her granddaughter. Olivia's hand crept into Sean's and squeezed it so tightly it hurt. It gave him hope. "We left Norton because I had to come back here to see Sofia. She called me home, and I could not deny her because she was dying."

"You talked to her?" Alessandro's face was bleak and frozen.

Nonna Lucia nodded. "I hadn't seen her for fifty-four years, a lifetime. Her betrayal changed the course of my life, and yet I couldn't deny her last wish. She wanted to make sure you'd be provided for, Alessandro. She wanted my help."

"I don't need your help," he said.

"Yes, clearly," Nonna said in a kind voice. "There's a crack in the Conti family," she continued, "a certain arrogance, a rashness. Too quick to action, the whole lot of you, and not particularly stable. I believe your mother's death broke Sofia's heart. She hadn't wanted her own child, but now her daughter was dead and she had you to raise too." Nonna shook her head sadly. "She cracked."

"She sold my birthright." His voice vibrated with suppressed fury.

"You weren't here to accept it, and she didn't want you to be alone, living your life in the shadow of her grief and a grudge that had already shaped the lives of too many in our families. Your grandmother made mistakes, and it was too late for her to fix them. She was ashamed. I forgave her. She didn't want to leave you alone with a run-down winery and more debt than she wanted to admit. Her spirit was broken."

Alessandro's fury seemed to disappear, leaving the husk of a dispirited boy. "So is my heart," he said softly.

"But you aren't alone." Nonna Lucia reached up to bracket his face in her weathered hands. He blinked at her. She grabbed the hand of the man who hovered behind her. "This is how I knew you." She took Alessandro's hand, connecting the three. "The cheekbones, sharp like the edge of a knife. The nose, so proud. I just knew. So many lives changed by a moment's indiscretion." She reached up to touch his cheek again. Sean saw Alessandro tremble beneath her hand. "It is said that age brings wisdom, but no. The gift of age is forgiveness. I regret I withheld my love and forgiveness from Sofia. I regret every year I could have helped raise your mother, every year I could have been there for you when your mother was gone. Now, it is too late, but you are mistaken to think you are alone in this world. You have Benito, your grandfather."

Alessandro shook his head and pulled away from her. "No."

The old man raised his head. The two men stared at each other, the resemblance undeniable. "Did Sofia tell you?" he asked Alessandro. The beseeching tone in his voice was startling. He was not a man to beg. "Did your grandmother tell you her secret?"

Alessandro's chin dipped once, a nod. "I know her secret, although she never told me herself. I found the birth certificates when I was a child, but what does it matter? A bastard is a bastard, no matter who the father is."

"Will you tell Lucia? Please?" Big Daddy's voice held a note of anguish.

Alessandro nodded again. He turned to Nonna Lucia. "There is a part of your story that is not true. According to my mother's birth certificate, this man is not my grandfather. My grandfather was Pasquale Capozzi." He looked at Big Daddy. "I assume he was your father too?"

Big Daddy nodded slowly, his eyes on Nonna Lucia.

She cried out. Gently, he grasped her shoulders. "*Amore mio*, I never touched Sofia. My father did." He switched to Italian. Sean couldn't understand a word he was saying, but the fact that Nonna was listening gave him hope. If Big Daddy could get Nonna to forgive him, maybe Olivia would forgive Sean.

———~~———

Olivia pressed her hands to her lips, unable to prevent her own sob. So many years, so much lost. She watched Big Daddy gather Nonna into his arms, cradling her against his chest. "We were so young, Lucia. And foolish. I couldn't betray my father's secret. He was so ashamed. It would have killed him. I know I am an old man now, but I have always loved you. I never stopped. Will you marry me?"

Lucia nodded, still crying.

"We'll do it tomorrow. We don't have any more time to waste." Benito turned his face to Alessandro. "*Grazie*," he said simply. "I hope you will forgive me for not contacting you sooner. I've been angry at my father for a very long time."

Alessandro bowed his head. "I am the one in need of forgiveness. I brought Vincenzo to Villa Farfalla. I paid him to find your father, hoping the secret to La Farfalla would help me reclaim my birthright. When Vincenzo discovered Pasquale was dead, he threatened to expose my identity if I didn't continue to pay him."

Alessandro turned toward her, shamefaced. "I am so sorry, Olivia. I shouldn't have tried to use you. I hoped that if we married…"

"I'd be stuck with you?" she asked.

"Something like that."

His repentant smile reminded her of the night after the opera, the night she had begun to like him. "No harm done. You did save my life after all."

A gruff chuckle drew their attention back to Big Daddy. "Vincenzo found more than he thought he did. I knew who he was as soon as he contacted me, of course. I didn't want him anywhere near Lucia's family here at Villa Farfalla. Men like Ferrari move in when they sense a weakness, but they aren't smart enough to look behind them. I have built an empire in America, an empire that has nothing to fear from a two-bit con artist like Vincenzo Ferrari. He will be running from me now. You have nothing to fear."

Gia strode over to Alessandro and punched his arm, hard. "You have plenty to fear from me. I can't believe you let me date such a jerk after I kept your secret. I can't believe I felt sorry for you. Once a punk, always a punk. I should have known."

Alessandro hung his head.

Gia looked like she might hit him again so Olivia took her cousin by the arm and pulled her aside. "I want wine," her cousin announced.

Abruptly, the last piece of the puzzle fell into place. Olivia looked at Big Daddy. "If Pasquale Capozzi was your father, does that mean you know the secret to La Farfalla?"

"Of course I do." His smile held more regret than joy. He reached into his pocket and held up an old-fashioned brass key. "It was my birthright."

———

Sean kept a tight hold on Olivia's hand as the crowd moved toward the tasting room, afraid at any minute she would remember she was mad at him. Big Daddy seemed to know where he was going, moving slowly but with purpose. Anticipation wound its way up his spine and curiosity fought with his desire to pull Olivia away from the crowd, fall on his knees and beg forgiveness. After hearing Nonna Lucia and Big Daddy's story, he didn't want to waste another minute.

Big Daddy disappeared around the end of the last barrel. Sean heard a clunking noise, then a slow creak. Big Daddy disappeared into the wall. After a second, light shone around the barrel and into the tunnel.

Big Daddy's muffled voice echoed into the tunnel as the crowd shuffled into the room behind him. "Barrels. Great big barrels the size of elephants. That is the secret of La Farfalla. Many kinds of wood have been used to make barrels for Amarone over the years. Light oak, heavy oak, charred oak, naked oak, but the secret of La Farfalla lies in the tradition of using enormous barrels. And not just made out of oak either. Cherry, chestnut, and beech were used, anything that was available at the time. Bigger barrels require longer aging, but they also give longevity to the wine. If you want a wine to improve with age, you can't rush it when it's young."

"That's it?" Sean asked. "The secret of La Farfalla is big barrels?" Surely there was more to it than that.

Big Daddy shrugged. "Big barrels and tradition." He gestured around the room, where gigantic barrels lined up in rows, dwarfing the crowd. Sean could almost see wheels turning in Paolo's mind as he looked around the room, balancing the variables, measuring the possibilities. Sean was doing the same thing as he watched Olivia's face.

"How long?" Paolo demanded. "How long did your father age the wine in this room?"

"Ah, well, perhaps there is a little more to the secret."

Big Daddy clapped him on the arm and gave him a grin that made him look every inch the mobster. The light bulb blew, darkening the room.

Big Daddy reached forward to flip the switch back down. "Better get the wires checked in here." The sudden darkness was unsettling. Big Daddy was the last to leave the room, so he pulled the door back flush with the wall and turned the key, handing it to Paolo.

"This is the year of La Farfalla." Olivia's father's nod was slow and certain.

Big Daddy put his arm around Nonna Lucia and led the crowd back down the long hall. Olivia pulled her hand away from him and followed them. Loneliness rose in a thin plume inside him. It poured from the edges of his soul, blinding him, choking him. He couldn't speak. The possibility of happiness hung between them like the grapes on the vines, fat with possibility, filled with sweetness, ready for harvest.

"Olivia?" he called softly.

She stopped, looked over her shoulder. He raced to catch up with her and held her back until the crowd left the tunnel. He took a deep breath. "I wanted you to come back to New York with me. I only said I didn't because you're so happy here, so at peace and cheerful in the kitchen. I couldn't ask you to go back to Norton. You were miserable there. I thought I was doing the right thing."

She raised her hand to his face. "I was happy here because of you, silly. You made me happy." Her green eyes were bright with unshed tears. "Until you rushed out of here like a bat out of hell and left me feeling cheaper than the manager's special in the meat department."

He pressed a kiss into her palm. "I never even considered that I might be the reason you were happy."

"Well, you're an idiot." She crossed her arms.

"That's not the first time I've heard that lately." He fingered the bruise on his jaw. "Colin called me a martyr and told me to get a life too. He's right. I never asked you what you wanted. I decided you were happy here, so I left. It was a stupid thing to do. If you're happy in Verona, we'll stay here. I don't care where we live. I just want to be with you." He felt like he'd been waiting fifteen years for a chance to say this to her. "I love you, Olivia. I hope it's not too late for you to love me too."

Olivia wrapped her arms around his neck and kissed him. "It's never too late for love," she said.

Gratitude and joy made him clutch her tightly and kiss her again. It was several long minutes before he remembered he had bought her a present in town tonight. He yanked the T-shirt out of his back pocket and held it up. "I promise to be less stupid in the future."

She burst out laughing and snatched the white T-shirt out of his hands. She held it up to her chest. "A perfect fit," she declared and he grinned at the elaborately scripted "I hate Romeo" emblazoned on her chest. "A man who has the insight to buy a shirt like this deserves my forgiveness. And my love." Her expression turned serious. "I do love you, Sean. So much."

She wrapped her arms around him, crushing the shirt between them.

He held her tight. "So," he began, "Verona or New York?"

"New York." She looked up at him. "I took my house off the market. Joe and Marlene are going to buy

Chameleon, and I'm going to open a bed and breakfast with Marilyn Russo. She's going to handle the business end and I'll take care of the kitchen. We'll do cooking classes and wine tastings—something a lot like Villa Farfalla but smaller."

"You've been busy," he said, loving her plans and the excitement in her eyes, but most of all just loving her.

She nodded. "A month ago, the idea of starting something new would have terrified me. I would have been paralyzed by fear and indecision, but not anymore. Part of that is thanks to you. I'm not afraid to take control anymore and start doing the stuff *I* want to do. Being with you taught me things about myself that I had never suspected." Her smile turned playful. "Some very interesting things."

"Hold that thought." He backed her across the aisle and boosted her up onto a barrel.

"There's whole hotel over there with beds and everything if you're looking to live out another fantasy," she said, when he stepped between her thighs.

"You are my fantasy, Olivia," he whispered, leaning down to give her a soft kiss.

He felt her smile against his lips. "*Perfetto*."

# Acknowledgments

The second book is a very different journey from the first! *Scrumptious* was inspired by my chef husband and fifteen years in the food industry. *Luscious* was a much more collaborative project. In fact, I kept a running list, lest I forget someone by the time I reached THE END.

*Luscious* was born when Dr. Michael C. Geraci walked into a patient consult room while I was editing the very first draft of *Scrumptious*. When I told him I was a writer and a chef, he spun tales of his fabulous Italian vacations. A year later, he and his wife, Dorie, graciously answered my questions and shared thousands of photos. I owe Villa Farfalla to their amazing memories!

My thanks to Robin and Duncan Ross of Arrowhead Spring Vineyards in Lockport, New York, for allowing me to help harvest the 2010 Chardonnay Vintage. I arrived at the vineyard and said, "I'm the chef who is writing a book." And Robin said, "I'm the farmer who is distributing bins." Sadly, I drove over one of those bins when they let me drive the tractor later that day. Sorry about that, guys!

I am grateful to Michelangelo of www.veronissima .com, who helped me place Villa Farfalla in Verona and whose lovely website educated me on Valpolicella and Amarone. It was my excellent fortune that my friends Molly and Dave Darnley toured Italy just as I was finishing *Luscious*, providing me with up-to-the-minute fact-checking resources. My heartfelt thanks to Anna Maria Park, a graduate of Universitá La Sapienza, Rome, Italy, who translated the Italian for me. Any errors are mine in revision!

Speaking of revisions, my editor Leah Hultenschmidt deserves daily cupcakes for the rest of her life for her insight, patience, enthusiasm, and excellent suggestions. It is a pleasure to work with her, Beth Pehlke, Aubrey Poole, Kristin Zelazko, and the rest of my awesome Sourcebooks team. A zillion thanks to my clear-sighted agent, Nalini Akolekar of Spencerhill Associates, for keeping me grounded. A lifetime of love to my husband and kiddies—for absolutely everything, especially the hugs.

My collaborative effort ends here, with you, the reader. Thank you for taking this *Luscious* journey with me. *Arrivederci!*

# About the Author

Amanda Usen knows two things for certain: chocolate cheesecake is good for breakfast and a hot chef can steal your heart. Her husband stole hers the first day of class at the Culinary Institute of America, so she married him after graduation in a lovely French Quarter restaurant in New Orleans. They spent a few years enjoying the food and the fun in the Big Easy before they returned to Western New York to raise a family. Amanda spends her days teaching pastry arts classes and her nights writing romance. If she isn't baking or writing, she can usually be found chasing the kids around the yard with her very own luscious husband. Visit her at www.amandausen.com if you'd like to chat about romance, writing, or recipes.